Gangstress 2

Gangstress 2

INDIA

www.urbanbooks.net

Urban Books, LLC
300 Farmingdale Road, N.Y.-Route 109
Farmingdale, NY 11735

Gangstress 2 Copyright © 2020 INDIA

ISBN 13: 978-1-64556-015-9
ISBN 10: 1-64556-015-5

First Trade Paperback Printing April 2020
Printed in the United States of America

10 9 8 7 6 5 4 3 2 1

This is a work of fiction. Any references or similarities to actual events, real people, living or dead, or to real locales are intended to give the novel a sense of reality. Any similarity in other names, characters, places, and incidents is entirely coincidental.

Distributed by Kensington Publishing Corp.
Submit Orders to:
Customer Service
400 Hahn Road
Westminster, MD 21157-4627
Phone: 1-800-733-3000
Fax: 1-800-659-2436

Gangstress 2

by

INDIA

Chapter One

The visit with Ace had my emotions all over the place. However, after receiving a text from Chucky requesting my presence at a meeting, I put my game face on. This was my first sit-down with all the players in his organization. I was nervous, to say the least. I didn't know how well the fellas would take to seeing a female at the table. However, I was quite anxious to find out.

Upon entering Snookers, a billiard spot off the I-96 freeway, I scanned the place for any familiar faces and saw Dog head past the regular patrons and then go through a door in the back. I followed behind him, went through the door, and found myself in a private room. The place was set up with several cocktail tables and one pool table. From the outside looking in, you would never guess all this extra space was back here.

"Yo, Dog, wait up," I called out, and he stopped walking.

He turned around and looked at me. "What's good, J?" He nodded. "I hear you and your girls have been doing the damn thing over at your spot. That's what's up."

"I told you we would." I nudged him playfully. Don't get it twisted. He and I weren't BFFs. However, he wasn't that bad, and right now he was the only person in this place that I knew to some extent.

"What's this meeting shit about?"

"I don't know, fam." After removing a bronze flask from his pocket, he took a drink, then sat at one of the tables. "Fox stated that Chucky wanted to sit down with the heads of each trap, but that's it." He shrugged.

I grabbed the empty seat beside him and sat down too. Quickly, the place began to fill up with hardened criminals. I caught a few niggas staring in my direction and gossiping like females. Yet no one had the balls to approach me . . . until one nigga actually did walk up.

"You must be the infamous Jane Doe," said the gap-toothed brother as he rested his Miller beer bottle on my table. "I heard you was getting it popping over on the Eastside."

"You could say something like that," I responded and smiled politely.

"That's unheard of, but I guess there's a first for everything. Right, homie?" He extended his fist to bump knuckles with Dog, but Dog didn't return the gesture.

"What do you mean by that?" I asked, feeling like this nigga was talking recklessly only because he saw me as a weak female, but he was going to learn today.

"I mean, back in the day the trap didn't have no place for a bitch, but I see things done changed."

"Ain't no bitches at this table," I smirked.

"Yeah, okay. There's a bunch I can say about that, but for now I'm going to let it ride." After grabbing his drink, he decided to move on to the next table.

Dog patted my back. "Don't let that nigga get you stressed," he told me.

"I'm not stressed." I brushed his hand away. The last thing I needed was to look like I was being consoled.

"Chill, J. I was only trying to let you know it was all right." Dog shook his head, and I felt bad for snapping, but I still stood my ground.

"I appreciate your concern, but if I were another man, would you be rubbing on my back?"

"Hell no!" he snapped.

"That's my point. Just because I'm a female, don't treat me like a pussy." I smiled.

"Point taken, Jane. I feel you," he replied and nodded just as Chucky came through the back door with a group of men on his trail.

"Who are they?" I whispered. The only person I recognized with Chucky was Fox.

"That light-skinned dude is Neal. Should something happen to Chucky, he's second-in-command. And the young nigga is Vito. He's Chucky's son."

"Did you say son?" My mouth dropped wide open. As long as I'd known him, I'd never known Chucky had children.

"Yeah, supposedly the little nigga has been living with his mother in Las Vegas or some shit like that. Until recently, Chucky didn't even know about him. Now that he's here, his spoiled ass gets everything he wants. He doesn't have to work for anything."

"How old is he?"

"About twenty or so," Dog whispered as Chucky took the floor.

"I called y'all here today for the monthly meeting, so let's get to it," Chucky announced. He paced back and forth in a Ralph Lauren polo and a pair of khaki shorts. "First and foremost, in case you haven't heard, we have a new member added to the team. Her name is Jane. She has the spot over on Charlevoix. After the meeting, stop by like gentlemen and introduce yourselves."

"I ain't introducing myself to no broad," someone joked, and everyone laughed except me and Dog.

Chucky frowned. "Don't get it twisted. Jane might be a girl, but she hustles like a man. This month her spot has outsold all of y'all. From what I heard, your spot is in jeopardy, so you better take notes from her, Nate." Now everyone was laughing except Nate. "Anyway, I brought y'all here to let you know we about to switch things up a bit."

Someone in the crowd asked the question that everyone else was silently wondering about. "What does that mean exactly?"

"In an effort to break the normal routine, I'll be rotating everyone," Chucky explained. "For instance, Jane and her crew will be moving to Rosemont. Vito and his crew will take over her spot and so forth."

Before Chucky could continue, I was up on my feet in protest. "Hold on! We've worked our ass off at that house. I'm not about to let anyone take our customers."

"Janelle, you and your crew have done an awesome job, but I'm relocating you, and that's the bottom line."

"So basically, you're giving your son everything I've worked hard for? Why not let him build up his own trap, like a real hustler?" I was pissed. A few men began to whisper, and some even snickered.

"Are you questioning me?" Chucky asked, in awe at my audacity.

"Are you stealing from me?" I retorted.

"Enough of that, Jane!" he snapped. "Keep on talking, and you'll be fined."

"Fuck you and that five-thousand-dollar fine." I removed a few green bills from my purse and made it rain all over the meeting room. On cue the entire room erupted in laughter, which pissed Chucky off.

"Are you fucking serious?"

"Are you?" I crossed my arms.

"Step outside . . . now!" He walked out the back door, and I followed suit, stepping over various denominations of money as I did so.

Once the door closed behind me, Chucky lit into my ass like a firecracker on the Fourth of July. "You won't last long in my circle by pulling stupid-ass stunts like that," he barked as he paced back and forth. "In fact, if it wasn't for the love and respect I had for your father, I'd take my belt off and whip your ignorant ass right now."

"Look." I exhaled slowly. "My bad about that. I was wrong for disrespecting you like that. Just tell me why, of all the spots you got, you want to take my spot?"

"It's simple, Janie." Chucky adjusted his collar. "Because I can!" Without another word, he opened the door and returned to his meeting.

I was too pissed off and humiliated to follow behind him, so I decided to leave. It was what it was, and there was nothing I could do to change his mind. Uncle Chucky had clearly drawn his line in the sand and had shown me where I stood. Unbeknownst to him, we were now on opposing sides.

Chapter Two

Chucky was a dummy if he thought I would bow down and kiss his ass like every other nigga on his team. My father didn't raise no fool. After all, before my daddy was murdered, he was the boss and Chucky was his flunky. Didn't he know that this street shit was in my blood? Both my mother and my father were gangsters in their own right. Chucky should've known better than to take my spot and give it to someone else—son or not!

When I got home, I didn't bother relaying the message to the girls right away. Since we weren't going anywhere, nothing was changing, which meant there was nothing to say about it. Instead, I took a nap to ease my pounding head. Regrettably, I was awakened later by the pounding of Alicia's headboard up against the wall and Keisha's high-pitched screaming. Promptly, I grabbed two pillows and covered my ears, but it was useless. After snatching the pillows off my head, I flung them across the room. Alicia and Keisha were getting it in like jackrabbits, and it was getting on my nerves. I hadn't had sex in several months. The batteries in my sex toys had been swapped out more times than I cared to count, and I was flat-out frustrated.

When I glanced at the clock on my nightstand, I noted that it was three o'clock in the morning, prime-time hours at the trap. As I got out of bed, I stretched my arms toward the ceiling as best I could without straining my belly. I was seven months pregnant, and my stomach was big, round, and tight. My due date was still two months away. Even so, I wished I had more time. The thought of going into labor and delivering without Ace by my side was sickening. I missed my fiancé tremendously. If I could turn back the hands on the clock, I would tell him never to get in bed with the Mob, since doing so would cost him twenty to forty years of his life.

I sauntered over to the dresser and removed a pair of sweatpants and socks, then put them on. Next, I went to the closet, took out a pair of Reebok flip-flops and put them on, and grabbed my purse. As I stepped into the hallway, Alicia's bedroom door opened and she emerged.

"Where are you going this time of night?" she asked as she stood there, her hand on the doorknob.

"I'm headed to the trap. I can't sleep," I told her. I was sure I sounded grumpy. I was irritated, no doubt.

"Oh, I'm sorry, Janelle." She turned her head and looked back into her bedroom. "Did we wake you?"

"It's all good. Don't worry about it. I'll catch you later." I took my keys out of my purse and left her standing there. It wasn't my intention to be rude. Today just wasn't one of my better days.

Coasting down I-75 in silence provided me the perfect opportunity to mull over the day's events. I didn't like my position with Chucky, so it was time to look elsewhere for employment. Furthermore, Alicia and Keisha were beginning to work my nerves. Maybe it was time we began looking into separate living spaces. Besides, I needed my own space when the baby came.

As I exited the freeway, my stomach began to hurt. Sharp pains hit me all of a sudden, and I felt weak in the knees. The feeling was so intense that I contemplated driving straight to the hospital. However, I ignored my intuition and continued to the trap instead. Michelle's car was parked outside when I pulled up, so I blew the horn once to let her know I was there.

As I waited for Michelle to open the door, I took a few deep breaths in and out and rubbed my stomach to soothe the pain. Michelle opened the side door a few minutes later, stepped outside, and walked down the driveway to my car door. I opened it.

"Jane, what are you doing out this late?"

"Auntie, I couldn't sleep." I grabbed my purse, swung my legs out of the car, and struggled to stand up.

"What's wrong?"

"That damn Ali and Keisha been sexing like rabbits, and it's making my stomach hurt," I groused. I laughed while rubbing my belly.

"So why didn't you just get a hotel room instead of coming here?" Michelle helped me from the car, and we headed up the driveway.

"This may sound weird, but I actually find peace here."

"You know, your daddy used to say the same thing." She shook her head. "You guys are so much alike, it's scary."

"I miss my daddy and my mama too," I admitted. There was so much I wished I could tell them and ask their opinions about.

"I miss them too, baby."

As we reached the side door, I saw movement in my peripheral vision. Before I could completely turn around, though, I heard gunshots ring out.

Bang. Bang.

"Aah!" I screamed as hot fire hit my knee, forcing me to the ground hard. My purse slid off my shoulder and fell behind the garbage can.

"Oh my God, Janie!" Michelle struggled with attending to my needs or running for shelter. Most people would've left me there in order to save their own ass. But she stayed behind and attempted to pull me to safety. My purse housed the gun I desperately needed, but it was out of reach.

"What's up now, bitch?" said the man who had shot me. He was standing several feet away from me now, close enough that I could see the mask on his face in the darkness. He pointed the gun at me and shot again, this time hitting my arm. His aim wasn't worth shit. If he were a real killer, I would be dead from a gunshot at this close range, but of course, I wasn't complaining. "Pick her up and get her in the house," he instructed Michelle, who was now covered in my blood.

"What's the matter with you! She's pregnant!" she screamed, with tears running down her face.

"Shut up and do what I said." The masked man walked right up to her, pointed the gun at her, then pressed it against her temple, and she shrieked. "Now hurry up!" he barked.

Michelle struggled to lift my body with her 135-pound frame. She carried me as best she could, stopping every few steps to catch her breath, until we finally reached the house. We both collapsed in the doorway.

"Where's the dope?" the gunman growled.

"We ain't got no dope," Michelle yelled through her tears. "Just leave us alone."

"Man, we don't have no dope! Please, just leave!" I mumbled while trying to apply pressure to my knee. Between it and my arm, my knee felt the worst.

"Bitch, stop lying." Once again, he pointed the gun at Michelle.

"I'm not lying. We ran dry over an hour ago," Michelle insisted.

"So, where's the money at?"

"It's already been delivered to the stash house," Michelle replied. I knew that was a lie.

See, me, I would've come up off the bread and lived to fight another day. Michelle, on the other hand, was from the old school. She would die before she gave a nigga anything. She knew once word got out that you did, they'd think you were soft. And that would be an open invitation to every Tom, Dick, and Harry to get at you.

"So, you want to be tough? Suit yourself. Both of y'all get into that closet," he barked. He pointed at the coat closet behind us.

At that moment I thought it was over, but just in case I lived to tell the tale, I concentrated hard on the sound of his voice, the pattern of his movements, and I memorized the shoes he had on. "Son of a bitch!" I said in a low tone, yet loud enough to be heard. "For real, dude, is that you?"

He was one of the local residents I'd had an encounter with a few days ago. Ali and I had stopped at the corner store for snacks. When we'd come outside, he and his homies had been leaning on Alicia's Lexus like they owned it. We asked them politely to move, but they decided to get ignorant. Dude actually tried to flex on me, until I revealed my gun and shot at his ass. I wasn't really trying to hit him, but now I wished I had. And now this man had the audacity to run up in my spot and try to rob me while wearing the same neon-green Air Maxs he'd had on the other day.

"Get in the closet!" he barked again as he snatched the mask off and threw it on the floor, no longer attempting to conceal his identity.

"You better kill me! If you don't, I swear on my mother, you'll wish you had," I snarled. With my adrenaline racing, I no longer felt the pain of my flesh wounds.

He walked over to me, grabbed the collar of my shirt, and dragged me into the closet. Auntie Michelle frantically tried to crawl away, but he shot her right in the ass. Screaming out in agony, she dropped to her stomach and lay flat on the floor. Old boy went over and pulled her by the legs into the closet with me.

Once he had closed the closet door, she wrapped her arms around me. "Janie, if only one of us makes it out of here alive, I'm gonna make sure it's you."

"We're both going to make it," I assured her as we heard his movement throughout the house. He had to be looking for drugs, money, or anything else to make his robbery worthwhile.

A short time later, the footsteps stopped. Soon, he increased the volume on the television to the max. I didn't know what the hell was going on until I saw the bullets tear into the closet door. The first two shots barely missed us. I was petrified yet pissed off, because I wasn't able to do anything about it. Michelle flung her body on top of mine as more bullets ripped into the wooden door. I wanted to scream as her body rocked from the penetration of bullets, but I knew better. If he was going to think we were both dead, then I had to stay still and remain silent.

Chapter Three

Too scared to move an inch or make a sound, I lay in the closet for hours, balled up like a baby, until the intruder left. The bleeding from my arm was minimal, but my leg felt like it had been set on fire. I yanked the laces from a pair of Nikes that had been left in the closet and tied them tightly around my knee. Truthfully, I wasn't sure if what I'd done was helpful or not, but I'd seen this done in the movies a time or two, to stem the flow of blood and prevent amputation.

The darkness of the closet made it hard to see Michelle, and I was thankful. I didn't want to know what she looked like dead, but I did notice that her temperature had dropped dramatically. Being this close to a dead body made me reminisce about the last birthday I had with my parents, the day they were murdered. Instinctively, I tried move away from Michelle, but my lethargy from losing blood and the stickiness of the floor made me stay put. I knew the blood pool I was sitting in was beginning to dry, and it smelled terrible. I felt hopeless, but I knew I was not about to die in the muthafucking coat closet. Taking a deep breath, I gathered myself and tried to think of my next move. Luckily, I didn't have to think long.

"Yo, is anyone in here? I'm trying to get serviced." The voice belonged to Leroy. He was one of the crackheads I served daily. Leroy was a middle-aged war veteran who had returned home from the war with a habit. After years of intravenous drug use, he had damaged skin, his teeth were decaying, and he was half out of his mind. Nonetheless, Leroy was harmless, and he was my savior at the moment.

"I'm in here." I was too weak to open the closet door myself, so I stayed put.

"Y'all really need to clean up. Look like a murder scene up in here," he rambled on while walking through the house.

"I'm in the closet, Leroy. Open the door."

"What in the hell is you doing in the closet?" He laughed to himself. "And they say *I'm* crazy." Slowly, he turned the knob and opened the door, and then he damn near leaped from his skin when he observed the scene before him. "Jane, are you all right?"

"No, Leroy. I need help. Please call Ali for me." Though he didn't spend big money, Leroy was probably my favorite customer. From time to time, he would wash my car and cut the grass for some free crack.

"I ain't got no phone, boss." He shook his head.

"My purse should be on the ground outside, on the driveway, by the trash can. Can you go get it and grab my cell phone?" It probably wasn't the best idea to send a crackhead to retrieve my purse. However, my options were limited at the moment.

Leroy was back in a flash and handed me my phone. Wearily, I put in the finger code and dialed Alicia.

She answered on the first ring. "I've been calling you all night, Janelle! Where in the hell have you been?" She was pissed, but now wasn't the time for that.

"Alicia, get over on the Eastside now. That nigga we had issues with at the corner store came over here and robbed us." Just as I finished my sentence, the uncomfortable sharp pains returned to my stomach. It was almost as if my baby knew it was finally safe to act up. "Ohhh," I moaned.

"What?" she screamed back. "Are you okay?"

"Yes, I'm okay." I spoke through short breaths. "He shot me twice, and he killed Michelle." The mention of her name caused me to finally look down at my aunt's lifeless body. Her eyes were still open. A wave of emotion came over me. However, I couldn't allow my tears to fall in the trap house. Besides, I had bigger fish to fry.

"I'm on my way."

"Get here fast. I think my water just broke." The liquid flowing from between my legs was a telltale sign that my baby was coming.

As I waited for Alicia and Keisha to get to the spot, Leroy did his best to keep me calm. "Just breathe, boss lady." Carefully, he pulled me from the closet. His breath smelled like hot beer and stale cigarettes, but at that moment I could care less. He was a saint.

"Leroy, can you look and see if the baby is coming out?" As I lay on my back, I slid my good leg over to the side for him to take a look.

"I don't want to see you like this, Jane. Just wait on the girls to come." Without further discussion, Leroy walked away and went into the kitchen.

"Fuck!" The pain was unbearable, and I began dry heaving. This had to be the worst day of my life. I didn't know if I was going to live or die. I didn't know if I was going to be handicapped, and I didn't know if my baby would survive the trauma of me being shot, on top of coming early.

"It'll be okay. Just hang in there." Leroy was back by my side with a cool, damp dish towel, which he placed over my forehead.

I must have passed out, because when I opened my eyes, Alicia and Keisha were struggling to carry me to the car. I winced silently at the pain, which rocked my entire body. However, knowing that help had arrived sent a wave of ease over me. After I was safely in the backseat, Ali went back and locked the house down. Keisha got in next to me in the backseat.

"What about Michelle?" Keisha asked.

Without a word, I cut Keisha a look that told her until I delivered this baby, I couldn't worry about Michelle. In a day or so, before the smell of death began to seep outside, I would send someone to clean up the spot and move Michelle's body to another location, just like I'd done in the past with Gudda. The only difference was, I had made sure they burned his ass to a crisp afterward. The coroner was probably still trying to make heads or tails of his ashes, especially since his teeth had been removed.

"So, you know for sure it was old boy?" Ali asked after getting behind the wheel of her car.

"Yeah." I nodded slowly. "He took his mask off." I grimaced in pain. My stomach was doing its own thing. I prayed like hell my daughter wouldn't be born in this car.

"I got that nigga, on the real." She beat the steering wheel.

Surely, he would get what was coming to him, but right now I couldn't concentrate on anything except having this baby.

"Janie, you know, once they see those bullet wounds, they're going to call the police." Keisha rubbed my shoulders. Until now, I hadn't thought about what I was going to tell the police; I had been too busy trying not to die.

"I'll just tell them I was robbed on my way to the corner store or something." I shrieked from the pain in my vagina and held on to the seat belt for dear life. It felt the baby was forcing her way down the birth canal at record speed.

"They're gonna want to know which store," Keisha continued.

"It doesn't matter. Pick one. Hell, you could be robbed at any one of the corner stores in this city." She was beginning to work my nervous system. Alicia registered the tension, so she turned on the radio. We rode the remainder of the way to the hospital in silence, with me gritting my teeth from the pain all the way.

When we got there, the emergency staff determined that I was indeed in labor, which trumped my bullet wounds. Therefore, they bandaged me up, then transported me to the maternity floor. On the way up, I thought of Gran.

"Can someone call my grandmother please?"

"I called her before I picked you up. She's on the way," Alicia said and squeezed my hand as my bed was rolled into an empty room. Quickly, a few members of the medical team began hooking me up to machines, while others began suiting up and prepping the baby station.

"Janelle, I'm Dr. Ruth." A white lady with blue eyes and white hair smiled as she flipped the cover off my feet back toward me. "You're almost there. Take a big deep breath, and then I want you to push for me, okay?"

"Ugh!" I grunted.

"Another deep breath and push again for me." Dr. Ruth was positioned between my legs.

Gran stepped into the room on cue and came over to be by my side. It meant so much to me that she was here. She was the only family I had left, besides my child. "Push, Janelle. Push, baby."

"Come on, J. You can do it." Alicia jumped up and down like a cheerleader on the football field.

"I can see the baby's hair." Keisha smiled from behind her cell phone. She was using the camera feature to record the birth for Ace. I was exhausted and drenched in perspiration. My lips were dry, and I felt cold. I was ready for my baby to make her entrance into this world.

"Janelle, just give me three good pushes. I promise this will be over and your baby will be in your arms." Doctor Ruth pulled a light down from the ceiling and placed it right over my vagina. Three nurses stood in the rear of the room—ready and waiting for my baby girl to arrive.

"J, you got this!" Alicia rubbed my shoulder.

"One." Dr. Ruth counted, and I pushed. She continued. "Two." I gritted my teeth, pushing until I was blue in the face.

"This is it, baby." Gran patted my arm.

"Three," Dr. Ruth said. I pushed like my life depended on it and felt something ooze out of me like a ball of slime. I watched as Dr. Ruth cut the umbilical cord and remove mucus from my daughter's mouth and nose.

"Eight o'clock on the dot," one of the nurses called out, noting her time of birth. Then she placed her on the digital scale to measure her height and capture her weight. "She's twenty-one inches and eight pounds, eleven ounces."

"Here's your big girl, Mommy." Another nurse placed my baby girl in my arms for skin-to-skin contact.

Immediately, I showered her with my tears and covered her with kisses. Seeing my daughter in the flesh was a bittersweet moment. Of course, I was happy that she was here, healthy and alive. However, I was overcome by the fact that she would never meet her grandparents. My mother should be right here at my side, and my father should be stepping outside to smoke a cigar in celebration.

"Happy birthday, Juliana Antonia Valquez. I love you," I whispered. I'd had her name picked out the moment I realized I was going to be a mom.

As she blinked slowly, I peered into her tiny face and acknowledged that her eyes held a hint of hazel and gray, just like her dad's. Truthfully, she looked like the mirror image of Ace. In that instant, I realized it would be exceedingly complicated to look at her every day and not be distressed. Ace was the love of my life. He had been hand selected by my father to watch over me in his absence. Ace had started out as a big brother figure, but over time things had escalated into love, which neither of us had seen coming. He was the yin to my yang. Every day that I raised Julianna without him would be nothing more than a reminder of how much time Ace had left on his shelf.

"She is absolutely adorable." Gran dabbed at a tear.

"J, you did so good." Alicia was crying as well.

"Congratulations on your miracle." Keisha rubbed Juliana's tiny hand.

"Thank you." Closing my eyes, I pretended that Ace was standing beside me and that they were his words I had heard rather than theirs.

Chapter Four

Though I had given birth three months ago, being a new mom, and a single one at that, was definitely something I was still getting used to. I had to figure out which diaper brand I liked better, which formula sat better in Julianna's stomach, how she should sleep, and what the perfect temperature of her bottle was. Some days were overwhelming, but with the help of Gran and Alicia, I was making it happen. They were my support system when I needed assistance. I even had Carol on speed dial, should I feel myself slipping into postpartum depression. Primarily, I kept Juliana with me. She was the apple of my eye; I loved her more than anything. Every day she was growing and changing right before my eyes, which saddened me to a certain extent, because her daddy was missing out.

Speaking of Ace, today I was taking Ju to visit him for the first time. To me, it was important for him to lay eyes on his daughter, as it would be a reminder of what he had waiting for him at home. The prison officials had tried to give me a hard time about the meeting. However, Richard Lennigan had pulled a few strings and had arranged the meeting in the lawyers' room, where nothing could be monitored or recorded.

When I got to the prison, I signed in, and then a corrections officer escorted me to the lawyers' room. *Beep!* The sound of the corrections officer swiping his badge to enter the room startled me a little and certainly

captured my attention. Just like the first time I was here
to see Ace, my stomach was in knots, and I was a nervous
wreck. Once I was inside the room, I took a seat at the
metal table and rested Juliana's car seat atop it. She was
napping quietly. Sitting up straight, I put on the best
smile I could muster.

"You all have fifteen minutes," the officer announced,
then turned and exited the somber white room. I imag-
ined this very room had seen many tears and fits of rage. I
was also certain this room had borne witness to more bad
than good news, but today I was there to brighten it up.

"Damn, Janie. You look nice." Ace stood in the doorway
and looked me over from head to toe. His eyes roamed
every inch of my body, like those of a lion ready to devour
his prey.

"Thank you, baby." I stood and performed a slow spin
for him to see what I was working with. Then I went over
to hug him. He grabbed me with so much force that I was
lifted off the floor. His shoulders were tight, and his back
was tense.

"Girl, I've missed you." Ace sounded sad, which in turn
made me sad. I was aware of the fact that prison was
definitely taking a toll on him. He even had a few gray
hairs on top of his head and wrinkles in his forehead. His
eyes were whitish red, which was a clear indication that
he'd been stressing. "What happened to your teeth?" He
frowned.

"They're called Lumineers. Do you like them?"

"It looks okay, but why did you get them?" Ace never
missed a beat when it came to me. Sometimes it was a
gift, and other times a curse.

"I had a run-in with Gudda, but it's been handled." I
hated even to say the name of the bastard who'd come
into my spot and beat my ass a while ago. He had kicked,
punched, and pistol-whipped me until I had had no
choice but to get new teeth.

"What happened?"

"Baby, let's talk about this some other time, okay?" I kissed his lips. Telling Ace about Gudda would enrage him, which was no good for anybody, especially somebody who was locked up. Going back to his cell infuriated would probably cause him to start a fight with the first nigga that looked at him wrong, and I needed him to stay on the straight and narrow. "I wanted to cheer you up, so I brought someone to see you."

He put me back down on the floor. "Who is it?"

"Her name is Juliana Antonia Valquez." I pulled him in the direction of the car seat.

"Oh shit. I didn't even see the car seat. I can't believe she's actually here." He was overcome with joy. "I didn't think I would see her in person anytime soon." Ace sat down in front of the car seat and smiled. "Oh my God, Janie. She's beautiful!" He rubbed her tiny leg. Ju smiled in her sleep, which made his day.

"I went into premature labor and had her early." I specifically skipped the horrific details about what had caused Ju to come early. Ace didn't need to know anything about it. "I would've brought her sooner, but I had to make sure she had all her shots first." I stood behind him and massaged his shoulders.

"I'm so glad you brought her. Thanks, baby. I really needed this today." He kissed her hand and rubbed her hair.

"Don't you want to hold her?" I asked.

"No. I have too many germs on me. This place is filthy." He shook his head and continued watching Ju sleep. I knew it had to be killing him that he couldn't even hold his flesh and blood, whom he was meeting for the first time. Regardless of being in a place like jail, he deserved to hold his daughter.

"Baby, I brought a bunch of blankets to cover you in. If you would like to hold her, trust me, it's okay." Juliana awoke just as I went to unlock the belt on the car seat. "See? She has your eyes." I pointed, and he smiled.

"She looks like the girl version of me."

As I handed him the blankets and then Ju, he was awestruck. I could tell by the way his hands were jittery that he was nervous at first, but within a minute or two, he was comfortable cradling her small body. I took out my camera phone and snapped a few shots of this moment for Juliana's photo book.

"Damn, J. She has stolen my heart already." He kissed her forehead while rocking her gently. I watched Ace with our daughter and wanted to cry, but I kept it together.

The rest of the visit went smoothly. While Ace held his daughter, I showed him the recording of the delivery so he could feel as if he'd been there. For a small moment in time, things felt normal again. Up until the officer came to inform us the visit was over.

"Time is up. Let's go."

"Can I have a few more minutes, please?" Ace's eyes begged the corrections officer for more time.

"Valquez, you know I can't do—"

"Please, sir, please! This is my newborn daughter. Can I please have a little more time?" Ace wasn't the begging kind, but today was different. I could see the fear of letting go in his eyes, and I could hear the desperation in his voice. I guessed the officer did too.

"Fifteen minutes, Valquez."

"Thank you, sir." Without removing his eyes from Julianna, he continued holding her in silence for the better part of seven minutes. After planting a few more kisses on her face, he placed Ju back in her car seat and strapped her in. "You know, when they took me down, they took the whole Pauletti family down, right?"

"Yeah." I didn't have anything else to say, so I let him continue.

"Well, I got word the other day that the wives of the men arrested have stepped up to take over the business in order to make sure the family stays afloat until this shit is worked out."

"That's what's up." I loved to hear about women handling shit.

"Well, Nicky Carmichael sent word, asking if I had someone willing to take my spot. I told him about you. If you're game, then you're on."

"So, you want me to go into business with the Mob?" I was shocked. Ace had never wanted me anywhere near the trap. Yet now he was handing me a Mafia connection on a silver platter.

"You said you had set up shop with Chucky in order to make money for us, right? Well, I figured if you were gonna take such a risk, then you might as well make it meaningful. The money they bring in is unheard of. If you do this shit like I know you can, then you'll be a millionaire in less than five years. Your new position with the Mob makes you the number one supplier on the streets in all the black community."

"Straight up, it's like that?" My mouth was wide open as I intensely considered what he had just said. On one hand, I wanted to be a better role model for Ju. Conversely, this connection could also be just what I needed to live the way I'd always dreamed I would.

"If you want the position, it's yours, J. Just say the word." He licked those perfect lips, which I loved to hate. "You know how I feel about you hustling. Especially now that you've got my seed. But I know you're a grown-ass woman and you going do your own thing regardless of how I feel. The coins you make with Chucky is chump change compared to Mafia money. So, if you going to do it, at least do it right." He had made a very valid point. I was hooked.

"Thank you, baby. Count me in." I kissed him.

"Before you get all excited, you need to know these fuckers don't play. If you mess up, they come for you hard."

"I promise I won't mess this up." I was excited about the new opportunity. It was time to take my crew to the next level; I couldn't wait to get started.

"I love you, Janelle. Please be careful." When he pressed his lips up against mine, I felt a shiver from the tips of my toes all the way to the top of my head, and a pulsation was happening in my vaginal area. "Do you still love me?"

"Of course I do." I looked at him like he was crazy.

"Say that shit, then. 'Cause a nigga need to hear it right about now," he demanded with a smirk, all the while rubbing my thighs.

"I love you, Anthony." I slid my hand down toward the bulge in his pants and fondled him.

"Damn. I miss this shit," he groaned softly.

"You'll be home soon, so don't worry." My nipples had hardened, and my body was aroused. Shit would've gotten real had the officer not come back to stop the party.

Before Ace left the room, he gave me a phone number for some woman named Karla and told me to call her.

Chapter Five

After the visit with Ace, I flew home in my car. I couldn't wait to tell Alicia the good news. When I arrived, Keisha was just backing out of the driveway. I pulled in, and with a quick wave to her, I parked, hopped out, and hurriedly unsnapped Ju's car seat. Alicia was standing in the doorway.

"What are you so excited about?" she called.

"Girl, you better sit down for this one," I said with a smile as Ju and I entered the house.

"What's up?" Ali flopped down on the sofa and waited patiently on the details.

"Today I went to see Ace, and he told me the Pauletti family wants to do business with us," I damn near squealed.

"The Pauletti family, as in the Mafia family Ace worked for?"

"Yes!"

"Shut the fuck up!" I could tell Alicia was just as excited as I was. "I wonder how that came about."

"Ace said the wives of the organization have stepped up to run the business in their absence. They asked if Ace had someone to take over his spot, and he gave them my name."

"We are in there like swimwear!" She jumped up from the sofa and did a little two-step. "Wait until the girls hear this shit!"

"Let's keep it under wraps until after the meeting. There is no need to get everyone excited until the deal is sealed."

Ali stopped dancing. "When is the meeting?"

"I need to call Karla and set it up."

"Bitch, what are you waiting for?" Ali laughed. "Go call her now, so we can get this shit popping."

"A'ight. I'll be right back."

The next morning Gran was at the door bright and early for her weekly visit to watch Ju. "I bought the baby some things," she said with a smile as I let her in. Immediately, she dropped three bags on the sofa and began pulling various pieces of clothing out. "Isn't this tutu cute?" She held it up for Ali and me to see. "I got it for only fifty cents. It was senior day at the Goodwill."

"Gran, I told you I don't like secondhand clothes. The tutu is cute, but you cannot put that on my baby!"

"You wouldn't even know it was thrift stuff if I hadn't told you," she said, fussing. "I spent twelve dollars on all this, and she is going to wear it!"

"Look, I don't have time to argue. I've got a meeting." When I checked the time on my MK digital, I knew we had to leave now. Karla's home was out in the boondocks of Romulus, Michigan, a good forty-five minutes away from Detroit. "Gran, please don't put that on my baby. Let me at least wash it first." I said that only to buy some time. I knew if I didn't, she'd be playing dress-up with Ju as soon as I walked out the door.

"Okay. Fine." She tossed the clothes back into the bags, and Ali and I headed for the door.

On the ride to Karla's house, we both remained silent. I couldn't speak for Alicia, but my silence was due to nervousness. I hoped the meeting went well, because I was ready to get that paper, but then again, I knew getting into bed with the Mob was on a whole other level than the low-grade shit we were used to. If shit went wrong with

Chucky, we could handle that, but if shit went wrong with the Mafia, we would all end up dead. They were known to cut off fingers and send your children through the meat grinder. Although I knew what my team was capable of, I knew there was virtually no room for error.

Almost thirty-nine minutes later, I pulled my whip up to the gates of the most magnificent home I'd ever seen. "Wow!" was all I could say as I marveled at the abode. The beautiful sight before me had me struggling to keep my bottom lip from dropping too low.

"Do you see this fancy shit?" Ali tapped me as I went to press the intercom buzzer.

"Hell yeah!" I nodded. Of course, we were used to nice houses, being from the suburbs and all, but this was no house. It was a real-life mansion.

"H-hello . . . hello?" someone asked, clearly fumbling with the intercom button. "Carmichael residence. May I help you?"

"Hello. My name is Jane. I'm here to see Karla." I tried not to sound nervous, as confidence was critical for sit-downs like this. However, the massive mansion that stood before me was quite intimidating, to say the least.

"One second."

"This is some boss shit for real," I whispered to Ali as the ten-foot wrought-iron gate opened and I pulled inside. The dark green lawn with sculpted shrubbery was immaculate; the red rose beds were impeccable. There was even an arch-shaped driveway made of cobblestone, with a white Rolls Royce parked out front. This home was the embodiment of how I wanted to live.

"Damn. I feel underdressed." Alicia straightened out her yellow one-piece capri jumper.

"Who are you telling?" I had on a simple orange maxi dress with sandals. This place was so fancy, I felt like I should've had on a big hat, an evening gown, and gloves or something. "Fuck it. We're here now, so let's do." After I parked the car, we both got out and approached the door.

"Hello, ladies. I'm Karla Carmichael. It's so nice to meet you." The perfectly tan woman with toned arms extended her hand. Her grip was soft yet firm, and her smile was sincere. In her eyes, I recognized the pain of missing a loved one. However, in her voice I heard the fortitude it took to bring that loved one back home.

"I'm Janelle, but you can call me Jane." I shook her hand and returned the smile. "And this is Alicia."

"Nice to meet you." Alicia smiled. "You can call me Ali, Mrs. Carmichael."

"Jane and Ali, I like that." She giggled. "Come on in, ladies, so we can get down to business." She gestured for us to enter the grand home, then closed and locked the door behind us.

The interior of Karla's home resembled something straight out of the home décor pages in *Vogue Italia*. The foyer and the hallways off it were an alluring combination of cream, burgundy, and gold colors. She even had a gold statue and a fountain in the foyer.

"This place is absolutely gorgeous!" Alicia said as she marveled at an oil painting in the hallway.

"Thank you, sweetheart. My husband, Nicky, and I decorated this entire place without a designer. We wanted it to be chic yet personal. It took us four years to complete the vision." She led us into a cream-colored kitchen with a lot of copper accents. The sink, dishwasher, oven range, and refrigerator were all made of real copper. It was the first kitchen I'd seen of its kind, and I was sort of feeling it.

"Well, kudos to you and Mr. Carmichael. You guys did your thing," I said as I ran my hand across the custom wall tiles. "When Ace is released, and after we save up enough money to buy a house, maybe you could help us decorate." I wasn't just gassing her up; I truly meant every word. Karla had mad talent.

"Oh, I would love to decorate for you, sweetheart. My husband speaks highly of your boyfriend, Anthony. He says he's like family and is a real stand-up guy." Karla pulled three teacups from the cupboard, then handed one to Alicia and one to me and kept one for herself. Then she went into a kitchen drawer and pulled out a small metal flask filled with a brown liquid and poured a shot into her teacup. "Girls, would you like a sip? It's aged brandy." She waved the flask. Alicia readily extended her teacup, and Karla poured a shot.

"None for me. I'm nursing," I said, declining.

"Well, since you can't have one, I guess I'll help myself to another." She winked and walked over to the kitchen table. "Jane, here is some hot tea, if you'd like some." Karla pointed at the tea kettle resting on the table. I wanted to decline that beverage as well. However, I didn't want to offend her. Therefore, I poured myself just a little.

"Thank you, Karla," Alicia and I said at the same time.

"No problem." She motioned for us to sit at the table, and once we had, she took a seat. "So, let's get down to business, shall we?"

"I must admit Anthony didn't go into much detail about this meeting. He simply provided me with your number and told me to call you," I noted. Ace had given me plenty of information. Nevertheless, I wanted her detailed version of the story so I'd have a better understanding.

"Well, in case you didn't know, my husband, Nicky, is a big part of the Pauletti family. Recently, they took a huge hit during a bust. As a result, the entire male population of the family is presently behind bars, awaiting trial, including Anthony." Karla sipped from her teacup. "Never in our history has every male under our umbrella been pinched at the same time. Naturally, with them away, we're losing money, as well as our respected position with the other families. Approximately two months ago, Constance Pauletti, the boss's wife, approached the rest of the wives with an idea to not only save the business on behalf of our husbands, but also to keep the family name up and running. Naturally, we all obliged, and we were then given our orders and respective positions within the organization. Although we've done well for amateurs, we've realized a substantial amount of our income comes from the urban areas. That's where you come in. We would like you to take over Anthony's spot with our organization until he comes home." She sipped from her teacup again while looking directly at me.

"In other words, you want me to be your black sales-girl?" I said. Then I also sipped from my teacup, with my eyes focused on hers. I knew how most Italians felt about black people, and she was probably no different.

Alicia looked as if her eyes were going to pop out of her head, but I didn't care. I would never be anybody's token nigga just to put a few dollars in my pocket!

"Jane," Karla smirked. "Not many people know this, but my grandmother was a black woman. So contrary to what you believe about me, when I look at you, I don't see color. All I see before me is a woman ready and willing to play her position until her man returns home—a woman just like me."

"Will this be a secret between you and me, or will I be introduced to the other ladies?" I wasn't a back-door bitch. If Karla wanted to do business with me, then she had better bring me to the table the correct way.

"It's funny that you should mention it, because the other women should be here any minute now. We get together every Saturday to eat, vent, and talk shop at Mrs. Pauletti's house, but today I invited them here to meet you." Again, Karla sipped from her teacup. "I know sometimes Italians have a bad rep when it comes to racism, but in this family, there is nothing like that. Especially once we bring you to the table, you're one of us." Karla refilled her and Alicia's teacups, and I relaxed a little. She made small talk about this and that until there was a buzz from the intercom. She then excused herself from the table, and Ali got straight to it.

"J, do you know what this means for us?" She smiled.

"It means a whole lot of trouble if we aren't careful." I shook my head. True, the Italian connection was just what we needed to dominate the dope game. However, more money and power virtually always came with more problems.

"They're here," Karla announced as she reentered the kitchen with four women in tow.

A heavyset woman held a Tupperware container, which she sat down on the counter. She was tall, with black hair, big boobs, and very full lips. In my opinion, she needed to have some of the Botox removed from her lips and to go down three sizes on the implants, but still I smiled.

"Hello, ladies. How are you?" she said.

Another woman carried a basket of bread and refused to acknowledge us. She was very tan and petite, and she had black hair. "I love what you've done with the place, Karla."

"It's hotter than an elephant's ass out there," said the oldest woman as she placed four bottles of champagne down on the table. "Hello, girls." At present, she wasn't much of a looker. However, I could tell that back in her heyday, in all probability she was a beauty queen.

"Constance, you better watch your mouth," said the fourth and final woman, who was carrying a box of pastries. She didn't look Italian to me. In fact, if anything, she appeared to be just a "regular" northern European woman due to the blond hair and blue eyes.

"I'm sixty-nine. So I'll say whatever the hell I want to say," Constance snapped and opened the refrigerator to retrieve a bottle of Fiji Water.

"Ladies, we have guests, so cut it out," Karla scolded with a giggle. Then she cleared her throat and announced, "Jane and Ali, this is Amelia, Ramona, Gia, and Constance."

"Hello," I said, while Ali simply waved. With the exception of Amelia, everyone seemed friendly. But I wasn't too concerned with her.

"For the meeting, we brought some penne pasta with sausage and tomato sauce, pinot grigio, and a loaf of freshly baked bread," Ramona said while pulling plates from Karla's cabinet. "Have some?"

"They don't have a choice," Constance joked. "If they're going to be a part of this family, then they have to eat like an Italian."

We all filled our plates and then moved into Karla's formal dining room. The spacious room housed a ten-seat cherrywood table, a four-tier chandelier, and a large china buffet with various family heirlooms atop it. We all took seats around the table, then participated in small talk for a little over an hour before getting down to business.

"Did Karla fill you girls in on what we are doing?" asked Constance, the boss's wife, as she used the last piece of bread to clean the sauce from her plate. Her husband had been the head of the family for over three decades. In the Pauletti family, she was something like a queen.

"Yes, she filled us in." I nodded. "But we haven't discussed percentages and payouts yet." It was time to get to the meat of why we were here in the first place. I'd had enough of the surface talk.

"Our family has a coke supplier straight from Mexico. Every Friday morning, we send a money truck across the border. In return, each Friday afternoon, they send back a shipment of pure cocaine at its finest." Constance wiped her mouth with a napkin from the table.

"Why is everything done on Friday?" Alicia asked.

"Friday is the border patrol's biggest day. They see over a million vehicles from sunup to sundown," Constance explained. "It's an arduous process to be thorough when they're attempting to move line upon line of waiting vehicles."

"I guess that does make sense." Ali shrugged. "So how long does it take the truck to get from the border to us?"

"It takes roughly four days." Constance took a gulp from her water goblet.

"Basically, we can expect the shipment to arrive at least by every Wednesday, right?" Alicia asked, continuing with her line of questioning.

I cleared my throat. "Forgive me if I sound crazy," I interjected, "but for clarity's sake, this isn't the same transportation operation that got everyone arrested, is it?" I was sure these ladies were smart enough not to use the same routine as the one that had got their husbands locked up. Nonetheless, I had to ask.

Ramona laughed heartily. "No, Jane. This is a totally different setup."

I shook my head. "Okay, cool. In that case, let's continue. How much coke am I expected to buy, and how much will it cost me?"

"I sell cocaine only in kilograms, and because I like you"—Constance smiled—"the cost for each kilogram is ten thousand dollars." Although Constance was the one stuffing her mouth with her bread, I was the one who almost choked. Her prices were splendidly low. Most kilograms cost between twenty to twenty-five thousand dollars. Hell, after we cut the coke and added filler, we could easily make a profit of at least sixty thousand dollars.

"Constance, I like your numbers. When can we get started?" I said. I was eagerly anticipating the bankroll that was sure to come. However, I wore my serious face, so that she wouldn't up her price.

"Jane, I'm ready to do business now. Do you have the money?" She pushed her plate aside.

On cue, Alicia excused herself from the table and went to the car to retrieve the "just in case" money we'd brought with us. We had actually anticipated a higher price. Therefore, we had put our money together and had come up with thirty thousand dollars.

After a few minutes Alicia was back with a duffel filled to the brim with neatly banded money stacks. "That's thirty K," I said as I unzipped the bag. Although no one said a word, I could tell they were impressed with the fact that we'd come to play ball.

"Count it, Karla," Constance instructed.

"Come on, Jane. Follow me," Karla said as she stood from the table. I did the same. She led me out of the dining room, down the hallway, to a room with a black door. "Excuse the cigar smell. This is my Nicky's office. No matter what I do, I can't get rid of the odor," she said as she opened the door. We entered the room, and once again, I was amazed. The large room had the exact setup of a room in the movie *Scarface*.

"This is so cool," I observed, in awe of the sleek vintage furniture and the draperies. Karla even had a red runner on the floor and a custom desk and chair.

"Nicky loves Al Pacino." Karla took a seat behind the desk and produced a money counter. I handed over the duffel bag and watched as she stuffed dollars into the machine. Within minutes the screen reflected the sum of thirty thousand dollars.

After finishing our business with the Pauletti ladies and loading three kilos of cocaine into the trunk of my car, we were once again on our way.

"So, what now?" Alicia asked as she put her seat belt on.

"As soon as we get back to the city, I'm going to holler at Chucky and give him first dibs on this shit." I put the car in gear and headed away from the mansion.

"Fuck Chucky!" Alicia spat. "That nigga tried to do us dirty by giving away our spot. He doesn't deserve first dibs on nothing!"

"I completely understand what you're saying, but you get more bees with honey. That nigga has Detroit on lock. If he's down, then all our shit will be in each of his traps, which will make his competition seek us out. Then we'll have even more business." I saw a bigger picture, but Alicia wasn't with it.

"Dude is shady. I still don't think it's a good idea." Ali shook her head. "Think about it. Your father was the king of Detroit. Chucky was his sidekick. He probably wanted what your father had, so he set him up. Next, Ace starts working for the Italians and becomes the man. Then, all of a sudden, he's behind bars. If we go in there telling him about our connection, something bad is going to happen, believe that!"

Chapter Six

Contrary to what Alicia thought, I knew I had to visit Chucky. Though her words and conspiracy theories had given me some doubt, I knew it was the right thing to do. After all, if we were to start supplying everyone with dope in and around the city without informing Chucky, the repercussions could be deadly for us. Ultimately, a move like that would be equivalent to taking food from his mouth. Most people would care less about stepping on the next person's toes, especially in the dope game, but not me. I believed unconditionally in doing good business, which was why I would alert Chucky to not only a new opportunity but to a potential partnership as well.

Since this matter was pressing, I rolled up to his usual bar choice unannounced and went directly to the back. As I suspected, he was bent over in a corner. playing dice.

"Hey, let me holler at you really quick," I said.

"I'll be done in a few. Grab a seat." He never looked up.

"Look, it's about business, and I don't have much time." I was ready to make moves, not sit here and wait on him. Those days were over.

"Speak then," he snapped, completely irritated with my presence.

"I got a connect on some uncut coke for the low-low. I want to plug you in, so can you make time to talk?" I watched him think for a second.

"How low are you talking about?" he finally said.

"I'm talking eighteen thousand a kilogram." I folded my arms and waited on his reaction. Even with the eight grand I had tacked on, the price was lower than what he was accustomed to paying, and I knew it.

Realizing the information I had was more important than the dice game, he stood up. "Where'd you get this connection from?" he asked.

"Come on, blood. You should know me better than that." I laughed, because he knew damn well that I wasn't going to give my connection up to him.

"Nothing personal. I just like to meet the people I do business with," he replied.

"You're doing business with *me*. That's all you need to know."

"How good is the grade?" He motioned for me to follow him over to a booth.

"I could hype this up all day, but I brought a sample for you to see for yourself." I tossed him a small baggie after we both sat down. After carefully reviewing it, he called one of the dice players over to the booth.

"Johnny, come here for a second."

"What's up, Chucky?" Though Johnny wasn't a bad-looking man, the yellowish brown in his eyes and the missing teeth were an indication that Johnny had indeed been through some things in his life.

"Test this for me, will you?" Chucky nonchalantly handed over the baggie, and together, we watched Johnny pour a small line of white powder onto his hand before taking a long sniff.

"Woo!" Johnny blinked rapidly and then coughed a little. "That shit is fire right there, Chucky." His nose started to run; I handed him a napkin from the table. "This is your best batch yet."

Chucky thought quietly for a second, then excused the man from the booth. Once Johnny had walked away,

Chucky had the nerve to ask me with a straight face, "Can you drop the price for family?"

"I'm sure I don't have to remind you that there is no such thing as family when we're doing business! Remember?" Those had been his exact words to me when I first started hustling for him at sixteen.

"Well, let me think on it, and I'll get back with you." He stood from the table with an attitude like he was dismissing me.

"Out of respect, I came to you first, Chucky. If you're not with my deal, then I'm on to the next one! There is no waiting in this game. You should know that." I stood from the table and grabbed my purse.

"Do what you feel you have to do. Just remember, your dope won't get far without my approval. I run this city. Ain't nobody fucking with you unless I say so." He laughed, then waved good-bye as I headed out the door without another word.

I didn't know why Chucky thought he had so much loyalty in these streets. Niggas in the dope game were only loyal to one thing, and that was the almighty dollar. It was time for plan B. After leaving the bar, I called Tyra and told her to close down the operation after she sold the last of what we had. Next, I sent Keisha to pass out one free sample to every dope fiend she laid eyes on. I was sure it was unheard of for dope dealers to pass out free dope. Yet I viewed the complimentary samples as advertising. After they tasted my product and got hooked, they wouldn't ever want to fuck with my competition again. Ultimately, this tactic would mean more money in my pockets. Finally, Alicia and I hit the streets hard to persuade some of the other dealers to join our rising empire.

The first stop I made was to see Dog. His spot was full of niggas playing loud music and hanging out on the porch, as usual.

"What brings you this way, fam?" he asked as he sat on the porch, with his feet inside a kiddie pool, and sipped on a bottle of water. Even though it was sizzling hot today, this Negro looked crazy as hell.

"I came to talk shop with you one-on-one," I told him. I took the vacant seat nearest him and placed the duffel bag on my lap.

"Do Chucky know you here?" Dog looked up and down the block, like we were under surveillance.

"Fuck Chucky!" I stated matter-of-factly. "Now, do you want to talk business or not? Because I got shit to do."

After giving my demand some consideration, he asked his crew to leave. With no time to waste, I got right down to business.

"Recently, I came upon a connection for cocaine. It's top grade, one hundred percent pure from Mexico. Since I'm trying to do things on a grand scale, I'm only selling kilos, and I want to put you down, if you're game."

"Damn. I usually don't fuck with that much weight. Normally, it's only ounces." Dog sat up in his seat.

"It's time to step your game up, fam." I patted the duffel bag. "Those ounces ain't going to do shit but keep you fly for a little while. I don't know about you, but I'm trying to be rich forever."

"If the price is right, then I might be down." He removed the cap from his water and took a gulp.

"I'm selling them for eighteen racks." I watched Dog's eyes widen as he removed his feet from the pool.

"Damn! I pay Chucky more than that for the processed shit."

"Come over to my side and you'll have not only more money in your pocket but a better product too." I watched as he pondered the pros and cons of doing business with me. Dog was a loyal dude, and I respected that. It actually impressed me that he wasn't so quick to turn on Chucky.

"You speak to your uncle on this?"

"Out of respect, I took it to him first, but he passed. So now I'm here. If you pass, I'll be on to the next one. It's just that simple." I shrugged.

"Let's say I do this. What's my take?" He finished the bottle of water.

"There are no splits. Once you buy your package from me at wholesale, you can sell it for however much you want. The profit is all yours."

"Square biz?" He was all ears now.

"Square biz!" I replied. "The way Chucky hustles is old and played out. Splits and all that shit is only going to keep his pockets laced, not ours. I'm trying to get us both paid. You feel me?"

"This sounds good to me, but are you sure you're ready to go toe-to-toe with Chucky? Once he finds out we crossed him, there's gonna be smoke in the city."

"I told you once before that I ain't ever scared, and I meant that shit! What about you? Are you riding with me or what?"

Dog nodded. "Yeah, count me in, J." Then we proceeded to conduct business.

After dealing with Dog, my confidence was so high that Alicia and I decided to conduct several meetings that same day with other dealers under Chucky's umbrella. The majority of the meetings pretty much went in our favor since most of the dealers were down with my prices. However, a small group was afraid of cutting ties with Chucky. Then there were a few of them who just flat-out declined my offer, stating they would never do business with a bitch. I respected the game and their decisions, but this was a decision they would soon regret.

Chapter Seven

News of my connection ripped through the streets of Detroit like a virus. Before I knew it, I was "the man," so to speak. Dealers from all over the Midwest and Canada began hitting me up for the goods. Within a year, we expanded the operation to Atlanta, Miami, and Los Angeles. The crew was bigger and stronger than ever, which amazed the Pauletti women on many levels. We were moving so much weight, they had to expand their delivery schedules in order to keep up with the demand.

Overnight, my crew became celebrities. Everywhere we went, people took notice. For fear of attracting the Feds, I didn't like all the attention. Yet Ali didn't mind it one bit. In her opinion, as long as we weren't caught with our hand in the cookie jar, there would be no harm and no foul. I knew better, but there was nothing I could do about it. My crew had made over 3.2 million dollars in a year's time. Everyone upgraded their whip as well as their address. I purchased a home in West Bloomfield; Alicia purchased a condo with Keisha. Tyra even managed to convince Tamia to join the squad as our accountant on a full-time basis. The first thing Tamia showed us was how to invest our money—the legit way. For doing so, we paid her well.

I invested in a chain of clothing stores in each city I trapped in. That way I could explain frequent trips and my paper trail, if it ever came down to it. The retail stores I owned were called Capa Donna and were set up in malls.

In Italian families, the word *capo* was used to describe the head of a crime family. The word *don* referred to a high-society man with money and power. Since I was not a man, I rolled with the female version of each word. If, for any reason, I was ever audited, my bank accounts were all linked to that business. Alicia chose to invest in a record company that would produce only some of the best female entertainers in the game. The company was called Grade A Entertainment, and she already had ten clients.

Money was pouring in at such an impressive rate that we were about to need dump trucks just to transport it. In my mind, things could only get better from here. Boy, was I wrong, and tonight was the reality check I needed.

"Oh shit! We've got the AFM in the building!" the disc jockey announced as we walked into Club Haze in Southfield. People began to stare at us and point. A few of them even raised their drinks in a toast.

"Who in the hell is the AFM?" I asked Alicia, who was in front of me. Tonight she had invited everyone out to celebrate the success of one of her artists, who had a single playing on the radio. Typically, the club scene wasn't for me. However, Gran had offered to watch Ju because I hadn't been out in a while, and I had agreed to go.

"It means the All Female Mafia," she yelled over the music.

I didn't know where he had gotten the name from, but it was kind of catchy. I liked it. Back in the day, Detroit had seen its fair share of drug dealers. The most memorable names were the infamous YBI, or the Young Boys Incorporated, as well as the BMF, better known as the Black Mafia Family. Those men mastered the game at different levels. It may sound crazy, but I was proud to be on the list. Never had a female-run organization been able to do what we did. This was only the beginning.

"This place is the truth," Tamia said in my ear.

I nodded in agreement. The club was packed with people dressed to the nines. The disc jockey was bumping the jams. Our bottle service kept the bottles of Cîroc and Grey Goose on deck. The funny thing about it was none of us were old enough to drink. Most of us were just a few months shy of our twenty-first birthday. All the same, when you had money, people did whatever you asked in hopes that you would look out for them. Favoritism was something I was learning to love when it came to being a hood celebrity.

"Yo, J, ain't that Chucky over there? What's his old ass doing up in the club?" Alicia laughed and then beckoned the waitress. When the waitress reached our table, Alicia said, "Here's five hundred dollars. Send that old nigga in the Kangol hat the best bottle of champagne you have in the building."

I stood. "No, please don't send that bottle," I told the waitress.

"Sweetheart, don't listen to her. Take this money and get his ass the most extravagant bottle you have at the bar," Ali said, slurring. She was already lit, and we hadn't been here for even an hour. "Keep this hundred for your trouble." She slapped the girl's butt. Keisha saw her do it but didn't say anything.

"Girl, why are you starting shit?" I yelled at Ali. I hadn't seen Chucky since he refused my deal. Presently, there was no bad blood between us, and I wanted to keep it that way.

"That nigga will be all right," she said, brushing me off. Then she went back to slow grinding on Keisha. I sat back in the cut and watched Chucky with a side-eye, wondering how he was going to react to Alicia's gift. If he accepted it, I knew we were cool. Unfortunately, if he sent it back, then we had problems.

"Grab your glass, Jane," Tyra said. Then she held hers up, along with everyone else, while Alicia's drunken ass made a toast.

"To the AFM, and fuck everybody else!" Alicia said, slurring.

With the exception of me, the entire crew repeated her toast. I was too busy trying to see what Chucky was going to do about the bottle of champagne. Unfortunately, I had lost sight of him in the dark room full of people. Maybe he left, I thought. I relaxed a bit and sipped from the glass. Usually, I wasn't a drinker. I didn't like being in an altered state of mind, but tonight was indeed a celebration. Besides, I needed to take my mind off of Ace. He was still behind bars, but Richard had assured me he would be home soon.

Keisha came over to where I was sitting. "What's wrong?" she said.

"I miss Ace, that's all." I offered her a smile, although it wasn't authentic. My man had been gone for sixteen months . . . too long. Every day he was missing out on Ju's big moments, which caused me to be despondent.

"He'll be home soon. His lawyer said it was looking good for him, right?"

"Well, yeah, he did say that, but they still haven't set a trial date." As we conversed, I noticed Chucky enter our VIP area and then head in my direction. My stomach hit the ground, but my game face remained unchanged. "Keisha, give me a minute please," I said, excusing her, and then I motioned for Chucky to take a seat. Back in the day, I would've stood to greet him. Except he no longer deserved that kind of respect.

"Look at you, all grown up, sending bottles and shit. What's this all about?" He was offended. "Are you trying to make me look bad or something?" Chucky placed the bottle of Ace of Spades on top of the cocktail table before me.

"First off, I didn't send the bottle. Nevertheless, it was sent as a peace offering." I grabbed the bottle and poured myself a glass. There was no need to let a good bottle go to waste.

"A peace offering for what? I didn't know there was an issue." He was mind fucking me, and I knew it.

"Look, Chucky, we just came here to have a good time. Sorry if the bottle offended you, but it really was intended to be a generous gesture."

"Well, I won't stop your good time. I just came over here to return the bottle and to give you a piece of advice." His smile made my skin crawl.

"And what piece of advice is that?" I sincerely wanted to hear what he had to say.

With a smug grin, he leaned down close to my ear and said, "Watch your back, little girl."

"What's that supposed to mean?"

"It means you may think that just because you've won the battle, the war is over, but not so. The streets are always watching." With those words, he excused himself from our region and vanished into the crowd of people on the dance floor. To say his words had me feeling some sort of way would be an understatement.

"What was that all about?" Ali asked as she wrapped her arm around my neck.

"Chucky didn't like your gift." I sipped from my glass. I wanted to tell the bitch I'd told her so, but it wouldn't matter. She was too drunk to pay attention.

"Fuck that old nigga! He's just mad because we're young boss bitches," Alicia declared. Then she turned her attention back to the crowd and went back to partying, leaving me in the corner, contemplating how to clean up this mess.

Thankfully, the night passed quickly, and before long it was time to go home. Outside the club, there was a line for valet parking. We waited good-naturedly, along with a few other partygoers.

"Baby, I love you so much." Keisha wrapped her arms around Alicia from the back and kissed her neck.

"I love you more, with your fine ass." Alicia palmed Keisha's ass like a basketball.

"Why don't you bitches get a room?" I teased.

"Yeah, don't nobody want to see that shit!" Tyra added, then cracked up laughing.

Alicia flipped us both the bird.

At last, one of the valets pulled my car up in front of the door. I tossed my girls the deuces and went to retrieve my ride. As I made it around to the driver's side, I heard the sound of screeching tires and then gunfire. Having no other choice, I dropped to the ground and lay flat. I heard screaming and saw everyone dispersing in one direction or another. The barrage of bullets appeared to go on forever. The moment it stopped, I was back on my feet, trying to make heads or tails of what had just occurred.

"She's been hit!" I heard someone say, so I checked myself for wounds, but there weren't any. "Call nine-one-one. She's been hit!"

This time I looked around to see who was hurt and to determine if there was anything I could do to help. My heart skipped three beats when I looked over and saw that Alicia's clothes were saturated with deep red blood. She was cradling Keisha like a baby. I knew this was bad. Leaving my car keys and purse right on the ground where I'd dropped them, I raced toward my friends.

"She can't die, J. Please make the bleeding stop," Alicia said as she looked up at me. Then she cried uncontrollably as she rocked her girlfriend. Looking down at Keisha, I knew there was nothing I could do. Only God could change this outcome.

Tyra kneeled down beside them with a cell phone glued to her ear. "Hold on, Keisha. The ambulance is on the way," she said.

"Baby, please don't die," Alicia whispered as she relentlessly rocked back and forth. "I love you, Keisha. Don't do this to me."

It broke my heart to watch this scene unfold. Alicia was a mess, and Keisha had already started to make that final transition. Her body had begun to shiver, her lips were practically blue, and her eyes kept rolling to the back of her head. We all heard the sirens approaching from a few blocks away. Even so, everyone knew it was too late. And then Keisha was gone in a flash. She died in Alicia's arms, with her eyes wide open. While Ali was rocking her lifeless body, I reached down and closed Keisha's eyes.

"We promised each other forever, J, so she can't be dead." Alicia cried huge tears.

"Baby, I'm so sorry, but she's gone," I told her. Sniffing back my own tears, I tried to be strong for my friend. This disaster was definitely a hit below the belt. The person responsible had taken one of our own. For that, this shit had to be rectified pronto.

Chapter Eight

Within an hour Club Haze was full of police, which made me uncomfortable. I had wanted to pull off before they got there, but Alicia had refused to leave Keisha. I had told the crew to get lost, but I had hung around to be there for my friend.

Alicia screamed and hollered like I'd never heard her do before when the coroner came to collect Keisha's body. The way she broke down caused my heart to hurt bad. I knew it would take a miracle for Ali to bounce back from this, if she even could. While I consoled Alicia, two men approached us.

"Hello. My name is Detective Price, and this is partner, Detective Walker," the taller one said. "We will be the detectives handling the case of your friend." He produced a business card. "Can we go to the station to ask you both a few questions?"

Alicia didn't take the card, so I did. "Detective, anything you want to ask us, you can do so right here." I wasn't going to the station, and that was that.

"Is there any reason someone would want Keisha dead?" Detective Price asked.

"No." I shook my head.

"Do you know who was shooting? Maybe one of you or someone else in your group was the target?" Detective Walker asked. Then he waited patiently for a response, with his pen ready to write the answers down in his notebook.

"What makes you think that my group was being shot at?" I raised a brow. It was now my turn to wait on a response.

"Well, Ms. Doesher, word circling among the other witnesses we've spoken to tonight is that you are a major player on the drug scene."

"Detective, I don't have a clue what you're talking about, and quite frankly, neither do you. I am a well-respected business owner. If you just check my background, as I'm sure you will, you'll find nothing drug related. Now, if you'll excuse me, I need to get my friend home." I reached in my purse and pulled out a business card of my own. "Call me if and when you find out who murdered Keisha."

Once we were inside my car, Alicia broke down again. It was so bad that she even had to roll the window down a few times and stick her head out to throw up. I knew my car would need extensive cleaning in the morning, but right now I wasn't concerned.

I pulled out of the parking lot and took off. We drove in silence, both of us lost in our thoughts.

"Where are you going?" Alicia asked after noticing that I had driven past her exit and was continuing toward my house.

"You don't need to be alone. Please come and stay with Ju and me."

"No. Turn around and take me home."

"Ali." I looked over at her with a sympathetic expression.

"Janie, I'm fucking serious. Take me home now!" She slapped her hand down on my dashboard.

"Why do you want to go back there? It won't be good for you."

"Janie, I'm going to ask you one last time. Please take me home, or I will jump out of this car and walk there."

Without any further argument, I took the next exit and turned the car around and headed back toward Alicia's place. I thought I knew what was best for her, but maybe I didn't. Everybody grieved in their own way, so I had no choice but to let my friend grieve in hers.

The days following Keisha's death were unnerving. My entire crew was on edge. And Alicia went silent. Days turned into a week and I still hadn't heard from her. I burned several tanks of gas going back and forth to her condo. She was either not at home or was refusing to answer the door. Both possibilities pissed me off, because I was worried that something had happened to her as well.

This morning I left Ju with Gran and drove over to Alicia's condo. Everything looked the same as it had yesterday. After stepping out of the car, I picked up a soggy newspaper from the sidewalk that had been drenched by rain and carried it up to the door.

I knocked and yelled, "Alicia, please open the door." When she didn't answer, I banged on the door and then rang the doorbell a few times. Next, I walked over to the window, tapped lightly, and called, "Ali, please, girl, come to door and let me know that you are okay."

For nearly thirty minutes I went back and forth, banging on the door and then ringing the doorbell, but there was nothing. I would've blown the locks off of that bitch and barged inside, but I wanted to respect her space. "I hope I'll see you later. I love you," I hollered, giving up.

Checking the time on my watch, I noted that Keisha's funeral would be starting in less than an hour, so I left the condo and flew over to the church. I knew if Ali didn't show up there, then I would have no choice but to put out an all-points bulletin for her.

Upon arriving at Bread of Christ Baptist Church, located on Wyoming, I parked in the first empty spot I could find, then gathered my composure before I headed inside. I didn't know what to expect, and I wasn't sure how I would feel seeing my girl laid out in a casket, but it was what was, and I had no choice.

Keisha's cousin Brandy walked over to hug me as I entered the sanctuary. "Thank you so much for coming, Janelle." Through my triple black Oakley shades, I couldn't help but stare at the skintight minidress Brandy had on. She was dressed more for the club than for a funeral.

"I wouldn't have missed it for the world."

"Is Alicia with you?" she asked as she looked behind me. "I haven't heard from her since Keisha died. I just wanted to make sure she was okay."

"Neither have I, but I'm sure she'll be here." I grabbed an obituary from the table along the back wall and proceeded into the viewing area. From a distance, I could see Keisha in a yellow suit, surrounded by yellow and white roses. Keisha was very popular and loved by many people. Although the place was small, it was filled to the brim with nearly one hundred people. At first glance, all the seats were taken. Then I spotted Tyra and Tamia waving me over.

"Girl, we got here early to save you and Alicia a spot," Tamia told me when I got to their row. She slid down so I could scoot in.

"Where's Ju?" Tyra asked.

"With Gran. I couldn't have her crying and disrupting the service," I responded as I took a seat. Then I opened the obituary and began to read about Keisha's life.

"The question should have been, Where's Alicia?" Tamia whispered just as the service was beginning.

I shrugged and then turned my attention toward the processional of family members going to view the body.

We were in the third row; I could see just fine from my seat. I preferred to remember Keisha the way she was. Therefore, I didn't want to see her up close and personal in that casket.

As the minister delivered his sermon on life and death, I periodically scanned the room for Alicia. She was still missing in action. A few people got up to say kind words about the way Keisha had always had an eye for fashion and about the fact that to know her was to love her. "Keisha could always make a friend out of an enemy with just her smile," someone remarked.

This caused me to wipe a few tears from my eyes, because it made me think of how she and Ali had hated each other in the beginning and then, out of nowhere, they had become lovebirds.

The family had decided to leave the casket open for the entire funeral, which was a bit much for me, because I didn't like seeing my girl that way. Though she looked damn good and appeared only to be sleeping, the sight of her was still a reminder that this was it for her. There would be no more tomorrows.

"Damn. My girl had her whole life in front of her. She didn't have to go out like that," I said, sniffing, and Tyra patted my back.

"She's in a better place, Jane," Tamia noted, which got me thinking about my own mother and father. I knew they were good people who did bad things, just like Keisha. Did heaven still have a spot for them? I didn't have time to dwell on that for long, since the minister soon announced the final viewing of the body. As I contemplated mustering the nerve to go up to see Keisha, my heart sank when I noticed Alicia standing in the aisle.

Time went in slow motion as she stood there, frozen. Everyone else had noticed her too, but no one had approached her. I watched as the tears began falling down her cheeks, and then she dropped to her knees. Instantly, I was out of my seat and consoling my friend.

"Why did she have to die, Jane?" she asked and looked up at me with eyes that needed an explanation. I felt horrible for Ali as I pulled her up from the floor and ushered her toward the back of the church.

"Keisha, I will get that nigga for you, baby. I promise!" she screamed for all to hear.

"You did this to her!" Keisha's aunt Eileen shouted. "You have no right to be here! You did this."

"I didn't mean for this to happen," Alicia responded, but this wasn't the time or the place for explanations. Forcefully, I, along with Tyra and Tamia, removed Alicia from the church before emotions rose any higher and things got out of hand. We put her in my car, and I got behind the wheel and then sped away. Tyra and Tamia followed behind us in their car.

After the funeral, I called an emergency meeting at my house that same afternoon.

The murder of Keisha had undoubtedly started a war between my squad and Chucky's crew. Alicia was in beast mode, and I could do nothing to tame her.

"So, what are we gonna do, Jane?" She paced my kitchen floor. "Somebody's going pay for this shit, no lie!"

"It's your call, fam. Whatever you decide, I'm riding with you."

"I say we hit that nigga in his pockets," Tyra said from her seat at the marble kitchen table.

"Fuck his pockets. After what he did to Keisha, I want that man dead!" Alicia slapped the counter, which caused Juliana to cry. She was sitting next to me in her high chair, so I picked her up and rocked her gently.

"Since they know we're coming for Chucky, he'll be under heavy protection for a while. I say we go after his crew one by one, until he's all alone and has no one to protect him," I commented. I handed Ju a Cheetos Puff and watched her chew with four little teeth the size of cooked rice.

"I'm with that! Let's brainstorm and make this shit happen." Alicia rubbed her bloodshot eyes. Poor thing probably hadn't slept in days.

For hours, we plotted about Chucky's crew and strategically calculated every move needed to make this shit successful. Our goal was to target his right-hand man, Neal; his son, Vito; and eventually, Chucky himself. Frankly, I was apprehensive to some extent about what was getting ready to go down. The odds were that beefing with someone as big as Chucky wouldn't work out in the underdog's favor. Nevertheless, for Alicia, I would go to hell with gasoline panties on. She had had my back on more occasions than I could remember. At this juncture, it was time for me to have hers. I just hoped we didn't mess up!

Chapter Nine

Much to Alicia's dismay, I had had second thoughts and had decided to put off the hit on Chucky for almost a month. Although our hearts had told us the time to avenge Keisha was right then, my head had told me to wait. They were probably expecting us to try something, and I knew if we acted to soon, it would end up being our own funerals instead of theirs. Alicia hadn't been speaking to me, and I had respected her decision and, therefore, had stayed out of her way. However, today was the day we'd been waiting for.

With a smile, I knocked on Alicia's door. She didn't answer. I heard the television and smelled something cooking, so I knew she was home. "Can I talk to you for a minute please?" I hollered through the door. Seconds later it opened. Ali stood there with looks that could kill, but I paid her no attention and sauntered into the home like I owned it.

"I don't recall inviting you in." She smacked her lips.

"Listen, I don't have time to play games." After flopping down on the couch, I grabbed the remote control and paused the television. "I came to talk to you about Keisha, so please close the door."

"I ain't got shit to say to you about Keisha until the plans we discussed about the motherfucker who took her from me are in play!"

"Tonight is the night we make that happen." I watched as her eyes lit up like a Christmas tree.

"What's the plan?" Eagerly, she closed the door and took a seat on the recliner across from me.

"First, let me start with I'm sorry for making you feel like I put your feelings and Keisha's death on the back burner. I also want to thank you from the bottom of my heart for not moving in on Chucky in spite of me. As the leaders of this organization, we have to think with level heads and play smarter than the opposition gives us credit for. The minute we would've tried to come for Chucky, he would've picked us off one by one, until there was no one left, and you know it."

"You're right. I see that now, but in the heat of the moment, it was what it was. I was ready to die anyway!"

"Facts." I nodded my understanding. It was hard enough losing Ace to the system. I wouldn't know what to do if I ever lost him for good.

"So, what's the plan?"

"First on our list is going to be Neal. I heard through the grapevine, he has a thing for junkies. I'm going to use that to my advantage and kill him when he least expects it. While I'm doing that, you'll be following Vito. On Thursday he usually runs errands to the bank and the grocery stores solo. As soon as he stops in a good location and is stationary for a while, I'll meet up with you, and we'll take him down. After that, we'll get Chucky." While speaking, I laid out all the surveillance pictures I'd acquired, as well as the keys to rental cars we'd be using for the day.

"Is it just me and you?" Alicia looked at me nervously.

"Yeah, it's just us. The fewer people involved, the better."

"J, I really appreciate you rocking with me like this." Alicia began to blink back tears. I wasn't in a crying mood today; therefore, I stood from the couch and walked the short distance to the bar caddy in the corner. After picking up the almost empty bottle of Don Julio, I grabbed two cups and poured shots. Then I walked back over to Ali and handed her one.

"To Keisha!"

"To Keisha!" Ali repeated, and together we downed the alcohol.

It was go time, and I was war ready.

Five hours later I pulled up to the mint-green house on Clairmount Street and blew the horn on my stolen old-school Camry. Patiently, I waited for someone to come out.

"Fuck you blowing the horn for? Get out of the car like the rest of the crackheads and knock on the side door," some nappy-headed little boy yelled from the porch.

I rolled the tinted passenger window down halfway and yelled back, "Tell Neal to come here really quick." The wig on my head and my sunglasses concealed my identity, for the most part.

"He doesn't come to dope fiends. Fiends come to him." The boy pulled a blunt out from behind his ear and lit it.

"Tell him it's Candy, and I need to make an arrangement, if you catch my drift." While doing my research on Neal, I had discovered he had to be one of the dumbest dope dealers on the planet. With his reputation for accepting head or sex from crackheads in exchange for crack, I knew he'd be an easy target. How in the hell Chucky saw fit to have him be his right-hand man was beyond me.

"Yeah, all right. Let me go get him." The boy knew what the deal was.

I smiled inwardly, because this plan was about to be executed beautifully. Just like clockwork, Neal was on the porch, with a smile on his face as big as Texas. Too bad for him it would be the last smile he'd ever have.

"Come inside," he yelled, but I stayed in the car. He motioned, but I didn't move. "Yo, Candy, come inside." I still didn't move. So he stepped off the porch and headed in my direction. That was when I rolled the window down completely and fired all seventeen shots from my nine millimeter at his bitch ass.

Pow! Pow!

As each bullet pierced his flesh, his body flew backward a little, until it landed on the porch. I didn't stick around to see his boys emerge from the house. It was on to the next location.

Quickly, I drove to a back alley ten miles away from the scene and pulled in. Then I jumped out of the car, grabbed the gas can from the trunk, and poured gas all over the Camry. Next, I struck a match and set the vehicle ablaze. Once I was satisfied with the fire, I ran down the alley to the awaiting Nissan I'd parked there earlier. Burning rubber, I sped away from the alley like my life depended on it. "Whew!" I hit the steering wheel, feeling such a rush. On cue, my burner phone started vibrating. It was Alicia. I answered in code.

"One down. Two to go."

"Any onlookers?" she asked, wanting to know about potential witnesses.

"Nope."

"Okay, cool. I'm following this other fool now. It looks like he's turning into a park or something. Is that a normal stop on the errand run?"

"No. I don't know what that's about. Do you think he made you?"

"No, not at all." She sounded confident.

"All right, cool. Let's keep it that way. Fall back just a little." I didn't want her to blow our mission in her haste to get at him.

"I got this!" she snapped, and I knew to leave her alone. "We're at Thomas Park. See you when you get here." She ended the call, and I plugged the location into the car's navigation system.

When I got to the park, Alicia was waiting near the entrance. Casually, she got out of her rented car, then got in mine. We drove through the large public park in search of Vito.

"This place is packed," I noted.

"Yeah, it looks like they've got a few games going on today."

"I wonder why he's here," I said before noticing his car parked near a fence. We pulled into a parking spot five cars away from his. The parking lot was semi full, and he was talking on the phone. I doubted he saw us. "I wonder who he's waiting on."

"With any luck, it's Chucky. Then we can kill two birds with one stone." Alicia patted the gun on her lap, with a crazed look in her eyes.

A few minutes into our surveillance, a blue Porsche truck pulled up beside Vito. Alicia clutched her gun. "I bet that's him. The minute these fools get out, I'm blasting," she said. She rolled down her window, and I knew there was no turning back. In order to make a speedy getaway, I put the car in gear. Never before had I pulled a stunt like this in broad daylight at a park, but there was a first time for everything.

With a frown, Vito stepped from his automobile and exchanged words with the driver of the second vehicle. We couldn't see who he was talking to, but the conversation was definitely heated. Then it seemed as if Vito looked right into our car before hurriedly moving toward the back door of the Porsche. I didn't know if he was getting a gun or running for cover.

"I think he saw us," I said, then reversed the car. On cue, Alicia lifted her weapon and fired multiple shots out the window in his direction.

Pow! Pow!

A young woman jumped from the driver's seat of the Porsche, letting out bloodcurdling screams. I screamed as well as I processed what was happening. In reality, Vito wasn't even thinking about us; he was only getting his son from the backseat of his baby mother's car. I watched in horror as bullets pierced both Vito and the child in several places. My heart begged me to stop the car and assist the little boy. Yet my instincts said to get the fuck out of Dodge, so that was exactly what I did.

Chapter Ten

We had barely escaped the scene without incident. A small mob of T-ball parents had even followed us all the way out of the park. They had attempted to take down our license plate number and snap pictures of our faces. Thankfully, my rental car had tinted windows, and it was registered to a dummy name on one of my fake ID cards. Ali and I both were shaken up. We knew the shit was about to hit the fan. Not only had we taken out Chucky's son, but we had also killed his innocent grandson. It was time for us to leave the D and lay low for a minute.

The very next morning, in an attempt to escape the madness, I packed Ju a diaper bag and headed to the airport with Ali.

"Where are you going?" I asked her as we both waited our turn at the ticket counter.

"I'm going to Cali. I promised to take Keisha one day, so it feels right to head there." She paused. "You and Ju should come too."

"Sorry, Ali. Cali isn't for me."

"What now, Jane? Will I ever see you again?" Alicia's eyes were moist with tears.

"Of course we'll see each other again. Just go to Cali, lay low for a while, and try to reinvent yourself. Stay out of trouble and check in with me daily. After some time passes, we'll discuss our next move." It was my turn at the counter. "I love you, Ali. You better take care of yourself, okay?"

"I love you, Jane, and you better do the same." Ali bent down to kiss Ju and then headed toward the other counter that had just opened up.

"I'll see you on the other side," I called over my shoulder.

"Yup, on the other side," she hollered back.

After purchasing my ticket, I hopped on the first Southwest plane to Atlanta, Georgia. I'd purchased a house there several months ago for the times I flew in to check on my businesses. During the flight, I was so visibly shaken that two flight attendants asked me if I was okay. Once we landed, I grabbed my things and rented a car to drive to my house. Thankfully, it was located in a gated subdivision in Alpharetta, Georgia, a suburb of Atlanta.

After pulling the car into the driveway, I grabbed my things and took Julianna inside. She immediately began playing with some toys I had left at the house the last time we were there. While she was playing, I went around the house, making sure that every door and window was locked. As I went, I thought about Vito's dead son. It had never been my objective to have an innocent child get caught up in our cross fire. Sadly, though, there was no take backs or redos when it came to death. All I could do now was ask for forgiveness for my sins. I took a seat on the sofa. I didn't quite know how to pray, so I called Gran.

"Praise the Lord," she answered in her usual manner.

"Hey, Gran." I tried to sound normal, but it was useless, as my voice trembled. My heart was terribly consumed with guilt.

"Janelle, baby, what's the matter?"

"Gran, I'm in trouble! Can you pray for me please?" I didn't know what else to say. For the first time in I didn't know how long, I was frightened beyond belief. Not only did I have to look out for myself, but I had to guard Ju as well. Just the thought of someone harming her in the manner we had massacred that defenseless child yesterday left me with bubble guts.

"What's the matter? Is my great-grandbaby okay?"

"Yes, ma'am, she's fine." I sniffed, completely broken and distraught. "I'm in trouble, and I need you to pray for me right now," I cried.

"Okay, baby. Do you know the Lord's Prayer?" she asked calmly.

"No, ma'am, I don't." It was funny that I had learned how to hustle, grind, steal, and even kill from everyone around me. Yet no one had ever taught me how to pray.

"Close your eyes, granddaughter, bow your head, and then repeat after me." Gran spoke softly and reassuringly. "Our Father, which art in heaven, hallowed be thy name. Thy kingdom come. Thy will be done in earth, as it is in heaven. Give us this day our daily bread. And forgive us our debts, as we forgive our debtors. And lead us not into temptation, but deliver us from evil . . ."

I gripped the phone tightly and allowed my tears to flow as my grandmother prayed for my forgiveness. Ordinarily, I hated to hear her preach, but today I needed those words. Maybe it was only in my head, but for the first time in my life, I actually felt a sensation in my body that I couldn't explain. I ended the call with Gran and knew exactly what I needed to do. It was time to walk away from the hustle game, change my surroundings, as well as my identity. I no longer wanted to be a hustler or a killer. All I wanted to be was an excellent mother to my daughter and wife to Ace. People were getting killed left and right; I couldn't handle one more funeral. My heart was heavy with grief, and my mind was no longer in the game. I picked up the phone to call Ali and inform her of my decision, but just then there was a knock at the door.

After placing my phone back down on the table, I grabbed a gun that I'd stashed inside of a vase in the living room, then went to the door quietly and peeked through the peephole. Had they come for me already? My heart raced as I wondered how the hell they found me so fast, and how the hell they had got past security at the entrance. However, when I saw Alicia standing there on my porch through the peephole, I relaxed.

I swung the door open with the gun still in my hand. "What are you doing here? I thought you went to Cali."

"I changed my mind and came here instead." She shrugged. "Anyway, that shit would be no fun without you and Keisha." Alicia looked past me and into my living room. "Plus, I would've missed Ju too much." She barged into the four-bedroom ranch-style home and reached for Ju, who was crawling around on the floor. "Auntie wants to take you shopping for toys. Do you want to go to the mall?" Ali got down on the floor, and Ju started clapping. "Come on, Jane. Let's roll up to Lenox Square." She picked Juliana up and kissed her forehead.

"How in the hell can you go shopping at the mall at a time like this?" I frowned. I didn't feel much like going anywhere today.

"We need to take our mind off that shit. Staying cooped up in the house will drive us crazy."

"Do you know what we did?" I looked at her sideways.

"Yeah, we did what we had to do. I'm sorry that the little boy got mixed up in his granddaddy's shit, but fuck it. Chucky took Keisha from us first, remember that."

Alicia was right, but I still didn't feel good about the situation. I knew we had different views on the matter because I was a mother and she wasn't. However, instead of going back and forth with her, I decided to oblige her request to go to the mall. Besides, I could use some new things for the house, since we'd be there for a while.

Chapter Eleven

The second I stepped from the crib, I sensed we had just made a terrible mistake. And the feeling stayed with me. There was something about the way a gray Ford Taurus followed behind us for the whole drive to the mall, and the way I kept seeing the same two men in almost every store we shopped in, even Bath & Body Works. I shared my thoughts with Alicia, but of course she blew me off. Her rationale was that no one knew we'd flown to Georgia, not even Gran or the crew. She was right, so I brushed the bad vibe off. Besides, my gun was outside in my car, and therefore, the safest place for us right now was in the crowded mall—or so I thought.

"J, are you good?" Ali waved her hand in front of my face. We were sitting in one of the booths inside the food court.

"Yeah, I'm good. Sorry. I was just thinking about this issue with Chucky, that's all. We need to eliminate his ass as soon as possible." I hated having loose ends. I surveyed the area, just in case.

"Don't worry about that nigga, J. After a while, this will all blow over, and when it does, we're gonna handle it."

"That's the thing . . . I don't know how to handle it, Alicia. We killed a child, for goodness' sake," I whispered. "If the roles were reversed, that could've been Ju."

"Jane, it was a mistake, and I'm tired of talking about it." She sipped from the Starbucks cup. "You did the right thing by flying here and getting Ju out of the D. I think you should bring Gran out here to help you care for Ju, so we can get back to Detroit and finish what we started."

"Ali, I don't know about that, especially right now. Detroit is probably a war zone right now."

"Fuck that. We came too far to pump the brakes now!" Alicia hit the table.

"I'm not saying forever. Just for a little while," I tried to explain. Alicia and I rarely had opposing views, but this issue with Chucky was a sore spot in our relationship. She was all gas, no brakes, because she had nothing to lose. I, on the other hand, wanted to live to fight another day, because I had everything to lose.

"Kill or be killed! This is the lifestyle we chose. So fuck the waiting. I'm ready to get to the action."

"Speaking of the lifestyle, I was just about to call you before you knocked on the door today." Not wanting to upset my friend or let her down, I paused before delivering the bad news. "Alicia, I think it's time for me to done with this life." I looked over at Juliana, who was in the stroller and was holding her bottle upside down, causing milk to drip into a puddle. "Stop, little girl." I removed the bottle from her clutches. She started to throw a tantrum. Therefore, I picked her up and placed her in my lap.

"What?" Alicia shook her head in disbelief. "You mean to tell me you want to give up everything we have? Shit, we're just getting started. There's so much more ground to cover. By the time we hit twenty-five, we could be multimillionaires." Alicia was dreaming if she thought money was worth sacrificing the lives of my family.

"Ali, when I first set out to do this, I never predicted it would turn out this way." To keep Juliana from pulling my earring, I shook my head at Alicia.

"What about the Pauletti family? Do you think they'll let us out of our business deal after all the money we made last year? I don't think so."

"I'll figure something out, but right now I can't worry about it." I stood and grabbed my garbage from the table.

"So, you just gone up and quit on me, J? Without Keisha, all I have is you and our hustle!" She was heated. I understood her frustration. In spite of that, you had to know when to hold and when to fold in this game. We had made enough money to be comfortable for quite some time, and thanks to Keisha, we had not only lucrative but also legitimate businesses. What else could you ask for?

"Alicia, just trust me on this." I ignored the roll of her eyes and walked over to the trash bin to discard my leftovers.

Juliana was on my hip, wiggling wildly. I suspected she was trying to get down. "Ju, are you ready to walk?" I smiled and placed her down on the shiny floor. At home, she was constantly pulling up on the furniture and standing still. She had yet to take one single step. Yet I was positive she would be walking soon. "Come on, Ju. Come to Mommy." I kneeled down in front of her and flung my arms open wide. My daughter stood there, smiling widely, with a slobbery mouth, flexing her small teeth. "Come on, Ju." I waved my hands, and she started clapping.

"Ju, walk to Auntie," Alicia chimed in from the table.

"Ali, can you record this, so Ace can see it?" As I turned around to face her, there were two masked men with machine guns approaching the food court. I tried to speak. However, my words were trapped inside my throat. All I could do was grab my daughter and attempt to take cover.

Chapter Twelve

Shots rang out, and people starting screamed for dear life. I watched in horror as parents snatched up their children and tried like hell to protect them. Senior citizens moved as fast as they could for cover. Some of them weren't fast enough. One elderly man was caught in the cross fire before he could roll away in his wheelchair. Clutching Juliana for dear life, I crawled to the other side of the trash bin. It wasn't an ideal hiding spot, but it was the best I could do in such an exposed space. The loud noise made Ju cry; I rocked her slightly. Glancing from side to side, I tried to find Ali and locate the gunmen, but I couldn't see shit except for people lying on the floor. "Fuck!" I mumbled. Chucky had changed the game by pulling a stunt like this. If I made it out of this situation alive, he would most definitely feel my wrath.

"Jane Doe! Where you at, bitch?" one of the men yelled.

My heart sank to my knees.

"Come out, come out, wherever you are," the other man taunted.

They sounded very close; I began to panic. *Should I continue hiding and let the scene play out, or should I stand and face the music?*

"Let's make a deal. If you come out now, I'll make it quick and easy," said the second man who had spoken. He laughed. I pressed my back firmer into the trash bin, as if it could somehow swallow Ju and me and make us invisible. Silently, I prayed for a miracle. However, I didn't foresee this concluding in my favor.

"Oh shit! Look at who I found," I heard the first man say as the sound of a table slid across the floor. "We got your partner now, Jane. Are you going to come out and save her?"

"I don't know what you're talking about." Alicia's voice was unsteady; I knew she was scared. "Jane ain't nowhere in this mall."

"Bitch, shut up!" I believed the man must've hit her, because I heard her yell out in pain.

"Jane, you've got five seconds to come out, or your girl is dead!" His voice was deep and firm. Therefore, I decided this was no idle threat. "Five. Four."

I took one last look at my daughter and regretted the life I had chosen for her. In a matter of minutes, I would be dead, and her father would still be in prison. Juliana would end up an orphan. It saddened me; she didn't deserve the hand she was dealt. With one last kiss to my baby girl's forehead, I sat her down on the floor and rose to my feet with my hands in the air. "All right. Let her go. You got me."

"So, you're the bitch that's causing all this trouble?" the first man said.

"I guess I am." I shrugged.

"Any last words before I send you on your way?" the second gunman asked, like this was a scene in a movie.

"You said you would let her go, so release her."

"I lied." He snickered while raising the gun to Alicia's head.

"No! Please don't," I begged and felt my bowels loosen.

"Don't worry about me. I'll see you on the other side, J." I could see the tears fall from Alicia's eyes as she pressed her head against the barrel of the gun. "Do it, nigga!"

"See you on the other side," I whispered as my own tears streamed down my face.

Before the man could pull the trigger, something or someone captured his attention. I looked over to see Ju crawling from behind the trash bin directly toward us. The first gunman, who was closest to me, walked over to her. Instantly, I lost it.

"Hell, no, muthafucka! Not my daughter!"

"Bitch, after what happened to Vito and his son, Chucky said ain't nobody safe!" He raised his weapon like the cold-blooded killer he was. I made a mad dash toward my daughter.

Pop! Pop! Pop!

I dove on top of Juliana like a football player trying to recover a fumbled ball. She hit her head slightly, but I took the brunt of the fall. As we tumbled on the floor, I felt fire rip through my body. I'd been hit. It took every fiber of my being not to scream. The pain was excruciating, but I dared not utter a sound. Silence was probably my best strategy. If the goons thought I was dead, maybe they would just leave me alone.

"Oh my God! J, please get up!" Alicia wailed. Then I could hear her begging me to give her some sign that I was alive.

However, I lay still on top of my daughter. It was all I could do to protect her as pain rocked my entire body. Keeping my eyes on Ju actually calmed my nerves. She was smiling at me, as if we were playing a game. Using every ounce of strength I could muster, I smiled back, reassuring her that all was well.

"Yo, man, go put one in that bitch's head and let's be out," the first man instructed the other. I was sure he knew the police weren't far away.

With every step the second gunman took in my direction, my mind raced a million miles a minute. *Will this be it? Will I go out in the middle of this mall?* The funny thing about it was I wasn't afraid to die. Hell, I welcomed death with open arms. On the other hand, I knew it wasn't my time just yet when I heard shots being fire from a different direction.

Boom! Boom!

"Ah, I've been hit!" The man coming to do me dirty was now howling in agony. I couldn't see what was going on, but I felt him fall beside me.

"Shit!" the other gunman cursed, then returned fire. After several bullet exchanges, he, too, caught some hot lead and dropped to the floor.

Several eerie seconds passed before I heard applause and cheers. When I looked up to see what was going on, I witnessed a group of people surrounding a short Asian man. He was holding some sort of pistol and was flashing a police badge. The guy had to be off duty. Nonetheless, I would be forever grateful that his ass was in the right place for us but at the wrong time for the assassins.

"J, thank God you're okay!" Ali exclaimed after coming over to where I lay bleeding.

"I've been hit in the back, but I'll be all right. Run them niggas' pockets, so we know who they are," I instructed Alicia.

Instantly, she went rummaging through their jeans. She retrieved two cell phones but no identification before coming back my way.

"Now take Ju and get the fuck up outta here," I told her.

She hesitated. "What about you?"

Gritting my teeth, I spoke through the pain. "What the fuck did I say?" I gave her a hard stare. "I'll call you when I get where I'm going, okay?"

"Okay." Alicia cautiously picked up Ju and disappeared into the crowd of distraught people. Though most shoppers had gotten out of Dodge, many still hung around the scene. I didn't know if they were hurt, helping those who were hurt, or were simply gawking.

For nearly twenty minutes, I lay on my stomach, waiting for help to arrive. My back was to the entrance to the food court. Therefore, I couldn't see what the hell was going on, nor could I hear much of anything. Slowly, I turned around and ended up staring right into the eyes of one of the deceased assailants. It startled me a bit, but it angered me even more. I wanted to spit right in his face but decided against it.

Then a voice said, "Ma'am, my name is Kobe. I'm an EMT." Finally, help had arrived. "Where were you hit?" the young man asked, as if he didn't see the blood pouring from my back.

"I think I caught two in the back," I informed "the professional."

He cut off my shirt and bra, then applied some type of gauze to the wounds. Next, he placed a neck brace on me, strapped me onto a board stomach down, poked me with a needle, and then asked if I could hold the IV attached to it. I didn't even respond. Instead, I snatched it from him. Afterward, he slid me onto a gurney, then hoisted me into the air.

"Where are you taking me?" I whispered.

"We're going to Grady Memorial Hospital." He began to roll me out of the food court. Inwardly, I smacked my lips. From what I had heard from people in Atlanta, "Shady Grady" was the last place you wanted to end up. Regrettably, I had no choice.

On the way out of the mall, I took note of all the innocent people who had been caught up in my shit today. When they had left the house this morning, none of them had been aware their day would end up like this.

An officer ran over to the gurney with a notepad and a pen. "Ma'am, do you know who shot you?" he asked as he jogged beside the gurney.

"No." I shook my head.

"Can you tell me how many shooters there were?"

"Enough with the questions! She needs to rest, but you can meet us at the hospital," Kobe snapped, cutting the interview short, and I was grateful.

As we rolled out of the mall, several news vans were already on scene, reporting the incident. A cameraman starting filming me, but Kobe turned him away as I did my best to cover my face. Somewhere between riding to the hospital and arriving there, I must've dozed off. When I woke up, I was in the hallway, on a hospital bed, in a hospital gown, and was still on my stomach, with my ass out for the world to see.

"Excuse me, nurse." I tried to reach for the lady walking past. However, she ignored me. "Bitch, I know you heard me!" I hollered and attempted to sit up.

"What's wrong, miss?" A young man wearing a white lab coat and glasses stopped in front of me.

"I'm trying to get some help around this bitch!" Was this fucker blind or deaf? "I've been in this hallway for God knows how long, with bullets in my back. I need to see a doctor."

"May I take a look?" he asked politely.

"Are you a doctor?" Lab coats didn't mean shit these days. For all I knew, this man could be a lab technician trying to get a free look under my gown.

"As a matter of fact, I am." He removed his badge and put it in my face. It read DR. BENJAMIN GARRISON, MD.

"All right, Doctor, take a look and tell me what I'm facing." I hadn't been given any medication yet. Consequently, the pain was still present and stronger than ever.

"Oh my. You need surgery immediately," he mumbled while snatching the clipboard off the end of my bed. "Excuse me." He stopped the same nurse who had just dodged me as she passed by again. Of course, she was still trying to act busy, but the tone in the doctor's voice indicated he wasn't fucking around. "Why is this patient still lying in the hallway when she has gunshot wounds?"

"Surgery is backed up, Dr. Garrison. More than likely, they won't be able to get to her until the morning."

"To hell with that! I can't wait until tomorrow," I snapped, causing the young doctor to place a warm hand on my shoulder to calm me.

"In the meantime, Nurse, can't we at least find her a room and remove her from the hallway, where she's exposed?" Dr. Garrison spoke in a soothing tone.

"I'll see what I can do," the nurse replied, relenting, and walked away.

The doctor glanced back at my chart. "Ms. Doesher, I apologize on behalf of the hospital for this inconvenience. Our emergency room is swamped, but I'll personally see to it that you're a priority." Although I was on my stomach, I could see Dr. Garrison clearly. His smile was warm, wide, and inviting. The brother was as fine as frog hair. He was tall, had a medium build, and resembled the basketball player Carmelo Anthony. "I'll have a nurse give you something to make you more comfortable, okay?" Again, he smiled, and I nodded.

As I waited on the nurse, I glanced at the tiled walls in the hallway and saw that they were in desperate need of renovation. The air in the hallway was stale, and the atmosphere was drab. I wanted to get up and walk out of this hellhole, but I couldn't. The shit was depressing, but it was not as bad as it could be. I could be in the morgue right now instead of in this hallway. Hell, my daughter could be in the morgue right now too. Just the thought of almost losing her caused my entire body to shiver. Not wanting to continued thinking about the what-ifs, I closed my eyes and tried to get comfortable.

Chapter Thirteen

The nurse must've given me some strong medication in that hallway, because it put me on my ass for the night. I didn't remember anything about the next morning, either, except someone coming in to prep me for surgery. I awoke in the recovery room, covered with a few heavy blankets but still shivering from the cold and anger in my heart. Everything was fuzzy, with the exception of my heart monitor and the conversation between two nurses at the desk across from me.

"Girl, did you see the shit that went down at the mall yesterday?" one of them said.

"You know I did," the other nurse replied. "I can't believe them crazy niggas just went on a shooting spree like that. Shit like this just don't happen in the A."

"I saw on the news that the shooters were from Detroit. I heard they were looking for one person in particular. You know niggas up north don't fuck around." The nurse had to be coming my way, because her voice got much closer. "My ex-boyfriend was a cop up there. I remember him telling me about the time a nigga went in and shot up the police station." As she pulled my curtain back, I closed my eyes and pretended to be asleep.

"I heard the police were up here earlier, looking to question some witnesses," the other woman conveyed as she walked past my bed.

Of course, my heart rate instantly increased. Did they know who I was? Were they looking for me?

My eyes popped open so fast, I think I scared the chunky black nurse. "Nurse, how soon can I get out of here?"

"Shit!" She jumped slightly and clutched her chest with pudgy little fingers. Her scrubs were so tight, I could count each roll on her body. I could also see the dimples in her knees. Afraid I had caused the poor woman to have a heart attack, I apologized.

"My bad. I didn't mean to scare you. I just need to get up outta here."

"I'm okay, Ms. Doesher, but you'll be here for at least a week." According to the tag on her top, her name was Leslie, and she was an RN. She began checking my vitals and IV.

"A week? I'm sure you can do better than that." Nobody had time to be laid up in this hospital when there were niggas trying to kill me and police trying to grill me.

"The surgeon removed two large-caliber bullets from your back. Although you don't appear to show signs of nerve or permanent damage, it's standard procedure to keep you under observation," Leslie said, enlightening me while lifting my gown and peeking between my legs. I was just about to ask what type of lesbo shit she was on, but then I saw the catheter cord. "We can't send you home too soon. You could hemorrhage, or worse." She put my gown back down.

"When will I get a room, then?" I tried not to sound irritated. It wasn't her fault I was in this mess.

"Actually, transport should be here any second to take you to your new floor. Is there anything I can get you? Like juice or water?" Leslie smiled genuinely. I could tell she really enjoyed her job.

"You got a cell phone I can use?" My question was accompanied with a smile. Gran always said you could get more bees with honey.

"Ms. Doesher, the use of cell phones isn't allowed on the floor."

"Please." I sighed. "If you let me use your phone, I'll make sure my sister tosses you something when she gets here." *Fuck it.* When you couldn't get bees with honey, you could surely get them with money.

Leslie glanced behind her to see if anyone was watching before slipping the cell phone into my hand.

"Thank you," I murmured while frantically dialing Ali.

She answered on the second ring. "Who is this?"

"It's me. Is Ju good?"

"Yeah. She's right here, banging on the table." I could hear the sound loud and clear. "What's up, J? Are you good? I've been waiting to hear from you since yesterday."

"I'm cool. Just had to have surgery, that's all. The nurse said I should be out in a week." I eyed Leslie, who was pretending not to ear hustle, before I started speaking in code. "I'm about to get a room here at Grady Memorial. Why don't you grab your overnight clothes and come through? You might want to come quick, because I'll probably have a lot of visitors real soon."

"I'll get Gran here on the next flight out, and I'll be there as soon as I can." Ali hadn't missed a beat. She understood that when I told her to bring overnight clothes, I was actually instructing her to bring me some street clothes. The "Come quick, because I'll probably have a lot of visitors real soon" was code for "The police were here and are surely coming to pay me a visit."

"Kiss Ju, and don't tell Gran shit. I'll tell her when I get home." I ended the call and handed the phone back to Leslie.

Approximately twenty minutes later, Dr. Garrison approached my bedside. "How are you doing today Ms. Doesher?"

"I'm cool, Doc." I spoke without really opening my mouth. Being without a toothbrush had me cautious. My shit had to be stank by now. "What are you doing here?"

"Well, I promised to make you a priority. For that reason, I'm here to transport you to your new room." He smiled again. I didn't know why, but my stomach did backflips.

"So, you're telling me you actually came here just to transport little ole me?"

"Yes." He nodded while removing my IV from the pole and laying it on my lap. "Why is that so hard to believe?"

"I just figured a fancy doctor such as yourself actually had real work to do." I laughed, and he did too.

"Unfortunately, you got the shaft yesterday, and I just wanted to make it up to you, that's all." As he rolled me past the nurses' station, Leslie damn near choked on a bottle of Diet Coke.

"I'll have my sister call your phone when she gets here," I called to her. I wanted her to know I saw her staring. Also, I wouldn't forget about having Alicia take care of her.

"Okay . . . ," she mumbled.

Another nurse standing near the elevator was staring hard too.

"Damn, Garrison. You got these hoes shook." I giggled.

"I was just about to say the same thing to you." He nodded at the nurse before pressing the button for the elevator.

"Why?" I looked back at him.

"Because you look ten times better than I do." The dimples in his jowls were gorgeous. I tried to think about Ace, but the shit wasn't working. Instead, I chose to focus on the lights in the ceiling while enjoying my personal escort.

Once I was all set up in the private room with two corner windows, I expected Dr. Garrison to dip. To the contrary, he took a seat and made himself comfortable. The smell of his cologne damn near had me salivating, but I kept it cool.

"Where are you from, Ms. Doesher?"

"You're making me sound old. Just call me Janelle, and I'm from Detroit."

"Motown!" He smiled. "I've been there a few times. My cousin used to live on Eight Mile." Most out-of-towners associated Eight Mile with the rapper Eminem. To us locals, it was just a street in our neighborhood. "Their last name is Wilkerson," he added.

"Okay." I nodded to be polite.

"His name is Tremaine. He played for Mumford High School back in the day. Now he plays professionally for the Chicago Bears." Garrison was obviously proud of his cousin, the way he rambled on. "That boy was the number seven draft pick."

"Garrison, no offense, but your cousin is the last thing on my mind." The pain meds were beginning to wear off. My shit was aching!

"I'm sorry. I didn't mean to talk your head off, Janelle." Garrison stood. The print in his scrub bottoms didn't leave much to the imagination. He didn't have the biggest dick, but it was more than a mouthful. "I'll send the nurse by to check on you, okay?" He paused like he wanted to say something else, but then he decided against it.

"Garrison, you're not bothering me, and I do appreciate the company. Since it seems like I'll be here for a while, come see me after your shift, okay?" Truthfully, I had no business flirting with this man, but it came naturally. He was easy on the eyes, intellectual, and had a little swag.

"Will do. Now get some rest." He winked before leaving me alone with my thoughts.

A million things raced through my head, including the Pauletti women, Ace, and that bitch-ass nigga Chucky. I had to make phone calls, set a plan in motion, and get the fuck out of the A. There was so much to do. For now, all I needed was morphine. Quickly, I pressed the call button and waited on the nurse to send me into medically induced paradise.

Chapter Fourteen

Tap. Tap.

The sound on the door caused my eyes to flutter for a second while I attempted to get my bearings. It took me a minute to remember that I was still in the hospital. My heart jumped slightly from paranoia. It could be anybody knocking—Alicia, Garrison, or some killer coming to do me dirty. Before I had time to keep guessing, the door swung open, and in waltzed two detectives. I wasn't thrilled to see the law, but they sure beat the hell out of a pair of killers.

Pressing the button on the side of the bed, I lifted myself. "Can I help you?" There was attitude in my voice. The cops hadn't said one word yet. Nevertheless, with the exception of Officer Bryant back home in Detroit, I hated all law enforcement. There was just something about them that rubbed me wrong.

"Are you Janelle Doesher?" the lady cop asked with a raised brow. The bitch obviously knew who I was.

"That depends on why you want to know." I played mind games back with her.

"Cut the shit, cutie. I know who you are and where you're from." She smiled smugly.

"Well, since you know so much, what the fuck you here for?" I was irritated with this bald-headed Barbie. Bitches killed me by cutting their hair damn near to the scalp, then wearing a face full of make-up. If they wanted to look so feminine, they should keep their hair in the first place. In my opinion, the only exception to the rule was someone with a disease.

"What's with the irritation?" the male officer asked.

"What's with the questions?" I rolled my eyes. When neither of them said anything, I added, "So are you going to stand there, or are you going to state your business?"

"What can you tell us about Bernard Talley and George Donaldson? They were the shooters from the mall," the female inquired, with a pen and notepad in hand.

"I can't tell you a damn thing. I've never heard those names a day in my life." That wasn't a complete lie. I had never heard or seen those cats before the other day, but I did know who had sent them.

"So why did they come to shoot you?"

I shrugged. "I was just in the wrong place at the wrong time."

"We have witnesses that can attest to the fact that one of the gunmen called you out by name in the food court before he started shooting." She flipped through her notes.

"And exactly what name was that?" This wasn't my first rodeo. I wasn't about to buck under pressure.

"I believe it was Jane Doe." The male officer smirked.

"That's not my name." Casually, I grabbed the remote and turned on the television. I knew they didn't really have shit on me, or they would've gotten down to the nitty-gritty the minute they hit the door.

"Janelle Doesher sounds pretty close to Jane Doe, wouldn't you say?" the female asked the male.

"There's no doubt about it," he replied.

"Look." I sighed, tired of the conversation. "We could sit here and guess all day about who Jane Doe is, but I'm tired. In case you didn't know, I just had back surgery."

"Okay, smart-ass! Tell me what you're doing in Atlanta?" The lady officer was getting frustrated.

"If you must know, I'm a business owner here. I own Capa Donna Boutique. Therefore, I fly in periodically to check up on my shit."

"Is that so?" the male detective asked.

"Just call one of my stores. They'll enlighten you." These clowns were horrible detectives. If they knew the first thing about their jobs, they would've found out everything about me before coming all the way up here and wasting a trip.

"Look, Janelle, I'm good at what I do. It will only be a matter of time before I dig all into your shit and discover why you brought this chaos to my city. When I do find out, you'll wish you had been more cooperative," the lady cop vowed as she closed her notepad.

"I guess we'll see when that day comes." I smiled. "As for now, please close the fucking door on your way out."

Without another word, they eyeballed each other, then honored my request. I was pissed. It was because of Chucky and his thugs that the cops were about to be all up in my business. He needed to be handled quickly!

I didn't have time to dwell on my beef back home, because my door opened again. This time it was Alicia.

"What up, doe?" She tossed a duffel bag onto the foot of my bed. I was glad to see her and ready to blow this Popsicle stand. "I just saw two cops at the nurses' desk. It looked like they were asking a lot of questions." After unzipping the bag, Ali laid out a pair of Hanes sweatpants, a pink T-shirt, and a pair of socks.

"Yeah, they just left here."

"What they say?" She grabbed the socks and slipped them on my feet.

"They told me they knew who I was and where I was from. This probably won't be the last we hear from them."

"Damn!" Alicia helped me slide on my clothes. "The lady officer was fine as shit, though. If she wasn't a cop, I would do some thangs to that ass."

"Girl, bye." I laughed as Ali helped me from the bed. While I was getting dressed, there was a light knock, and then the door swung open. My ass must be popular today.

"Going somewhere?" Garrison stood there, with an amused expression.

"Home," I replied. Alicia remained silent but stared Garrison down. "He's cool." I had to reassure her, because my girl was about to go in.

On cue, Garrison extended his hand for a shake. "I'm Dr. Garrison, one of the doctors here." He waited for Alicia to introduce herself, but she didn't. Instead, she gave him a brief nod, then went back to getting me dressed.

"Come on, Jane. Let's go!" she said when she was finished.

"May I ask why you're leaving?" Garrison questioned.

"Damn. Who the fuck is this nigga?" Alicia was annoyed with all the questions.

"I can't explain right now. Just know that I have to do what I have to do," I told him. I felt bad about Alicia snapping on him. His questions were out of concern, but she thought he was being nosy.

"I'm sorry, but as a medical professional, I cannot allow you to leave." He was adamant.

"Dr. Garrison, I am leaving whether you like it or not."

"Before you leave, then, I need you to sign a document releasing the hospital of responsibility for any harm to you resulting from you discharging yourself." Raising his hands in defeat, he left the room to go retrieve the document.

"Thank God," Alicia sighed after he left the room.

After sliding on my shoes, she helped me walk toward the door. My legs felt like noodles, and my feet tingled bad. The gravity pulling me down had my back on ten. Dr. Garrison was standing outside the door with a form and a pen. Quickly, I glanced over it and signed it.

"Be sure to see about that wound. You don't want to risk infection," he advised.

"Thank you, Garrison." Through the pain, I forced a smile, handed back the form, and followed Alicia, leaving him standing there. He was one of the nicest people I'd met in a very long time. I only wished our encounter had occurred under better circumstances.

Once we were down the hallway, my heart started racing. Less than twenty feet away stood the police officers, who were now speaking with the nurse on duty. She was holding a chart, which was mine, I was sure. In order to get on the elevator, we had to pass by them.

"Fuck!" I said under my breath.

"No worries. Just be cool." Alicia pulled me toward the stairs. I was glad she was calm, because my nerves were all over the place.

"I can't take the stairs. I'm too wobbly," I told her. My legs felt numb, and it was hard enough to walk, so there was no way I could manage the stairs.

"I got you." Alicia kneeled down in front of me, indicating that I was supposed to get on her back and travel piggyback style.

"Alicia, I'm not getting on your back." This girl had me by only twenty pounds or so. There was no way she would be able to carry me down several flights of stairs. One wrong move and my stitches were sure to come loose.

"Come on and stop playing, before they find us."

"All right, but your ass better not drop me!" Nervously, I hoisted myself onto Alicia's back as best I could through the pain. She took each step slowly and cautiously until we arrived at the bottom. Finally, we strolled casually past the front desk and out into the warm night air.

Chapter Fifteen

The dark ride home from the hospital was silent. I didn't know what was on Alicia's mind, but heavy on my mind was how I was going to rectify this situation with Chucky. Before he'd come for me at the mall, I was ready to walk away and let him have the game, but now there was no fucking way I could let him live.

As if she was reading my thoughts, Alicia spoke. "So, what's next?"

"First things first. I'm on the next plane headed back to the D. Me and that bitch Chucky has some unfinished business." I was hell-bent on paying that nigga back for trying to body me and my fucking kid. They said that hell hath no fury like a woman scorned. If he knew like I knew, he should've already been trying to get the fuck out of Dodge.

"Speaking of Chucky, he's been blowing up one of the phones I took from the shooters." Alicia lifted up her bottom and retrieved the phone from her back pocket, then handed it to me.

I scrolled through the missed calls, as well as the text messages. One had just come through an hour ago. It read, Is it done? Did you finish that bitch?

Knowing that he couldn't have a clue about the shooting so quickly, I replied. She's done! Then I hit SEND and waited for him to respond. Right away, the phone started buzzing. I rejected the call, then sent another text. No phone calls. This shit could be traced.

"What if he knows we have the phone? Do you think he's playing us?" Alicia asked.

"Chucky is an old-school nigga. He doesn't have social media, and he doesn't watch television unless it's a football game. He doesn't know shit."

After a few seconds, Chucky texted back. I need to know it's done. Where's the proof?

"Shit!" I cursed.

"What's up?" Alicia asked.

"He wants proof that I'm dead. I don't know what to do." I looked at her for an answer. Together, we pondered until I had a bright idea. "Stop by the grocery store."

"What? Why?" Alicia looked at me sideways.

"I need you to grab a few things." I was sure Alicia thought I was crazy, but there was a method to this madness.

Seconds later, she pulled up and parked at the Publix around the corner from my crib. "Go inside and grab a few large bottles of Hershey's chocolate syrup and ketchup. Also, grab some powder foundation from the make-up aisle. Park by the door, and leave the car running. I'll wait here."

Within fifteen minutes, she was back in the car, with a devious grin. "What do you have planned?"

"You'll see. Take me back to your hotel." Alicia was staying not far from my house. I would've gone home, but I knew Gran was there, and I didn't want her to ask any questions.

On the ride to Alicia's hotel, flashing lights came out of nowhere. "We're being pulled over," Alicia said. Once she had brought the car to a stop on the side of the road, she fumbled through her purse to find her license and registration.

"Is this car dirty?" I asked calmly while we waited for the officer to approach our vehicle.

"I have two guns in the dash, but that's it." Alicia rolled her window down. Both of us realized that two guns carried a four- to ten-year sentence if convicted. Well, it was what it was. All we could do was play it cool.

"Good evening, miss." The female officer leaned into the window. Due to the high beams shining behind us, it was difficult to see. Despite that, I recognized her as the same officer from the hospital. Bewildered, I tried to figure out how she had gotten up on us so fast.

"Hello." Alicia smiled while handing over her paperwork. "May I ask why I'm being stopped?"

"You were doing eighty-five in a seventy," the officer lied. I knew Alicia had barely been doing sixty-five miles per hour, because I'd looked at the dashboard minutes ago. "I'll be right back." She strutted away with Alicia's identification.

"That's the bitch from the hospital." I tried to move my body just enough to peer out the side-view mirror.

"I know," Ali replied. "How should I play this?"

"Just sit tight," I advised. "Besides, there's no need to speed away. The bitch has your identification, and we ain't from here." We wouldn't know which way to go, and we didn't have anywhere to hide.

Several moments later, the officer returned, this time walking up to my side of the car. I rolled down my window.

"Ms. Doesher, I wasn't aware that hospitals discharged patients this late at night."

"Are we under arrest?" I asked without even looking up at her.

"Not yet." She laughed.

"Well, please just give my friend a ticket, so we can be on our way." I sighed.

"Where are you two headed tonight anyway?" she continued, as if she hadn't heard me.

"Home!" I tried to remain calm, but it was unnecessary shit like this that put me out with cops. Utilizing their shields, they tried to bully people and make them feel powerless. However, I knew my rights.

"What's with all the anger?"

"What's with all the questions?" I retorted. She appeared shocked by my boldness.

"Do you know who the fuck you're talking to?"

"Lady, you don't intimidate me!" Although I was fresh off the operating table, I would've whupped this girl's ass in a Detroit minute and suffered the consequences later.

Lucky for both of us, a call came over her radio, and her partner yelled for her to come on. Without another word, she tossed Alicia's stuff into the car and walked away. I was certain this would be the first of many pop-up visits. Already Atlanta was proving to be too hot for me.

Once we were inside Ali's plush suite at the W Hotel, she helped me take a seat. "So, what's the plan? Why did you have me buy that stuff?"

"Give me one second." Moving slowly, I took my shopping bag and headed into the bathroom. Once inside, I began covering my face with just enough powder foundation to look dead but not like a ghost. Next, I popped the top on the chocolate syrup and ketchup and poured them on the T-shirt beneath my hoodie. Together, the two ingredients created the perfect color and texture of blood. Alone, the ketchup would've been too bright and too thin. When I came back into the living room, Alicia smiled, comprehending what I was up to.

"Damn, that shit looks real!" she exclaimed.

"Come on. Let's get this over with." Combined, the ketchup and chocolate had an awful odor.

"Okay, lie on the floor and I'll take the picture." Alicia helped me down, then grabbed the phone. Although my back was hurting, I lay on the carpeted floor and tried my best to appear dead. Ali snapped so many pictures, you would have thought we were doing a real photo shoot.

"Okay, I just sent a picture." She helped me get up off the floor.

While I was in the bathroom, cleaning myself up, the phone buzzed. I wasn't sure if my plan had worked, but I prayed like hell it had.

"What did he say?" I asked Ali, who was reading the text message. She didn't say anything. She just turned and handed the phone to me. I read Chucky's message aloud. "Good work, but you should've closed casketed that bitch!" By "closed casketed," he meant I should've been shot in the face, so my family would have no choice but to have a closed casket funeral. Although his words were grim, I found his antics amusing. At least he thought I was dead. Now he would let his guard down long enough for me to reach out and touch his ass in the worst way.

After Alicia drove me home, she helped me out of the car and to the door. Once I slid my key into the lock on the door, I told her good night and walked in. The place was silent. I figured Gran and Ju were asleep, but I was wrong.

"They released you already?" Gran asked from the sofa. She was sitting in the dark, like a crazy person. Then I realized she was only meditating. It was something she had done every night when I lived with her.

"Hey, Gran. Thank you for coming so fast." I closed the door and took a seat on the adjacent chair.

"When your friend called and said you were in a car accident, I came running." Gran looked concerned but relieved to see me alive and well.

I felt bad for having Alicia lie about my injury. However, there was no way in hell my grandmother could ever find out I had been shot. Gran and I were making progress. I didn't want news that I'd been shot to remind her about my father and set our relationship back.

"Speaking of your friend, where is she?"

"Ali is staying at a hotel."

"How are you feeling? Can I do anything for you?"

It was unusual for Gran to make a fuss over me. None-theless, I liked it. "No, I'm okay."

"Janelle, would you like to talk about our conversation yesterday?" Gran was referring to the call I had placed in which I'd asked her to pray for me. Alicia and I had just killed a child by accident, and I had been seeking forgiveness. In that moment, I had needed to know God was real. Then I'd been ready to wash away my sins and start anew.

Today things were different. Chucky had come for me and had placed my daughter in harm's way. Hate was in my heart, and forgiveness was nowhere to be found. He had to pay for what he had done. If that meant I was foregoing my seat in heaven, then so be it. God forgave, but I didn't.

"Good night, Gran," I said as I stood there, dismissing myself. Then I left the room.

Chapter Sixteen

Early the next morning, while Ju was still sleeping, I got dressed in a loose jogging suit and packed a bag. After placing a kiss on my daughter's lips, I walked down the hallway and knocked on the door to the bedroom Gran was sleeping in before entering.

"Janelle what's the matter?" Gran said as she lay in bed.

"Gran, I have to go back to Detroit, but I'll be back soon. There is food in the cabinet, and I scheduled a fresh food delivery for this afternoon. Money is on the dresser in my room. Call me if you need anything."

"Granddaughter, what is going on? Why are you going back to Detroit?" Gran was now sitting up.

"We'll talk more about it when I get home, but for now get some sleep before Ju wakes up." Without another word, I closed the bedroom door and inched myself toward the front of the house. I headed into the kitchen, where I grabbed a bottle of extra strength Tylenol from the drawer, took three, and put the bottle in my purse.

I left the house and met up with Alicia at her hotel. From there, we headed to the airport. Two hours later we boarded the plane, and by 1:00 p.m. the flight had landed and Alicia and I were in a rental car and heading to our hometown of Detroit.

"Are you okay? I'm sure the ride was brutal," she said as we drove.

"I'm all right." Honestly, I was experiencing some discomfort, but not enough to deter me from the task at hand. After pulling out my phone, I dialed a familiar number.

Gambino, one of my associates, answered on the second ring. "Hello?"

"Hey. It's Jane. I need a favor."

"Jane?"

"Yeah, nigga, it's Jane. Fuck you sounding all surprised for?" I said.

"My bad, li'l mama. Word on the streets is the nigga Chucky took you out. What's good?" Gambino was a major gun distributor for the Midwest. He dealt in everything from .22s to choppers with banana clips. Gambino and I had met through Ace. They were very good friends.

"As you can hear, I'm far from dead, but I can't say the same for Chucky much longer."

"I get your drift. What you need?" He already knew what time it was.

"Set me up with three Alpha Kappas." That was the code name for AK-47 assault rifles.

"When do you need them?"

"Now," I replied.

"Oh shit. You going to the funeral with guns blazing!" He snickered. I didn't know what the fuck he was talking about. Therefore, I probed him for additional information.

"Whose funeral?"

"Chucky's son, Vito's funeral is today at eleven," Gambino explained.

Inwardly, I smiled. I couldn't have asked for a better situation. Chucky would have his guard down; he would no longer see me as a threat. Moreover, his emotions would be all over the place due to his grief. This was the perfect time to catch him slipping.

"Where are the services being held?"

"House of Salvation on the Eastside." As Gambino reeled off everything he knew, I jotted it down on a piece of paper from my purse.

"Okay. I'll be there in a few," I told him once I had written everything down.

"All right. They'll be ready when you get here," he said, and then we ended the call.

"So, we're just going to roll up in the funeral on some gangster shit, huh?" Alicia burst into laughter.

"Hell yeah. Straight like that!" For some reason, my adrenaline was now pumping. I couldn't wait to send Chucky to hell.

Roughly half an hour had passed before we were pulling up to Gambino's place in Waterford. It was a nice, large two-story brick house with a white picket fence, a wraparound porch, and a porch swing. He lived out in the boondocks. His closest neighbor was nearly half a mile away. Due to his occupation, he valued privacy.

After stepping onto the porch, I pressed the doorbell and tried to stand as straight as I could. Several seconds later, the door was opened by a little boy. I'd never seen this little boy before, but I could tell Gambino was probably his father by the thick unibrow and the strong jawline.

"Boy, what in the hell did I tell you about opening up my door? Do that shit again and see what I do to you." Gambino scolded the toddler, who ran off crying into another room. "Jane, what's up? I'm glad to see you're okay." He pulled me in for a tight hug, which, of course, made me wince. "You good?" Gambino pulled back.

"Yeah, I'm good. Nothing major," I lied.

"What's up, Alicia?" He slapped her a five. "Man, I heard you was out of here, Jane. Damn. I thought you was dead."

"I'm one hundred. As you see, them fucking niggas were just practicing when they came for me." I chuckled.

Truth of the matter was, they would've laid my ass down had it not been for the hero at the mall that day.

"I know that's right." Gambino nodded before leading us downstairs into the basement, which served as his storage facility. "I got your AKs right over here," he said after flipping on the light. The finished basement had painted white paneling and plush gray carpeting. It was covered from wall to wall with various gun safes and boxes of ammunition. Even the one gray sofa was covered by boxes. "I also have a few nine millimeters and Glocks, just in case the AKs weren't enough."

"No, this is all I need right here. What's my ticket?" I replied.

"Normally, I sell them for three grand a piece. Since you my peoples, just give me six for all three."

"How much for the bullets?"

"I'll sell you fifty for five grand."

I was cool with the price of the guns, but the bullets cost just as much, which didn't make sense to me. "Can we do four grand on the bullets and call it an even ten?"

"Damn, Jane. I already cut you a deal." Gambino rubbed his hand down his face.

"How about ten grand, plus five hundred? Truthfully, that's all I have in my purse."

"All right. That'll work."

I appreciated the hook-up. Without delay, I dropped the cash in his hand, collected my shit, and was back on the road in no time. Showtime was right around the corner. I couldn't wait for Chucky's demise.

Chapter Seventeen

After leaving Gambino, Ali and I headed over the church, where the service was scheduled to start at 3:00 p.m. We had thirty minutes to spare, so we decided to wait outside the church and watch for a minute from a distance. It was 2:30 p.m., and the church parking lot was only halfway full. I didn't know if people were on "CP" time or if Vito just wasn't that loved.

About ten minutes later, Alicia looked at me and said, "You ready?" Eagerly, she put her hand on the door handle.

"Not yet." Something in my stomach just didn't feel right. "Let's give it another thirty minutes and go in once the service has started." I needed to make sure Chucky was already inside before making my entrance.

"Fine," Alicia huffed. She was ready to put in work, but she stayed put, obeying my directive. My eyes were fixed on the small church with the brick exterior and stained-glass windows. I watched and waited for a sign that it was time to move. The last thing I wanted was to be caught off guard.

Finally, after forty-five minutes of waiting, Ali had had enough. "Girl, the funeral is going to be over by the time we get in there." She had a point, so I relented.

"Okay. Let's go."

After stepping from the car slowly, I slid a red ski mask over my head, and Ali did the same. We walked across the parking lot like two women on a mission. Although our faces were concealed, we did nothing to obscure the large AKs both of us toted. With a deep breath, I pulled the doors of the church open and headed inside, Ali on my heels. From the entryway, we could hear the faint sound of an organ playing. I looked back at Ali, raised my hand, and counted to three before opening the doors to the sanctuary.

Inside the small room were only about thirty people, most of them women. Therefore, it was easy to spot Chucky sitting on the front pew, with his head lowered. He was dressed in all black from head to toe.

"You watch the door, and I'll get Chucky," I said to Ali.

Everyone was too busy reading obituaries, gossiping, or staring at the dead corpse to notice me. Rapidly, I made my way up the aisle and yelled, "Don't nobody move and won't nobody get hurt!" Those words were enough to send everyone into a fit of terror . . . except Chucky. Women started screaming and grabbing their children. The pastor ducked behind the podium, and a few of the church nurses dropped to the floor.

"You got a lot of nerve, Jane," Chucky stated calmly after lifting his head. The tears on his face were fresh, and his eyes were red. "You killed my son, and then you show up to disrespect his funeral."

"You think I give a fuck about you or your son!" I yelled. This nigga, his son, and his tears meant nothing to me. "You killed my friend in cold blood, and then you sent your goons to kill me, so fuck you!" I spat.

"So, what you gone do?" he challenged me.

"Keep talking and you'll find out a lot sooner than later," I replied.

"You think you bad now?" He stood, daring me to make a move. "Don't forget who made your young ass!"

"I didn't come from your dick! You didn't make shit, except that pussy nigga laying in that casket." My choice of words was harsh; they cut Chucky deeply. Instantly, he lunged for me. Luckily, my reflexes were A1, even after the surgery, which allowed me to leap out of the way. In my condition, I probably wouldn't have gotten a away from a younger man. Thank God Chucky wasn't a younger man.

"Shoot her!" He looked up toward the ceiling. That was when I noticed a hefty-sized man standing in the balcony and pointing something at me. From such a distance, I couldn't tell what type of gun it was. Nevertheless, I could definitely detect a little red dot dancing near my chest.

Pop!

It was the last sound I wanted to hear at the moment. Looking down at my chest, I expected to see blood, but there was none. Relieved, I looked up just in time to see Chucky's goon fall face forward over the railing into the crowd of mourners. Chucky used the distraction to try to escape, but I was on his ass like white on rice.

I raised the gun, then closed my left eye to focus. Before I could squeeze the trigger, two men barged into the sanctuary, blasting. *Boom! Boom!* The shit they were shooting sounded like canons. Hastily, I dropped to the floor and immediately winced from the agony. Seconds later, part of the pew I was under blew up into small pieces. People were scattering like roaches, but I stayed put. *Boom! Boom!*

"Shit!" My heart raced like that of a horse on a track. Frantically, I attempted to crawl to safety. *Pow! Pow!* It seemed as if bullets were raining down on us. From my vantage point, I could see Alicia lying flat on the floor. I was unsure if she was hurt. At any rate, there was nothing I could do to help her right now; I was trying to save my own life.

After several minutes of silence, I lifted my head slowly. It appeared that the shooters had retreated. There were several bloody bodies sprawled across the church. Plus, someone had knocked over Vito's casket. I scanned the scene of the massacre for Chucky, but like a magician, he had disappeared.

"Ali," I called out before making my way over to her. That was when I spotted a nigga hiding under the organ, with a gun. No doubt he was one of the shooters. Without hesitation, I lifted my weapon and fired.

Pow! Pow! Pow!

The bullets sprayed from the AK so fast that I emptied the clip before I knew it. Just like that, the man was toast.

"Ali, it's me. Come on." I kneeled down and tapped her. We needed to get moving if we didn't want to run into the law. She remained still, and I began to worry.

A second later, she said, "Shit. I was playing dead." She laughed. "Where did they go?" Alicia sprang to her feet like a jack-in-the-box.

"I don't know, but let's get outta here."

Wherever Chucky was, he was probably plotting against my ass, or so I thought until I saw him lying on the floor near the overturned casket. "There he is!" I pointed. "Help me grab his ass."

Alicia and I went to work carrying Chucky out of the church. He must've taken a shot to the chest, because he was covered in blood. However, I knew he wasn't dead by the way he wiggled around.

"You don't know what you just did!" he snarled before I unlocked the trunk to the car and tossed his ass inside it.

Chapter Eighteen

After Ali pulled away from the church, I got on the phone and put in a call to some of my girls who had handled a good amount of dirty. We needed a place to finish what we had started with Chucky, and they had just the place. They told us to meet them in back of an abandoned house in Highland Park.

When we pulled up, my girls, Patrice and Rocky, two bad bitches I kept on the team, were standing outside. By *bad bitches*, I didn't mean pretty, thick, or any of that shit. No, these bitches were pit bulls in skirts. They packed a mean punch and probably had a higher body count than most niggas. They were my version of Snoop and Chris from the HBO show *The Wire*. I'd found these thoroughbreds through a friend of a friend. After watching how they got down for the very first time, I'd signed them exclusively to my team.

"Fuck we got here?" Patrice asked after I unlocked the trunk. She glanced inside before smiling and rubbing her palms together. Patrice got off on shit like this.

"Get this nigga out of the trunk and bring him inside," I instructed. My ass was tired, my back was sore, and I had to sit down. At this point I was beginning to feel like my stitches were coming loose or something, because my shirt felt wet. I knew it had to be blood.

Patrice and Rocky lifted Chucky, who struggled, but he was no match for my heavyweights.

Inside, the smell of the abandoned house was stale and rank. The stench was so bad, Alicia and I both had to cover our noses.

"Y'all kill somebody in this bitch?" Ali asked after Rocky and Patrice sat Chucky in a folding chair.

"Do you really want to know?" Rocky asked with a raised brow.

Alicia shook her head, indicating she would pass on the information.

"Y'all bitches wild!" I laughed, but I was genuinely happy they were on my team.

"And you know this man!" Patrice replied, imitating Chris Tucker.

We all shared a laugh before I turned my attention to Chucky. He was slumped over in the chair. The loss of blood had him weak.

"Wake up, nigga!" I screamed before I grabbed a half-empty glass of liquid off the counter and splashed it in his face.

"Hey!" Rocky yelled. "That was my drank!" Her Southern accent was thick. She was originally from Georgia.

"Don't worry. I got you," I told Rocky. "Wake up!" I yelled again. Chucky still didn't respond, so this time, I threw the whole cup at him. Slowly, he blinked and tried to lift his head. His eyes were weak, and I was cognizant of the fact that he needed medical attention. Unfortunately, I didn't give a fuck. He was going to die today!

"What you waiting for?" He glared at me before glancing around the room. When his eyes landed on Patrice and Rocky, he shook his head. Chucky realized then that shit was about to go down in a major way.

"I got a few questions first," I answered. There were two things burning a hole in my head; I needed answers before this fucker drew his last breath.

"What kind of questions?" He scowled defiantly at me.

"Did you set Ace up?"

"I got better things to do than to set up some kid who learned his game from me and your father." I could detect by the way he shifted his eyes that he was lying. Even so, I left it alone and moved on.

"Speaking of my father . . . did you set him up?" For years, I had wondered who had played the key role in my parents' murders. From day one, Chucky had been atop the list of suspects. Typically, it was the people closest to you that brought you down.

"Are you fucking joking?" Chucky went into a coughing fit. Although blood was now dripping from his mouth, his eyes remained on me. "Your father was my brother and best friend. Don't ever let that thought cross your mind again. I would've died for my brother if I could've." The conviction in his voice indicated he wasn't lying this time. Even though his revelation put me at ease, the feeling was short lived. All his words meant was that the person who had really set my father up was still lurking around somewhere. "If your interrogation is over, then get down to the matter at hand!" he yelled.

"Not a problem." Rocky left the room.

"Y'all better put these on." Patrice tossed Ali and me two hazmat suits.

I wanted to ask what the hell was about to happen just as Rocky returned with a chain saw. She was wearing a pair of safety goggles and a devilish grin. Everyone's eyes widened in surprise, including mine. She was really on some psycho shit. Without another word, she revved up the large tool and went for the nigga's kneecaps. The sound of the saw against his bones reminded me of a wood chipper.

"Fuck!" Chucky screamed out in pain as Rocky struggled to disconnect his lower leg from his thigh. After several minutes of the chain saw's ridges struggling against the bones, Chucky's lower leg was finally severed and fell to the floor in front of us. Patrice kicked it aside, grabbed the chain saw, then went to work on the other leg.

In less than an hour's time, Chucky had been dismembered from limb to limb. Only his head remained attached to his torso. Alicia stood there, quiet and stunned. I, on the other hand, was intrigued.

"Let me do the head," I said.

"Are you sure?" Rocky asked, and I nodded. Carefully, she handed over the massive weapon.

The vibration against my hands felt good; I felt powerful. Even though Chucky was already dead, his eyes were open and staring straight at me. Most people would've closed them, but I wanted him to see me. I wanted him to know that I was smiling while beheading his bitch ass.

The neck had big muscles; therefore, it was resistant to being cut. At first, I struggled, especially because of my back. The shit was much harder than it appeared, but after a few minutes, I found my rhythm. Gradually, I forced the blade down until Chucky's head rolled off with ease. After cutting the engine, I stood and stared down at my handiwork.

"Y'all head out. We got the rest," Patrice said as she removed the chain saw from my clutches.

Alicia and I took off the hazmat suits in silence. I could tell she was a bit shaken up, but I was fine. It was just another day at the office. Seeing Chucky die and knowing for sure he was never again going to darken my doorway was a relief. I thought Alicia would be relieved too, but she didn't appear to be. So I decided to give her time to process the whole thing.

Before leaving, I laced my girls with a hefty payment and put Alicia in a cab to the hotel and promised to check on her later. As for me, I headed back to the airport like nothing had happened. I was so calm, it was spine tingling. Something about that day had ignited a fire within me that I had never realized was there. Killing that innocent child was not one of my finest moments, but I was finally realizing that losses of war happened daily. If it hadn't been that boy, it could've been Ju, and if it hadn't been Chucky, then it could've been me. It was at that precise moment that I graduated from a bad girl to a gangstress!

Chapter Nineteen

After catching the seven o'clock flight back to Atlanta, I didn't get home until 8:30 p.m. There was still a little sun out, and I was happy because I knew Ju would still be up. After unlocking the door to my home, I called out for Ju and Gran. When no one responded, I pulled out my cell phone to give Gran a call. That was when I saw the note taped to the television.

Janelle,
I took Ju out for an evening stroll. We'll be back shortly.
Love, Gran

I balled up the paper and headed toward my bedroom to get comfortable. It had been a really long day, and I wanted nothing more than a shower. But with open wounds, I had to settle for washing up in the sink. Before removing my clothes, I shot a quick text to Ali, informing her that I had made it home. While I was removing my shoes, the phone rang. I answered it on the second ring.

"Hello."

"You have a collect call from a Michigan State inmate," a familiar computer voice said into my phone. It was a call from Ace. I didn't wait for him to speak his name before I accepted the charges. I hadn't spoken to my baby in days. Ali had said he called while I was in the hospital. She hadn't been sure if I wanted him to know what had happened, so she hadn't answered his call.

"I miss you, baby." Smiling, I waited for him to respond.

"Where the fuck you been!" he snapped. "I called you four times the other day! What's up?"

"Whoa, nigga. You better calm down!" I looked at the phone's screen, as if Ace could see me.

"Where the fuck you been?"

A nigga in jail was a jealous-ass nigga. I started to mess with his emotions but changed my mind. "I got into some beef with my people and decided to fly south until things calmed down." I was speaking in code, but Ace knew what I was saying. "When I got to my destination, trouble was waiting for me, which is why I couldn't answer the phone."

"Are you all right?" Now he was exceptionally concerned.

"I caught two hot ones, but I'll be straight in a few days."

"What? Who did this?" His tone was excited again.

"Calm down, Ace, before they take away your phone privileges."

"Who did it?" he asked.

"Don't worry. It's handled. I swear on Ju, I'm good." If I could tell Ace the real, I knew he would be pissed but proud of the way I had handled things.

"How is my baby girl?"

"She's good. Gran came down to help with her until I get better."

"That's good, I guess." Ace sighed. I could hear the heaviness in his voice.

"How are you holding up?" The last time I'd spoken to Richard Lennigan, Ace still hadn't been given a trial date. Sometimes when the caseloads were backed up, it could take years for a trial to begin.

"I'm good. I just wish I was out there with you." Ace rarely displayed vulnerability. "I feel like I let you and Julius down. I promised to take care of you, Janie."

"Baby, you haven't let anybody down. We're going to get through this, I promise." Of course, my eyes were watery, but I didn't want him to know.

"I ain't no good to nobody up in here."

"You'll be home in no time," I sighed. "Just hold tight, boo."

"Janie, I took a deal." While his voice was low, mine was caught somewhere down in the pit of my stomach, and I couldn't respond. "Hello?"

"What kind of deal, Ace?" I finally said. I gazed up at the ceiling; it felt as if it was caving in on me. My emotions were all over the place. I was both pissed and saddened by the news.

"The DA came back and said if I pled guilty, he'd lower the sentence to fifteen years."

"Fifteen years?" I repeated. "That shit sounds like an aeon to me. The last deal they offered you was only five years. What happened?"

"I decided to take the wrap for the Paulettis. In return, they promised to look out for you on my behalf and reward me upon release."

"I don't give a fuck about the Paulettis or what they promised to do," I snapped. Sure, where we came from, his act would be considered commendable. But I was downright pissed. "You have a family! What about your fucking daughter? What about me?"

"Jane . . ." Ace didn't get a chance to finish, because I ended the call right then and there.

"How dare he make a deal without discussing this shit with me? Fuck him and his fifteen years!" I said aloud to myself. I was angry beyond words and wanted to blow off a little more steam. However, the sound of the doorbell interrupted my ranting. With an attitude, I flew down the stairs and swung open the door. Standing there, like a sight for sore eyes, was Dr. Garrison.

"Janelle, don't think I'm crazy." He smiled. "I've been worried about that back of yours. I know your dressing needs to be changed by now."

"Aw, Garrison, you're so sweet." He was right; my dressing did need changing. "Come on in." I nodded for him to follow me.

He glanced around. "Your place is nice."

"Boy, stop!" I laughed. The living area was barely furnished, though it did have a sofa, an area rug, and a television. I felt the need to explain. "I live in Detroit. This is my second residence. That's why it's so empty."

"I can tell it'll be nice when you finish decorating." Garrison sat his medical satchel on the sofa. "Have a seat and I'll hook you up."

"Thank you for coming over and doing this."

"No worries." He winked and immediately went to work on me. I watched him remove the gauze bandages. Next, he wiped my wound gently to clean the dried blood. Then he put new bandages on. "Try not to get this wet, and it should hold for another week. If you like, I can come back then."

"Thank you so much. Can I pay you anything?" I said.

"Your money is no good here. I'm just looking out for a patient." He shook his head, causing the scent of Versace to hit my nostrils.

"I owe you one, then." I smiled seductively. There was definitely some flirtation taking place on my end.

"A brother could use some grub. Can you cook?"

"I haven't really tried to cook, but tell me what you like and I'll whip it up."

"By 'whip it up,' you must mean you'll have it delivered," he joked, causing us both to erupt with laughter. "Tell you what. Since you're not from here, let me take you out to dinner this Friday. My treat."

"I'd like that."

"Cool." He licked those juicy lips of his. For some reason, I couldn't help but wonder how they tasted. "Hey, the other day, two cops were up at the hospital, asking about you." His words ejected me from the daydream.

"What?" I stuttered. "What did they say?" I asked.

"They wanted an address on you after you bailed from the hospital." He must've noticed the mortified look on my face. "Don't worry. Under HIPAA, we can't provide that information unless they have a warrant." Garrison began collecting his belongings from the sofa.

"Thank you . . . Thank you." At least he had bought me some time. Sorry to say, I knew they would resurface, sooner rather than later.

"Don't thank me. It's the law." Garrison smiled.

"I don't know what you may think of me, but . . ."

"Janelle, whatever it is, it doesn't concern me. I don't care about any of that." Garrison headed for the door. "You seem like a good person, and that's good enough for me."

I wanted to tell him that I wasn't a good person. In fact, after having just participated in the murder of a man by way of a chain saw, I was rotten. All the same, I mustered a smile and responded, "I'm no angel."

"Me either," Garrison countered. "See you Friday at eight, okay?"

"Okay," I gushed before he walked out and I closed the door.

Inside, I knew I shouldn't have agreed to the date with Garrison. However, Ace shouldn't have agreed to accept the plea. In my eyes, we were even.

Chapter Twenty

The days following Chucky's murder were a blur, as our business thrived like never before. His death was the end of his organization, which meant more money for us. His runners were experiencing a drought, which caused them to come our way for re-ups. Niggas knew we had that hot shit! Even with our prices now doubled, they eagerly signed on to join the team. Currently, we were the number one supplier on the streets of Michigan. The demand was overwhelming, but Alicia and the others handled that shit with finesse in my absence.

Part of me really wanted to be there for my crew, but I needed a break from Detroit. There were too many bad memories there. It was time to start expanding the AFM legacy. With my newfound confidence and gangstress mentality, I was ready to kick shit up a notch here in Georgia. Besides, I'd already been through the worst. What else could happen?

On Friday I placed a call to the Paulettis, and Karla Carmichael answered the phone. "Jane, how are you holding up?" She sounded much happier than she had in the past. I guessed that having your man home would do that to you.

"I'm maintaining." My response was short and to the point. I didn't have any beef with her. I just wasn't the type of chick to go crying on the next bitch's shoulder.

"What Ace did was very stand up," Karla said, and I could tell she was beaming.

"Thanks, Karla. I wanted to tell her what Ace did was selfish, but I wasn't stupid. "Hey, I was calling to see if we could set up a meeting next week. I want to talk to you about expanding."

"My husband would be happy to meet with you. I'll set it up and send you the details." Now that the Pauletti men were home, the ladies were back to being regular Mob wives.

"Cool." I ended the call and tossed the phone on my bed.

Today was my dinner date with Garrison. I should've been at the mall, finding a cute outfit or getting my nails done. However, I had business to handle. Although I hadn't yet gotten the clearance to proceed, I took it upon myself to call a meeting with a few of Georgia's best female hustlers. Being that this was Rocky's stomping grounds, she was able to point me in the direction of four women well known for the way they got down in the streets.

After grabbing Ju from the bed, I eased her up onto my hip, careful not to rip the new dressing on my back. "I love you, Ju."

"Mommy! Mommy!" She bounced up and down, which irritated my back. Her hair was a curly mess, tamed somewhat by the purple headband she wore. The Baby Couture onesie and jean skirt exposed her chubby thighs, and the small baby doll shoes on her feet were to die for. Normally, I would take a picture of her on my phone to show Ace at our next visit, but I wasn't even thinking about visiting his ass anytime soon.

"Are you leaving, Janie?" Gran asked from the hallway. My bedroom door was open, and I saw her standing there, rearranging my linen closet. I liked sheets on one shelf and towels on another, but Gran liked everything color coordinated, no matter if it was bed linens, towels, or extra blankets. Her method didn't make any sense to me, but as long as it preoccupied her, it was okay with me.

"Yeah, Ju and I are going to visit one of my shops."

"I would like to see one. Can I go?" Gran smiled like a proud grandmother.

"Um . . ." I paused. "I don't see why not. Grab your purse and let's go." I didn't know how I would play it off, but I would certainly figure something out.

We entered the boutique half an hour later.

"This is nice." Gran hadn't made it past the OPEN sign, but she was already in love. "Look at this mahogany wood flooring and recessed lighting. You must've spent a pretty penny on this place," she observed, marveling at the interior.

"It's just a little something."

"Don't be modest with me, girl." Gran laughed.

I had to admit the place was nice. It was very neat and organized, just the way I liked it. All the new merchandise was on display at the front of the store. The racks were filled with color-coordinated clothing; the seasonal clearance pieces were in the back. Accessories adorned the showcase beneath the cash register, and several custom kicks lined the wall.

Iesha, one of my sales associates, greeted me at the entrance. "Ms. Doesher, you have guests waiting for you in the office," she informed me.

"Thank you, Iesha." I nodded. "This is my grandmother. Can you show her a few pieces while I finish up in the back?"

"Absolutely!" Iesha smiled before escorting Gran toward the section of the store best suited for her. Capa Donna didn't exactly have Gran's style of clothing. Hopefully, Iesha could show her something fun and sexy.

"Ms. Doesher, would you like me to hold the baby?" Brielle, another associate, asked.

"No thank you." I smiled and proceeded toward the back.

Upon entering the office, I could hear an argument under way.

"Bitch, fuck you and that nigga!" shouted a girl with a short red Mohawk.

"I will kill you about mine," yelled a light-skinned girl with a blond sew-in. She then jumped up after producing a switch blade.

I looked down at my daughter before placing my fingers in my mouth and whistling as loud as my lungs would allow. Ju thought I was being silly and tried to imitate me. "Everybody, just calm the fuck down!" I slammed my purse down on the black desk, then sat Ju in the chair behind it. "What's the problem?" I inquired of the roomful of women.

"Evidently, this one was fucking this one's baby daddy, or some shit like that," one of the other women explained with a smile. All she needed was a bag of popcorn, because she was definitely enjoying the show.

"Can y'all put this shit on ice until after the meeting?" I said as I took a seat at the conference table. I was starting to have second doubts. Females always had some type of beef going on. Why couldn't we uplift one another, instead of always tearing each other down?

"I'm sorry, but I don't play about mines." The blonde stared Mohawk down.

"Girl, I keep telling you don't nobody want his little-ass dick but you," Mohawk retorted while demonstrating with her fingers how small it was.

"Bitch!" Blondie stretched her hand out and sliced the shit out of Mohawk's face. Blood squirted everywhere.

"Goddamnit!" screamed the girl next to Mohawk as the tissue in ole girl's face parted like the Red Sea.

"Bitch, you cut me?" Mohawk grabbed her face in disbelief.

"Talk that shit now that you got two sets of lips." Blondie calmly wiped the bloody blade across her jeans before closing it and taking a seat. Her actions spoke volumes to me. She wasn't a talker, she was a doer, and I liked that shit. I realized then that she definitely had a place under my umbrella.

"Bitch, I got you." Mohawk went for her purse and removed a .22, ready to pop a cap.

"Hey, we aren't going to have nobody getting shot in my place of business!" I yelled. These two bitches were crazy. But, again, I liked it. Ju was entertained by these clowns as well. She was sitting in the chair, smiling and clapping her small hands together. "You want to shoot her, then do it on your time, not mine." I hit the table. "I came to talk to y'all about money. All this other bullshit can wait. If you're in, let's get to it. If you're out, then there's the fuckin' door." I pointed. When no one moved, I continued but not before getting up, going over to the desk, reaching into the desk drawer where I kept the cleaning supplies, and tossing Mohawk some paper towels. They definitely weren't going to stop the bleeding, but I couldn't have this chick bleeding all over the white sofa she was sitting on.

"You straight?" I asked as I took my seat at the table.

"Yeah." Mohawk nodded while staring her adversary down.

"Let's go around the room and introduce ourselves, starting with Blondie," I said.

"My name is LaShay. I'm from South Fulton." She looked like a black porn star, with a face full of makeup, plump lips, and curves in all the right places. She was Alicia's type. Too bad my girl wasn't here.

"Your turn, Mohawk."

"My name is Najae. I'm also from South Fulton. I'm a natural-born hustler and ready to put in work." She was still holding her face. Blood slowly oozed between her fingers and trickled down her hand. I was certain her shit was hurting, but she was handling the pain like a boss.

"Your turn, li'l bit." The third girl couldn't have been any taller than four feet, three inches. She was a little on the chubby side and had a baby face. Were it not for all the tattoos and piercings on her face, I would've guessed she was about fifteen.

"I'm Honey, and I come from Buckhead." Her voice was small, just like her. She was adorable. Then again, it was evident she didn't play.

"Your turn, baby girl." I pointed to the last girl, who was really fidgety.

"My name is Asia. I was born and raised in South Atlanta." She spoke without making eye contact with anyone in the room. Where I came from, that was a bad sign.

I showed that bitch the door pronto. "Asia, I'm sorry, baby girl, but you're dismissed."

"Huh?" Asia asked, as if she hadn't heard me.

"I said good-bye," I announced as I waved. The other girls snickered. I could tell Asia was embarrassed, but oh well. Once Asia was gone, I got down to business.

"My name is Jane Doe, and my partner is Ali." I saw no need in dropping government names this early on. "Together, we head the largest female-based drug organization in Detroit, Michigan. Currently, we're expanding our franchise. For that reason, we need a few brave hearts to assist us. I did some research. Each of you is here based solely on the work you've put in here in Georgia. I understand that you all have your own teams and a good clientele. The plan is for us to supply you with our products for the low. Then you guys will flood the streets, doing what y'all do best. The goal is to put every other nigga out of business by next year."

Najae expressed her concern. "What about the suppliers we already have? If we stop using them, it'll start a war."

"I hear you, and I understand your apprehension. However, we'll cross that bridge when we get there. It won't be the first time, and it won't be the last, either. Are there any other questions?" I said.

"When do we get started?" Honey was already counting money.

"Fuck that!" Blondie interrupted. "Before we get started, I need to know what you're expecting us to sell. I also need to know how low your prices are to see if this is even worth it."

"LaShay, we push everything from cocaine to heroin. As far as prices go, we get our shit straight from the source. With the middleman eliminated, I can guarantee you'll be making more than you've ever made in your life." I must've said a mouthful, because Blondie sat back in her seat and remained silent. "As for when you can get started, we're looking to be up and running in one week, tops."

"Cool," the women said in unison.

"Now, I don't have to tell you that loose lips sink ships. Keep your fucking mouths closed, and things will go as planned. The minute I hear someone running their mouth or doing some shit to violate your alliance with us, we won't hesitate to come see you." I made it a point to look each and every one of them directly in the eye. They needed to comprehend that I wasn't made to bitch up or one for backing down. "I will kill any nigga or bitch before I let them take me down or bring harm my way. Are we clear?" I said.

No one spoke, but everyone nodded.

I went into my purse and handed each of them throwaway phones. "I'll be in touch."

As the women gathered their things and prepared to leave, I asked Blondie and Mohawk to stay behind. In order for this to work, they needed their own personal lecture. I could see their hate for one another in their eyes.

"Hey, look, I'm not you guys' mamas, and I'm not trying to be," I told them. "However, if y'all plan to work for me, it means working together is mandatory and not a request. From this day forward, I don't want to see either of you fighting over a nigga who's probably out fucking the next bitch as we speak. He ain't worth losing out on this opportunity. As women, we need to stop being crabs in a barrel, constantly dragging one another down. As an alternative, we need to be the ones pulling our sisters up. Can y'all squash this?"

"I'm not going to lie. You are asking a lot from me, especially after she just cut my face." Mohawk looked over at Blondie.

"But you fucked her baby daddy, so let's call it even." I laughed.

"I'll let it go if she can." Blondie extended her hand. "Raynardo ain't worth all this, and you're right. His dick is little."

"It's done, then." Mohawk extended her hand as well then, and the ladies shook on it.

Chapter Twenty-one

Today had gone extremely well. After leaving the boutique, Gran and I had grabbed lunch at Justin's. Next, we had taken Ju to the famous Georgia Aquarium, then had stopped at the King Center exhibit. On the way back to the car, we were approached by a large black man wearing a chef's hat and jacket.

"Hey, ladies. My name is Dr. Kenneth Willhoite, but you can call me Mr. Soul Food." The man extended his hand.

"Mr. Soul Food?" I repeated with a smile. Something about the man was warm and inviting.

"Yes, darling! Mr. Soul Food, of the Soul Food Museum." He nodded back at the storefront. It was alongside several other businesses. "Did you know the icebox was patented by an African American?"

"Really?" Gran was all in.

Swiftly, Mr. Soul Food placed his hand on the small of her back and ushered her inside. I followed behind them. The place was small but packed with everything from celebrity pictures, old kitchen fixtures, and various food items.

"Why, sure, sweetheart." He laughed. "Did you know that eggplant and black-eyed peas were brought over to America from Africa?"

"No, I didn't," Gran answered. I remained quiet, but I loved the impromptu history lesson Dr. Kenneth was teaching us.

The tour lasted just under an hour; by the end, I was impressed. To be honest, some of his stories seemed a bit far-fetched. Even so, I liked the man's personality, and his hustle was impeccable. There was a tip jar at the door. I reached into my purse, removed two one-hundred-dollar bills, and dropped them in the jar.

Back at the house, I scrambled to get ready for my date. Everything I pulled out to wear was either too dressy or too casual. Dr. Garrison would be arriving in less than twenty minutes, and I hadn't even attempted to do my hair. As I stood in the walk-in closet, revisiting my options, the phone rang. I dashed across the room to retrieve it, but the caller hung up before I got there. It was a private call, so I probably wouldn't have answered, anyway, but I did wonder who it was. After placing the cell back down, it buzzed, which indicated I had a message. Quickly, I picked it up, tapped the screen, and saw the message. It read, You a dead bitch!

With a frown, I stared at the phone, trying to figure out who the fuck was playing on it. As far as I knew, my enemy was dead, so this shit had me puzzled. I dropped the phone down, and it rang again. This time it was Alicia.

"You got that crazy call too?" she asked before I could say hello.

"Girl, yeah! This nigga talking 'bout I'm dead. What the fuck is this?" I went back into the closet.

"I don't know, my nigga, but I been hearing some wild shit out here on the street. I would've called you earlier, but I knew you were hanging with the fam."

"What you hear?" I grabbed a black, sheer top and a pair of black skinny jeans.

"Niggas talking 'bout Chucky had something like a will in place," Ali explained.

"What does that have to do with the call?" After slipping on and buttoning the top, I slicked my hair up into a bun, with baby hair around my edges.

"The will states if ever he was murdered, his estate would pay one million dollars to the person who executes his assassins." Alicia paused to allow me time to comprehend her words. "They're gunning for us, Jane."

"Fuck!" I snapped. With a bounty of that caliber on our heads, everybody and their mamas were liable to come looking for us. "Look, you need to hop on a plane and get the fuck outta there. Don't tell anyone. Not even Patrice or Rocky!"

"I know." Alicia sounded nervous. "What about you?"

"I'll figure something out." The sound of the doorbell invaded my thoughts. "I gotta go, Ali, but hop on a plane and call me when you land."

"All right." She hung up.

Hastily, I slipped into a pair of black and cream wedge pumps, grabbed a cream Michael Kors bag, and sprayed on a little perfume.

"Janelle!" Gran yelled up the stairs.

"Here I come," I said before rolling a little nude lipstick across my lips and stepping into the hallway. On the way down the stairs, I tried to put my issues behind me.

"Hello, gorgeous." Dr. Garrison smiled. Although there was a small gap between his teeth, his smile was perfect.

"Hello, Doctor." My stomach fluttered. "Gran, this is Dr. Garrison. Dr. Garrison, this is my grandmother." I was nervous yet eager to be in Garrison's presence. His intellect fascinated me. It was also nice to be around someone who was cut from a different cloth.

"This fine man has already introduced himself." Gran gawked at Garrison like he was the last buttermilk biscuit on the dining table.

Leisurely, I roamed over his body with seductive eyes. The pair of red Mauri gator gym shoes, black denim 501 jeans, and the red hoodie with a gator print throughout had Dr. Garrison's swag on ten. He had to be fresh from the barber: his lineup was razor sharp. The diamonds in his ears shimmered whenever the light hit them; the chain around his neck was icy too.

"Damn, Garrison. If I didn't know you were a doctor, I would swear you were a dough boy," I joked to break the ice.

"I get that a lot when I wear my regular clothes." He laughed before extending four roses toward me. Each of them was a different color—red, white, pink, and yellow.

"Thanks." I thought it was a weird combination of colors. However, the thought was all that mattered.

"I didn't know which one was your favorite color, so I grabbed them all." He laughed again.

"Aww, that was so sweet," Gran crooned. She was smiling so hard, you would've thought the flowers were for her.

"Shall we?" he asked, and I nodded. We both said good-bye to Gran and headed off into the warm night air.

Anxiously, I walked to the Infiniti truck. This was my first date with a man who wasn't Ace.

"Since I'm treating, tell me where you want to eat," I said. I expected a man like Garrison to say something fancy, but he surprised me.

"I was thinking chicken and waffles. What did you have in mind?" Garrison replied.

"Actually, waffles sound perfect. Can we go to Gladys Knight's place?" I had received positive feedback about the soul-food restaurant.

"Sure." He held the door open for me, then walked around to his side of the SUV and climbed behind the wheel. I saw Gran staring out the front blinds with a smirk. She approved of Garrison.

"What type of music do you listen to?" Garrison started the vehicle with the push of his finger.

"Rap. What about you?"

"I listen to a little rap, but mostly old school." Just then a song by Anita Baker came on. "What you know about that youngster?" Garrison teased.

"You are not that much older than me." I flipped him the bird.

"I'll give you a fifty-dollar bill if you can name this song."

"Fifty isn't nothing to a boss like me." I laughed, trying to play off the fact that I really didn't know the name of the song.

"Yeah . . . yeah! You're still wet behind the ears."

"Whatever!" I laughed before reaching for the dial and turning it to Atlanta's hip-hop station. An old song by Ciara was on.

"I know you know the rules." Garrison stared at me.

"What rules?"

"Never touch a black man's radio." Garrison reached for the preset button and turned the radio back to old school.

"What do you have against rap music?"

"No offense, but most of that shit sounds retarded." Garrison started pretending he was a rapper. "Bitches be on my dick like the laces on my kicks!" He laughed. "That stuff makes me feel dumber by the end of the song."

"That's true." I laughed.

"I get tired of hearing us referred to as niggas. I get tired of hearing our women referred to as bitches and hoes." Garrison shook his head. "So, tell me what you like about rap music?"

I shrugged. "I come from the streets, so I can relate to most of the lyrics."

"I feel that." Garrison nodded. "I came from the streets too."

"You're kidding, right?" I wanted to laugh.

"Girl, I'm from the South Side of Chicago." Garrison was proud to share his story. "I grew up in the trenches!"

"I just find that hard to believe."

"Why so? Because I'm a doctor?" He glanced over at me. "My mother was a junkie, and my father was her pusher. Trust me, I know what it's like to go days without eating and to not have running water and electricity."

"Wow!" He was the true definition of never judging a book by its cover.

"When I was ten, I came to the conclusion that it was up to me to make a better life for myself and my family. That's when I decided to become a doctor or the next Michael Jordan. Well, your boy can't dribble a ball worth a damn, but I was good at school." He laughed.

"That was deep, Garrison. Thank you for sharing."

"It's not easy telling people where I come from, but it's my story. I'm not proud of my beginnings, but the things I went through made me who I am today. What's your story?"

"You want the truth?"

"Uh . . . yeah!" He laughed.

"My father was a hustler, and my mother was his bottom bitch! From the time I came into this world, the streets were calling me." I stared out the window while speaking. "My parents were killed when I was sixteen. By seventeen, I was stealing cars, and by eighteen, I was pushing dope throughout my city." I chose not to elaborate any further, for fear of incriminating myself.

Garrison didn't say anything for nearly two minutes. I just knew he was going to stop the car and tell me to get out. "I didn't expect you to say all that, but thanks for being honest," he finally said before whipping into a parking spot behind the restaurant.

"Thanks for not judging me." I smiled before stepping from the car.

"Baby, I leave the judging to God." Garrison placed his arm around me as we walked toward the restaurant.

Chapter Twenty-two

Over a table full of waffles, fried chicken, fried catfish, macaroni, and grits, the conversation continued.

"Man, if this don't taste like Inez Martin's cooking, I don't know what does," Garrison commented.

"Who is Inez?" I smiled just watching Garrison eat his food like it was going out of style.

"Inez was the best cook this side of the map." He dabbed his mouth with the end of a napkin. "She was my grandma."

"Aw, snap. This food is good, so Grandma Inez had to be a beast in the kitchen, then."

"Man, what? *Beast* isn't even the word. I used to look forward to Sunday dinner every week when she was alive. Old and all, that woman would lay out a spread for twenty people, although most days it was just us. Hot water bread, collard greens, dressing . . . Oh my God, her dressing was the best!" he cooed.

"I don't know about that. Monica had the best dressing in the world." I licked my fingers to drive home the point.

"Who is Monica?" Now it was Garrison's turn to smile at me.

"That was my mom. She wasn't Betty Crocker, but she had a few good dishes up her sleeve, and dressing was definitely at the top of the list." Just the thought of my mom at that moment made me miss the days when I would sit at the kitchen counter and watch her cook on rare occasions. She used every dish in the kitchen, which drove my father crazy, but he never said anything. I would watch as she drank her wine and made a show of seasoning the food. Just the images in my mind of her tossing salt and sprinkling pepper made me giggle.

"What's so funny?" Garrison asked.

"Talking about my mom made me think of the production she put on every time she got the urge to cook."

"My grandmother was the same way. I remember her taking all the seasonings she needed and spreading them out over the counter. Next, she would cut on some gospel music, lace up her apron, and then she was off."

"Grandma Inez sounds like a lady I would have loved to meet, especially on the days she cooked like this."

"I would have loved to meet Mrs. Monica too, especially to taste that dressing."

As the night progressed, Garrison told me a little more about himself. Surprisingly, I did the same. Garrison made me feel extremely comfortable. I liked being in his company. It felt good to speak openly and have someone just listen. He filled the companionship void I hadn't noticed was present until now.

When we left the restaurant about an hour and a half later, Garrison put his arm around me again. "I had a lot of fun, Janelle. We should do this again sometime," he said as he held the passenger door open and waited until I was inside the SUV.

"Me too!" I exclaimed.

"My next off day is in twelve days, so pencil me in." Over dinner, Garrison had told me he worked twelve twelve-hour days at a time at the hospital and then had only three days off in a row. There was no way I could put up with a schedule like that. Despite his grueling schedule, he was very passionate about his job. Thus, it didn't even faze him.

"Where are we going now?" I asked when he had climbed behind the wheel. I wasn't ready to let him go just yet.

"Where do you want to go?" He looked at me curiously.

"Take me to your house." The seductive tone in my voice was a telltale sign of what my agenda was. Garrison didn't say a word. However, I did notice the speedometer on his car increase several notches as we drove away from the restaurant.

In no time, we were pulling up to a semi-attached condo. Garrison used the remote in his car to open the two-car garage. As soon as he had pulled in and had put the car in park, I leaned over and pressed my lips against his. Although he was unprepared for the kiss, Garrison didn't miss a beat. His big hands instantly reached over and gently pulled me onto his lap. Reaching to the side of him, I pressed the button to slide the seat back, then positioned myself right on top of his manhood. Though both of us were still fully dressed, I could feel the rising heat from his dick, which caused the walls in my vagina to contract. The thumping against my panties was nearly too much to handle. I was horny, and Garrison was about to get it!

From the side of his neck to the firm six-pack, I left a trail of soft kisses. "Mmm," Garrison moaned as I unfastened his Gucci belt. His eyes were closed as I unzipped his pants and reached inside his boxers. The moment the large, curved dick was in my hand, my nipples hardened and the juices began to drip from between my legs. Slowly, I moved my hand up and down, jacking him slightly. "Shit!" He bit down on his lip, which, in my mind, was an indication that he enjoyed what I was doing.

"I'm ready for you, baby," I whispered.

Garrison opened his eyes, then began to unfasten my pants. I wanted him inside; I wanted to feel good. However, the second Garrison stuck his finger in my panties, all I could do was visualize Ace. Up until this very moment, he was the only man who'd ever touched my vagina. Being in this car now with Garrison, I felt like I was betraying the sanctity of what Ace and I had. Instantaneously, I tensed up.

"What's wrong? Do you want to go inside?" Garrison asked.

"It's not that." I sighed, lifting myself up off of him.

"What's wrong, then?" Garrison leaned in. With his lips less than an inch away from mine, I smelled the peppermint gum on his tongue. When I didn't respond, he continued to pry. "Is this about your man?"

"No. Yes. I don't know." I put my head down. In spite of Ace's decision to take a fifteen-year plea, I was immensely committed to him. He was the love of my life. What I was doing with Garrison was wrong, yet it felt right.

"I can respect that." Garrison raised his hands and backed away. I wanted to pull him by the collar of his shirt and press my body against his, but I resisted. "Do you want me to take you home, or would you still like to come in?"

"I'll still come inside, if you don't mind."

"It's fine by me." He got out of the SUV and headed toward the door of his condo like nothing had happened. I wasn't sure if he was pretending not to be mad or was just really cool about the situation.

I followed behind him like a child, unsure if he was upset with me. "Garrison, I'm sorry. It's just that I'm a loyal person. I love Ace."

"Janelle, you don't have to explain to me." He unlocked the door that opened into the kitchen. After flipping on the light, Garrison dropped his keys on the gray granite countertop and opened the stainless-steel refrigerator to retrieve a can of beer. "Would you care for water or something?"

"Yes, please." I nodded. After handing me a bottle of water, he took the time to fix his clothes. "You have a nice place," I commented, trying to make small talk.

"Thanks, Janelle." He took a sip from the beer can. The way his neck muscles moved when he swallowed turned me on. "Come on. Let me show you the rest."

I followed Garrison as we toured the den, living room, dining room and, finally, the upstairs, which consisted of three bedrooms. One of the bedrooms was being used as a library. Garrison had to enjoy reading, as there had to be over two hundred books on the shelves. The second bedroom was a guest room. Then there was the master suite, which was painted gray and accessorized with black furniture and a white carpet. It was nice, but it could've used a light cleaning.

"Excuse the mess." He tried to straighten up the newspaper scattered across the bed and the dishes on the dresser. "I don't have much time to clean."

"It's cool." I went over to assist him with the untidiness by neatly lining his shoes up along the wall and tossing his scrubs into the hamper near the closet.

"See? That's why I need a woman. Your man is lucky." Garrison grabbed the remote to the television and turned it on.

"He doesn't deserve me sometimes." I wanted to tell him details about Ace's situation, but that was way too personal.

"I know the feeling." He took another sip from the can, then stretched out across the bed.

"Do you still talk to her?" While at dinner, Garrison had told me about his last relationship. Her name was Ella; they had been college sweethearts. She was a teacher and had been the love of his life. They had been engaged to be married. Regrettably, two months before the wedding, Ella had turned up pregnant by another man—his fraternity brother.

"Fuck her!" he spat, finally losing his good boy manners. "You'll find someone who's worthy of having you."

"I don't know, Janelle. I'm too busy to find love."

"Let love find you," I said before crawling into his bed and lying beside him.

Even though the setting was perfect, neither of us did anything sexual. Instead, we simply talked well into the night. I didn't realize we had fallen asleep until I heard glass breaking downstairs. Startled, I sat up and went for the nightstand.

"Shit!" I realized I wasn't in my own bedroom. "Get up!" I nudged Garrison hard.

Garrison stirred. "What's up?"

"Someone's in your house," I whispered.

"What? Are you sure?" Garrison was now sitting up and wiping sleep from his eyes.

"Listen." I placed an index finger to my lips. The sound of footsteps coming up the stairs was apparent. Garrison leaped from the bed, reached beneath the mattress, and retrieved a silver revolver with a black handle.

"Stay here," he mouthed and headed for the door. I was never one to act cowardly. Hence, I eased off the bed.

"Whoever is up in my shit better know they got ten seconds before I bust a cap in that ass!" Garrison yelled before leaning his head out the doorway.

Pop! Pop! Two shots whizzed past his face and got lodged in the drywall. Garrison ducked back into the bedroom.

"Jane, come out, come out wherever you are," a female sang from the hallway. At the mention of my name, Garrison's eyes widened in surprise. "You better come out, or the good doctor will die."

I looked at Garrison and had to make a hard decision. "Give me the gun!" I urged, but he shook his head.

"I got you, Janelle. Fall back," he told me. He wanted to protect me, but I couldn't let him die for me. He had too much good left to do in the world.

The female began counting. "One."

"This is my battle, so give me the fuckin' gun!" I reached for it, intending to snatch it out of his hand, but he raised his arm higher.

"Two."

"Jane, I said fall back!" This time, Garrison shoved me so hard, I flew over the end of the bed.

"Three!" Just like that, the female assassin shot six bullets through the bedroom wall. Garrison took them all.

"No!" I screamed while watching his body drop to the floor. Frantically, I crawled over to him and cradled his head in my lap. On his face was a look of utter shock and confusion.

"What happened?" He rubbed his stomach and then raised his hand to inspect the blood on his hand. It was pouring profusely from his body.

"You've been shot, Garrison."

"But why?" he asked through a mouthful of blood.

"Just for being my friend." Tears slipped down my face as I held on to the man who had done nothing but befriend me. He didn't deserve this. It was all my fault.

"Jane, it's your turn." The female, wearing an all-black catsuit, stood less than three feet away from me, with her gun pointed at my dome. Oddly, she looked familiar. Then I realized she was the one I had dismissed from the meeting this afternoon.

"Who sent you?"

"Does it matter?" she asked.

"Well, it is common courtesy to tell a nigga who sent for them before laying them out, don't you think?"

"I guess you're right." She smirked. "Tamia sent me."

"Tamia?" I couldn't believe the same bitch I had put on was the same bitch trying to take me out.

"When she found out about Chucky's last will and testament, she put me on you. After leaving the store, I watched you and that old bitch go to lunch and the museum. Then I watched you and the doctor on your little date. Tamia said she and I will split the million dollars if I kill you." All of a sudden, this bitch had diarrhea of the mouth.

"A million dollars?" I smacked my lips and tried to create doubt. "Is that all she said?"

"What are you talking about?"

"My girl Ali called and told me the bounty was three million," I lied. The look on the girl's face was priceless. While the wheels turned in her head, I used it as a distraction to snatch her to the floor by her ankles.

"Shit!" she yelled. On the way down, her head hit the wall, giving me the opportunity to grab the gun from her.

Pop! Pop! Pop! Pop! I lit that bitch up like a man at the gas station smoking a cigarette.

From Garrison's bedroom window, I could see the neighbor's lights turning on. "Fuck!" I grabbed my purse off the bed and searched ole girl's pockets for a cell phone. "Bingo!" I slipped the phone into my back pocket and made a beeline for the first level. I didn't know if it was in my head, but it seemed like I could hear sirens already blaring in the distance. Realizing I was too far from home to walk, I scanned the kitchen for Garrison's car keys. It was dark, but I dared not turn on any lights. In an effort not to leave fingerprints, I felt around the countertop with my arm.

As soon as I spotted the silver glimmer of hope shining beneath the plug-in night-light, a knock came from the front door. Garrison had glass panes in the door, and I could see an elderly couple peeking inside. My heart raced at such a rapid pace, I feared I'd suffer a heart attack.

"Dr. Garrison, it's Betty and Joe from next door," the woman called through the door.

"Betty, we should probably go home and wait for the police," the husband replied. I prayed like hell his wife took heed. I would hate to kill them, but I would if it came down to it.

"You can go home, but I'm going to use this key he gave me last year in case of an emergency." I could hear the key dangling, then the knob turning. Hurriedly, I backed myself into the corner of the kitchen that was concealed by darkness. Apprehensively, I gripped the pistol, prepared to let loose.

Thank God I didn't have to. Instead of coming into the kitchen, the couple headed for the stairs. Once I was certain they were all the way up, I grabbed the car keys and ran for the garage. Without even waiting on the garage door to lift, I put the whip in reverse and burst through the garage door like a bat from hell.

Chapter Twenty-three

I drove the car for approximately five blocks before deciding it was a bad idea. His shit probably had a GPS tracker, which could lead police right to me. After coming to a stop near a burger joint, I wiped down the steering wheel, then hopped out, leaving that bitch running, keys and all.

"You left your car door open, lady," shouted some fat kid riding his bike around in circles. His ass should've been home, in bed.

"That ain't my car, kid," I replied without making direct eye contact with him.

"Whose car is it, then?" He rode faster, trying to catch up to me. My ass was power walking.

"It's yours if you want it."

"For real?" He smiled. "Why are you bleeding, lady?"

"What?"

Without a word, he pointed. While giving myself the once-over, I noticed that my clothes were painted in Garrison's blood. "I spilled something."

"You capping!" This was his way of calling me a liar. "Fuck all that, though. Can I have the car for real?"

"Tell you what." I stopped walking. His ass was out of breath, and so was I. "You give me the bike, and you can have the car."

"It's yours!" He hopped off the bike like it was on fire and fled back to the stolen vehicle.

I rode that mountain bike until my legs burned, probably over an hour. I had no idea where I was, but the neighborhood looked pretty rough.

"Yo, ma, let a nigga know what's up?" someone catcalled from a passing car. I ignored them and pedaled even faster. All I wanted to do was get home.

Unfortunately, the odds were stacked against me. The front tire began to deflate, causing the bike to become more difficult to maneuver, which in turn made my back feel the worst it had in days. I looked down to see several shards of glass from a broken bottle on the ground. "Fuck!" After getting off the bike, I let it fall and kept walking.

From a distance, I spotted a bus stop. No one was over there, and the bus looked to be the safest option at the moment. Therefore, I headed over. After an hour of waiting, I realized the bus might not run all night. For the first time in a long time, I was scared. I was accustomed to having Ali with me; now I was alone. I didn't have any allies in Atlanta except Garrison; now he was dead. With my head down, I felt my mind race as I tried to figure out how I could get out of this jam. Then it hit me that I did have someone to call. After pulling out my phone, I scrolled through the contacts and found Blondie's cell number. I dialed.

"Hello," she yelled over music. She was probably at a club.

"It's Jane. I need you to pick me up." Just like that, the fear was gone and I was back in boss mode.

"Where you at?"

"I don't know, but let me tell you what I see." I started to rattle off landmarks in my area.

"I think you're near Magic City. Stay put. I'm on the way."

Blondie definitely knew her city; she pulled up to the bus stop within twenty minutes. When I hopped in the passenger seat, she said, "What's up, Jane? What happened to you?" She was a bit taken aback by my attire and the blood.

"I got into some shit earlier. I need to take a shower and put on a change of clothes." There was no way I would dare walk into my house covered in blood. I didn't want no smoke with Gran.

"Okay. I got you." Blondie pulled off without another question. I didn't say anything, but I liked her style. She was a real bitch inside and out. Not too many people would do what she was doing for me.

"I'll look out for you on this first thing in the morning," I told her.

"Jane, you don't owe me anything. Earlier, you said us ladies had to stick together. Being in your organization is going to be the closet thing I have to family besides my kids, so I got you." Blondie reached into the ashtray and removed a fresh blunt. "I don't know what went on tonight, but I'm sure you did what was necessary."

During the ride, Blondie and I had an opportunity to get to know one another a little more.

"What's your story?" I asked her.

"What do you want to know?" She looked at me for clarification.

"Just tell me who Blondie is. Start from the beginning."

"Well, if you must know, Blondie is the product of rape. Although my mother carried me to term, she put me up for adoption at only three days old. From there, I was transferred from home to home, until I finally ran away." Shifting in her seat, Blondie continued. "In the beginning, I sold my body to make money—starting off as an underage exotic dancer, then ending as a flat-out whore. It wasn't until my twin boys were born that I started to view life differently. After giving up a promiscuous lifestyle, I tried to live on government assistance for six months. However, the handout wasn't enough. Under the tutelage of my old boyfriend, I got into the trenches and hustled. Once my old boyfriend became a permanent resident of the Georgia State penitentiary, I stepped up as the leader of our crew and the rest is history." She shrugged.

I was impressed with her story, because it was almost parallel to mine. Making a way out of no way was something that I could definitely relate to. There was a connection between her and me. Nonetheless, I wouldn't call us friends just yet.

"We're here." Blondie stopped the car, and we got out. The small duplex was nothing fancy, but you could feel the love seconds after stepping inside.

"Mommy!" two boys shouted in unison before tackling their mother at the door.

"Terry and Tyler, what are you doing up this late? It's almost one in the morning. You should have gone to sleep hours ago." She smiled. From the look of the older lady knocked out on the couch, it was obvious the boys had put their babysitter to bed.

"We missed you, Mommy," one of them said as he reached up for his mother, while the other tugged at her foot.

"I missed you too," Blondie replied. "Jane, let me put them to bed. You can use the bathroom in my bedroom. It's the one at the end of the hall." She pointed.

As I walked down the hallway, I glanced at all the pictures on the walls. Some of them were in frames, while others were colored pictures taped to the wall. I turned the knob to the bedroom at the end of the hall and hit the light switch on the wall. Two naked bodies lay in the spooning position. My nerves were on edge. Therefore, I whipped the pistol out without a second thought.

"What the fuck!" yelled a male with a shriveled-up dick as he jumped up, causing the female to open her eyes.

"I'll be damned!" I exclaimed. I couldn't believe the bitch in Blondie's bed was none other than Mohawk. I wanted to pistol-whip her ass on GP, but lucky for me, Blondie barged in.

"For real, Daryl? I know you ain't fuck this bitch in my house . . . in my bed . . . with your mother in the fucking living room!" Blondie yelled.

Daryl looked like he wanted to lie, but his ass had been caught with his pants down, literally. "LaShay, let me explain."

"Fuck you and this bitch!" Blondie snatched the gun from me.

Now, I was not the one to interrupt a murder when it was deserved. However, I knew Blondie didn't want it to go down like this, especially with her children home. Calmly, I put my hands over hers.

"Not only are your boys here, but their grandmother is too. Don't do it! They're not worth it," I told her.

"You're right, Jane." She handed me back the gun before diving on top of the bed and going to work on Daryl. I watched with amusement as Blondie put the hammer down on his punk ass. Mohawk eased out of the bed, then grabbed her belongings off the floor. After slipping into her panties, she called herself walking past me. I knew it was none of my business. However, Blondie had come through when I needed someone the most. For that, I had her back.

"Bitch!" I slapped that ho with the front of the gun, causing her wound, which she obviously had had stitched up earlier, to rip open. "Where you think you going?" I asked as she fell to the floor.

"I—I . . . ," she said, stuttering.

"I, nothing! Yo' ass better sit right here until she's done with him." With my gun pointed at her, she dared not make a move.

When I tell you Blondie kicked both of their asses up and down every square inch of the bedroom, you better believe it. She stopped only because her arms had gotten tired. By then, they were more than happy to leave without a commotion.

"Thanks, Jane," Blondie said after I handed her a bag of ice from the kitchen.

"We are family, remember?" I winked. Hell, me and this girl had been through more shit in two hours than I cared to count.

"I need to get up out of Georgia before I fuck around and kill someone." Blondie shook her head.

"I'm leaving for Detroit the day after tomorrow." After the stunt Tamia had pulled, I had to holla at her ASAP. "Maybe you can come with me, just to catch a break for a few days and clear your head." I knew firsthand that pressure could bust pipes.

"Maybe that's a good idea." Blondie nodded, happy to have found a friend.

After taking a shower in the en suite bathroom, I dressed in the pair of leggings and the T-shirt that Blondie had left me on the bed after she'd changed the sheets. She offered to drive me home, but I knew it was too late, and besides, we'd both had a long day. I told I would crash there if it was cool, and she obliged. While she went to bed in the kids' room, I slept in her bed. For the first hour or so, I tossed and turned. Every time I closed my eyes, they would pop open as thoughts of another home invasion crept into my mind. Yet sometime around 3:00 a.m. I finally dosed off.

Chapter Twenty-four

"Where is my Ju at?" I asked after unlocking the door. It was nine in the morning when Blondie took me home. Therefore, I knew both Ju and Gran would be up.

"Mommy!" Ju screamed and stumbled toward me. Outwardly, it appeared as though my daughter had changed overnight. Gran was sitting on the sofa, folding laundry and watching the Food Network.

"I missed my big girl." After kneeling down, I enveloped Ju in my arms. After all I'd been through, it felt good to squeeze my daughter. My heart always felt empty when she wasn't nearby.

"We need to talk," Gran announced.

"Yes, ma'am, we do." I released Ju and focused on Gran.

"What's going on with you? Are you in trouble or something" Her eyes were attached to the floor; she knew more than she was letting on.

"What makes you ask?" I slowly walked over and took the seat beside her on the sofa.

"For starters, I know you weren't in a car accident, Janelle!" Her eyes met mine. I didn't say a word, so she continued. "In case you didn't know, most old people watch the news. I know you were shot up at the mall."

"I'm sorry I lied about the car accident. I just didn't want you to panic."

"You had my great-grandbaby with you. What if something would've happened to her? What if you had been killed?" She was wiping her eyes now. "Sweetheart, when you live fast, you die fast. Janelle, you've got to slow down!" Gran paused and took a deep breath before placing her hand over mine. "I also saw the story about the doctor you left here with last night."

"Gran, I . . ."

"Regardless of what you think, I love you. I may not always show it the way I should, but I love you, and I never want to see you in harm's way." Instinctively, she pulled me into a tight embrace. My back throbbed, but I didn't say a word. This hug between me and my grandmother was long overdue. It was a moment that would forever be etched in my mind. "What happened last night?" she asked as she released me from her embrace, then stared at me.

"I can't tell you." I wiped my own tears.

"Are you in danger?" she asked.

I nodded.

"Dear Lord! I can't lose you, like I lost your father. You and Juliana are all I have left in this world, Janelle. If something was to happen to either of you, I would be no good." She shook her head from side to side.

"Gran, that's what I wanted to talk to you about. I'm in need of a huge favor." I sniffed. Last night I had had time to think about my life and the life I want for my daughter. She didn't need to know her mother was a gangster and her father was a hood nigga. Juliana didn't need to grow up glamorizing my lifestyle, the way I'd done with my father. She needed substance and balance, two things that I couldn't give her at the moment.

"What is it, Janelle?" Gran searched my face for a clue.

"Would you take temporary custody of Juliana until I can do better for her?" Every word I spoke felt as if it were caught in my throat. I didn't want to give my daughter away, not even for a short period of time. She was my baby. On the other hand, I knew my sole responsibility in life was to do right by her.

"Janelle, are you sure?" Gran was outdone.

"I don't want to sign any papers or anything like that, but I'm sure." Once you abdicated your parental rights and signed them over to another individual, it was difficult to regain custody. "I just need a little time to get some things in order, that's all." The lifestyle I lived was fast and furious. I would die before I put my daughter in danger ever again.

"Well, baby, you know I would do anything for you and Juliana." Gran smiled.

"We have to shake on something first," I informed her while wiping my eyes again.

"What is it?" she asked cautiously.

"You have to agree to stay here in Georgia and let me take care of you financially. I don't want my daughter eating Vienna sausages, I don't want you to throw away her clothes, and I don't want you treating her the way you treated me when my parents died." I eyed Gran prudently. "These rules are nonnegotiable, so you better think about it long and hard before you agree."

"You have yourself a deal." Gran extended her hand without hesitation. Simultaneously, I experienced joy and sorrow. Even though I felt I was making the right decision, it weighed heavily on my heart.

For the remainder of the day, I spent as much time with Ju as I could before packing up her belongings and moving her and Gran into a deluxe condo in Midtown Atlanta, at the Twelve. The place had a total of fifteen hundred square feet of living space, and there were two bedrooms, two bathrooms, and a gourmet kitchen with granite countertops and stainless-steel appliances. It was too upscale for Gran. In spite of that, she didn't protest. In a day's time, I furnished the entire place and even snuck in a trip to the grocery store up the street. The fridge was stuffed, along with the cabinets and the pantry.

Toward the end of my visit, Gran started to cry, which caused a domino effect. Before I knew it, both Ju and I were crying as well. I was sure Ju didn't comprehend why she was crying. Then again, it did feel like she sensed I was leaving her.

"Mommy go bye-bye?" Her beautiful eyes were sad and glossy.

"Only for a little bit, okay?"

"No." She pouted.

I wanted to renege on my agreement altogether, but I couldn't. It was the right thing to do. "Gran, all my numbers are in the notebook in the kitchen drawer. I left a credit card in the drawer, too, and some emergency cash. Please use them."

"Can't you just stay with us?" Gran was now the one not wanting to let go.

"I can't." With a deep breath, I grabbed my purse and kneeled down to give Ju the longest kiss ever. "Mommy will be back to visit every month. I love you." After standing back up, I looked at Gran. "Please take care of my baby." Without another word, I headed out the door. Walking away from my baby girl was extremely difficult, but it was necessary.

The minute I stepped into the hallway, it was game time! No more tears, no more emotions. Feelings were useless in the game; therefore, I left my heart right there at the condo and went to meet Blondie at the airport.

Once we were in the air, I heaved a sigh of relief. As far as I knew, no one was looking for me in connection with Garrison's murder. It was time to deal with Tamia.

Chapter Twenty-five

"Damn. Who is that?" Alicia stared Blondie down while she placed her luggage in the back of the car.

"That's my girl LaShay from the A," I replied after closing the passenger door.

"Shorty is straight!" Alicia replied.

I shook my head as Blondie got in the backseat.

"Hello. I'm LaShay, but you can call me Blondie. Jane does." She extended her hand to Ali, expecting a handshake. However, Ali had other plans.

"I'm Ali." She kissed Blondie's hand. The expression on Alicia's face was one of discomfort, but she played it off.

"Let me call and check on my kids." Blondie reclaimed her hand and quickly made the call.

"Want me to take you to the hotel first?" Alicia asked me as she pulled off into the flow of traffic.

"Hell no! Take me to Tamia's ass now." It was time to body that bitch!

It took us approximately forty minutes to arrive at an empty warehouse near the Eastern Market. On the way over, I sent a text to both Tamia and Tameka, requesting their presence at the warehouse. Rocky and Patrice were waiting inside with everything I needed.

When we got to the warehouse, Tamia was the first to come over and greet me. "What's up, Janie? I missed you."

"Everybody, let's go inside," I said, ignoring her comment.

"Is this the new spot?" Tameka asked. She thought we were here to show them a new location for the organization.

"Yeah. I just wanted you guys to see it and tell me what you think," I said as we all stepped inside. The place was dim, with little lighting entering through the skylights. It smelled bad too, like rotten food and backed-up sewage. Thankfully, I didn't plan to stay long.

"I like the location, but the odor in this bitch is foul!" Tamia held her nose.

"I guess you would know," Blondie scoffed.

"Fuck you say?" Tamia was on defense now.

"Bitch, I said if something is foul, you would know!" Blondie bucked.

"Who is this bitch?" Tamia looked at me.

"It doesn't matter." I stopped in the center of the large space.

Tameka frowned. "Jane, what's up? Why are you acting all funny?"

"I'm sorry, but I get like that when friends try to collect a bounty that's on my head."

"What?" Tameka was clueless. Yet Tamia knew exactly what I was talking about.

"Go ahead, Tamia. Tell your sister why she's about to die." I stared at the twins.

"What is she talking about?" Tameka said frantically, begging her sister to explain.

Tamia said nothing.

"Here. See for yourself." I handed Tameka the cell phone I had taken from the shooter at Garrison's place. On it were several messages from Tamia's phone, some of which had my picture attached to them. With friends like her, who needed enemies?

"Why would you do this? Jane is our friend." Tameka tossed the phone and hit her sister in the chest.

"Jane, I'm sorry. I allowed greed to get the best of me. Punish me, but don't punish my sister," Tamia said, finally finding her voice.

"Birds of a feather," Rocky said as she emerged from the shadows, with Patrice at her side.

Without delay, Tameka began to cry. Whenever you saw those two, death was certainly around the corner.

"I have two questions before we get started." I eyed Tamia. "How did you find out about the bounty?"

"Chucky's lawyer, Billy Kensington, put the word out." Tamia's voice trembled from fear of what she had coming. "What's your second question?"

"Who wants to go first?" I extended my hand to Rocky and retrieved a Louisville Slugger bat.

"Jane, please don't hurt my sister." Tamia dropped to her knees.

"You should've thought about that long before now." I shook my head. "Look at your twin and apologize for killing her."

"Tameka, I'm sorry . . . I'm so sorry!" Tamia cried, and Tameka did too.

I nodded for Patrice to do her thing, which she did.

Pop! One shot between the eyes dropped Tameka where she stood.

Tamia flew into a state of rage, screaming and crying. The bitch was giving me a headache.

Wham! I slammed the bat so hard into her face that the sound of her jawbone breaking echoed through-out the building. *Wham! Whap! Wham!* Repeatedly, I bashed her head in, until all that remained was a completely flat surface. Lifting the bat, I prepared to strike once more, but Alicia stopped me.

"That's enough. She's dead, Jane."

After dropping the bat, I walked away without so much as a peep. Alicia and Blondie headed out behind me, while Rocky and Patrice hung back to clean up.

The next morning, bright and early, I headed to the law office of Billy Kensington with Blondie. It was time to put an end to his shenanigans once and for all.

"May I help you?" the receptionist asked when we walked in. Ignoring her, I proceeded to the back of the office. On instinct, the receptionist jumped up from her seat. She thought she had the power to stop me. That is, until I removed a Desert Eagle from my jeans and pushed it against her temple. "Go ahead. He's in the last office on the left." She gave up the goods without me even asking.

"Watch her!" I barked at Blondie. "If she tries to dial the police or hit any panic buttons, shoot that bitch." I tossed the gun to Blondie before bum-rushing the back office. Billy was sitting behind his desk, reading over some type of document.

"What the hell? Nancy!" he yelled with a voice over-flowing with fear.

"Nancy ain't coming, pimp." Instead of sitting on one of the burgundy office chairs, I sat on top of his desk.

"Who are you?"

"You know who I am. Let's not play games." I wagged my finger.

"I swear, I don't." His hands rose in surrender.

"Does Jane Doe ring a fucking bell?" I charged at him and wrapped my arms around his throat. Billy was stronger than me and could've easily pushed me off like a bug. Yet terror kept him planted in his seat.

"I didn't know who Jane Doe was. I just did what my late client asked me to." This nigga was beginning to sweat bullets.

"I need you to call the bounty off!" With every word, I squeezed harder, digging my nails in real deep.

"I can't do that." He shook his head.

"Oh, I think you can." After releasing his throat, I pointed to the computer. "You might want to log in and check your surveillance cameras at home."

"What have you done?" Anxiously, he pounded the keyboard.

"I haven't done anything *yet*." With a smile, I watched as three camera views came on the screen. The first one revealed Rocky leaning over a baby's crib, wearing a ski mask. The second image was of a masked Patrice watching a little boy sleep, and the third one was of Alicia. She was masked and had a gun aimed at the woman sleeping peacefully in Billy's bed. Unfortunately for Billy, members of his family were not early risers.

"You better not touch one hair on their heads!"

"It doesn't feel so good to be hunted, does it?" I laughed.

"I'll do anything! I swear!" he pleaded.

"Call that shit off, Billy, and I mean it." I headed for the door. "Try to play me, and a member of your family will lose their life! Don't believe me, just watch."

My final warning was one I hoped he took seriously.

Chapter Twenty-six

Although I was certain Billy had gotten my drift, we had made sure to drive the point home by showing up at his church service, the grocery store he frequented, and even his doctor's office. Things had been quiet for almost two weeks, and I was back to getting money.

"I hate that I gotta go home. I had so much fun up here with y'all." Blondie sipped from the straw in her cup.

We were sitting at one of the booths in the Coliseum, a popular strip club in Detroit. Today was finally our meeting with the Mob about expanding the business to Atlanta. For the occasion, Ali and I had rented the entire venue strictly for Mr. Pauletti and his crew. The Mafia liked privacy. More importantly, after coming home from prison, I was certain all a nigga wanted was a big booty and a beer. Italians pretended not to favor black pussy, which was why I had selected the Coliseum. The women in there comprised various flavors.

Anthony Pauletti approached the booth with two men at his side. "You must be Jane Doe," he said.

"Mr. Pauletti, it's a pleasure to meet you." I stood to hug him. He kissed both sides of my face; then we all sat down.

"Is all of this for us?" He stared around the club in amazement. The place was empty, yet every dancer in the building worked as if the place was standing room only.

"All for you," I answered, then beckoned the waitress and told her to bring an oversize bottle of Ace of Spades that was chillin' on ice.

"I like your style," Mr. Pauletti commented. He then waited until after the waitress had filled everyone's glass before raising his in a toast. "To new beginnings."

"To new beginnings," we all repeated.

"*Salute!*" He smiled before tipping his glass.

"Why do you think Atlanta is a good place to expand?" asked a younger male to the left of Mr. Pauletti. He didn't appear to be happy about the meeting.

"The city of Atlanta is surrounded by thirty-nine counties in North Georgia, with an estimated population of six-point-one million people. A good number of these individuals are actors, ballplayers, and lawyers with big habits and even bigger bank accounts. Once we set up and acquire a consistent buyer's market, the money will practically come to us in dump trucks." I sipped the champagne before continuing. "I don't know about you, but I like making money that I don't have to work for." The table erupted into laughter.

"What sets you apart from every other nigga in Atlanta who is trying to get fast money?" the young man asked. I swore the room got so quiet, you could hear a cotton ball drop.

After looking each man in the eye, I chose my words carefully. "Call me a nigga again, and I'll show you what sets me apart."

"Come on, Luis!" Mr. Pauletti shook his head disapprovingly. "Watch your mouth."

"But, Dad—"

Whap! He backhanded the boy with a closed fist. I later learned that Luis was Mr. Pauletti's son from a previous marriage. He was the black sheep of the family business and would become a major thorn in my ass. The more money we made for the Pauletti family, the more he resented me. I guess he was mad that a black female was running circles around his spoiled ass.

On that day, the AFM had elevated the game and had earned a permanent seat at the Pauletti table. Within a year, not only did we have a booming business in Atlanta, but we were getting money in Texas, New York, and Florida. Our organization was handled by the best bitches in each state. Our net worth was roughly fifty million dollars.

With so much of my life dedicated to the AFM, time had truly gotten away from me. The monthly visits with Gran and Ju had become less frequent, and my letters to Ace had been nearly nonexistent. I hadn't done it on purpose. They said, "Out of sight, out of mind." The longer Ace was locked up, the more distant we became. In spite of everything, I still loved him and wanted to ensure he knew it. For his birthday, I wanted to do something special. He needed to know I was still his chick and would hold him down from now until eternity if I had to.

"Are you sure this is what you want to do?" Alicia stood beside me in the prison waiting room. She wore a baggy pair of denims, a white button-down shirt, and some low-top red Vans. Her hair was in the beginning stages of locking up. Dreads weren't my thing, but I liked her new look.

"Yeah, I'm sure." My plan was to surprise Ace with a visit today. However, this wouldn't be a regular visit. I had a reverend and Alicia as my special guests. Ace and I were going to get married! In my mind, it was the only way to certify my loyalty.

"Ace is my nigga. I'm just saying you should think on it." Alicia put her hand on my shoulder. Her rose gold Rolex glistened in the light. "He's looking at a very long time up in here, J. At least let someone else tap it one time before you get married."

"Ali, I appreciate your concern, but I got this." If there was one thing I knew in this world, Ace and I were made

for each other. I didn't care if I lived three lifetimes.
There would never be another him.

Alicia, the reverend, and I waited in the private room
for fifteen minutes before Ace came through the door.
When he finally did, my mouth dropped slightly. My baby
had definitely seen better days. The bags under his eyes
were deep and dark. His frail face matched his body; he
had to have lost at least twenty to thirty pounds, but it
didn't matter to me.

"Hey, baby! Happy birthday!" I couldn't wait to kiss his
lips. Sadly, kissing was forbidden until we completed our
nuptials.

"What's up, Janie?" He mugged me. "You look good."
Ace paid close attention to the diamonds protruding
from my ears as well as the ice around my neck and wrist.

"I've been missing you like crazy." I beamed with
excitement.

"I thought you forgot about a nigga." His voice was
calm; however, I could tell he was pissed. Those gorgeous
but weary eyes of his told it all.

"How could I forget about you?" I wanted to be offended by his statement, but he had a point, so I let it ride.
"Anyway, I came with a surprise today."

"What's the surprise?" He looked from Alicia to the
unfamiliar reverend. Before I had the opportunity to
respond, the door opened again. In walked some hood
rat in a minidress and a pair of five-inch stilettos.

"This lady is here for you too, Vasquez. I brought her
back so she wouldn't miss the wedding." If the corrections officer could see the expression on my, Ace's, and
the new bitch's face, he would know something in the
milk wasn't clean.

"Who the fuck is this?" homegirl and I inquired in
unison.

"You came here to marry me?" Ace smiled, oblivious to the drama that was about to go down.

"Bitch, who the fuck is you?" I repeated. I no longer could give two shits about the wedding.

"I'm Felicia." She smiled with a big gap between her teeth. "You must be his ex."

"Ex?" I looked at Ace for clarity.

"Felicia, chill the fuck out. Ain't nobody said shit about having an ex. This is my lady." Ace tried to clean up his mess, but I was done.

"Your lady? I thought I was your bitch?" Felicia said. "That's what you've been calling me every time I come up here to see you. That's what you called me in your letters, and that's what you called me when I paid the guard fifty dollars to give us some alone time a few days ago." Felicia didn't have to go any further; I had heard enough.

"Fuck you, Ace! You ain't shit but a slimy-ass nigga," I yelled. The rage in my heart wouldn't permit a single teardrop to fall. I wanted to cry, but this nigga wasn't even worth the tears. "Come on, y'all. Let's go." I nodded at Alicia and the reverend.

"Jane." Ace grabbed my arm, but I snatched it away.

"Fuck her! You need to be concerned with me," Felicia said as she stepped up into Ace's face.

"Get the fuck on." He shoved Felicia.

"How dare you put your hands on a pregnant woman!" she screamed.

"Pregnant?" I said. It felt as if the wind had been knocked out of me.

"Don't believe her." Ace shook his head wildly.

"Why shouldn't I believe her? After all, it's obvious you been fucking her," I retorted. If looks could kill, Ace's ass would've been dead in a matter of seconds.

"Janie, please don't leave. Let me explain." Now Ace was the one with tears in his eyes.

"Fuck her!" Felicia spat.

In a split second, I turned around and kicked that bitch right in the stomach. Thinking back, it probably wasn't the best thing to do, but I reacted in the moment. As she fell to the floor, screaming bloody murder, I took the opportunity to kick that bitch again and again, until the prison guards pulled me off her. As the reverend prayed, they put me in handcuffs and hauled my ass off.

I was escorted to a small holding cell. Sitting for over three hours did nothing to calm me down. My adrenaline was pumping; I was ready to tear into someone else's ass. Lucky for me, I was in a cell by myself.

"Doesher, you made bail," a male officer announced as he unlocked the cell. I stood and stretched before heading out.

Officer Bryant was waiting for me in the hallway, with his arms folded. He was always the person I called when I found myself in a situation with the law. "Why can't you stay out of trouble?" he asked me, with a stern look on his face.

"Thanks for coming." I gave him a hug. Over the years, he had become like a big brother. "What did they charge me with?" Years ago, I had vowed never to end up back in jail. But today was sort of out of my control.

"They wanted to hit you with attempted murder of a fetus. Lucky for you, the girl isn't actually pregnant." His news came as a relief, but I was still upset that Ace had even put me in that situation. "Jane, I'm going for sergeant next month. I can't pull any more favors." Bryant pulled me toward the stairwell.

"Fuck that mean?" I frowned.

"It means that you're becoming hot out here, and I can't associate my name with some hot shit," he whispered. "The AFM is slowly climbing up the food chain. Once you get on the Feds' radar, can't nobody help you but God."

His comment resonated with me. His prediction wouldn't come to pass for a few years, but I should've taken his warning seriously right then and there.

Chapter Twenty-seven

The next two years went by in a blur. Though Ace made numerous attempts to contact me, he was the furthest thing from my mind. After everything I'd been through, the last thing I needed was a disloyal-ass nigga. Ali and I threw ourselves into work, and the shit was paying off tremendously. Not only had we taken over the game in Detroit, Atlanta, Texas, New York, and Florida, but we were also now moving weight in other major areas, like New Orleans, Virginia, and California. Most of our affiliates were making an average of five hundred thousand dollars in profit every day after my and Alicia's cut. Shit was good!

"Have you seen my bag?" I asked Alicia after watching the luggage from our plane go around the carousel for the fifth time.

"Nope. That's why I told you not to bring one. You're a rich bitch. You can pop tags everywhere you go. We need swimsuits anyway." Though we were in Las Vegas on business, Alicia had talked me into taking some downtime to relax.

"I had some good pieces packed, though." I pouted.

"It's your birthday. Fuck them bags. Let's go shopping."

"But—"

"I'm treating, so come on." She practically pulled me to the cabstand. While we waited, she blew my ear off about this and that as I pretended to listen. She didn't even notice I wasn't paying her any mind, until we'd gotten to the mall and she was asking which store I wanted to visit first.

"I'm sorry, Ali," I said, apologizing, as she stood in my face, looking at me all crazy. "Let's hit Fantaisie." It was a very upscale French franchise, and the name was French for "fancy." The swank retail chain had storefronts only in Las Vegas, Hawaii, and Los Angeles.

"Oh, I see you're trying to run up a check on your girl. It's cool, though." She wrapped her arm around me, and I followed suit. Together, our goofy asses headed toward the store.

"Damn. They got the boys right outside. Nobody better try that fuck shit in here, I guess," Alicia said as we passed the officers at the entrance to the store.

"I need to get a few rent-a-cops to stand outside of Capa Donna. These little hoes be stealing."

"Damn. Look at these." Alicia flew over to a pair of shiny gold rain boots. "These bitches are six hundred dollars, but they're dope." After removing one of her shoes, she slid her foot into a boot and then modeled it. "Aw, they even have some baby ones for Ju."

"Girl, you better not even think about getting someone that's still growing some six-hundred-dollar shoes," I warned. As Alicia continued looking through the boots, I made my way over to the clothes. Most of them were simple, with a few crystals, and some of them had real leather embellishments. Either way none of them were worth the amount on the price tags.

"Janie, look at the bullshit here." Alicia waved a plain white shirt in my face. "This muthafucking shirt is three hundred seventy-five dollars. I ought to get it and walk around with the price tag sticking out just because."

"Girl, let's go. I've seen enough of this place."

"When is the last time we've been on vacation . . . ? Don't worry. I'll wait!" Alicia looked at me with a grin.

"I'm a girl from the hood that ain't ever had shit. I'm buying this shirt and these flashy boots just because I can."

"Well, rock on with your bad self," I told her. As I followed behind her to the register, I stopped to look at the studded belts. My mouth almost hit the floor when I saw that they cost over two thousand dollars.

A tan woman with a brunette bob stared at Alicia from the other side of the counter. "Before I ring this up, can you afford these items?"

"What?" Ali snapped, and I knew shit was about to go left. Quickly, I looked back to make sure the police outside the door weren't alerted.

"You tourists come in here and have us ring all this stuff up. Then, all of a sudden, you can't find your wallet or whatever."

"Bitch, I can buy just about everything in this bitch, including you, if I wanted to." After reaching into her book bag purse, Alicia produced several wads of rolled and rubber-banded cash, then slammed them down on the counter one by one.

"Come one, Ali," I said.

"Nah, fuck that. I ain't ever been so disrespected in my life. This bitch is gone learn who the fuck I am today." Alicia was fuming. "Ring my shit up, cashier!" she spat.

I placed the money back in her book bag, then zipped it up and pulled her away from the counter. "Why give her the commission? She just shit on you, and now you want to give that ho a bonus check? Nah. Let's go spend that money where our business is appreciated."

As Alicia and I walked out of the store, I gave the cashier and the camera two middle fingers.

Chapter Twenty-eight

"Come on, Jane! I'm ready to play the machines." Alicia pulled the sleeve of the Armani blazer she'd gotten me earlier, along with a few other things. We had so many bags, we had to have the stores courier them back to the hotel. "It's your birthday. Come on!"

"It's my birthday, so I should be the one calling the shots, right?"

"Janie, you're in Sin City. Let's go play the slots." Alicia had been addicted to the casinos ever since she turned legal last year.

"Ali, I just want to have dinner and sip something before we meet with this new buyer. All that shopping wore me out." Truth be told, my birthdays were always bittersweet. Seven years ago, my parents had left me in the worst way. Therefore, I never made a big deal about turning a year older.

"Let's just play a bill or two. It's relaxing." Ali brandished a wad of one hundred-dollar bills.

"One bill!" I relented. "Once that's gone . . . we're gone."

The Bellagio was grand in every sense of the word. It was an award-winning, luxurious five-star resort, best known for its dancing fountains and light shows. Some travelers had even described it as having the best casinos in Vegas, while others appreciated its upscale shopping and numerous restaurants. Still, I was uninterested in and unimpressed with my surroundings as I followed Alicia with my head down. I was reading a text message, and I practically ran someone over.

"I'm so sorry, sir!" Mortified, I apologized profusely.

"It's all good." With a smile, the stranger wiped the liquor that had spilled from his cup off the front of his snakeskin hoodie.

"Let me find you some napkins."

"It's cool, Ma." He chuckled while looking me over from head to toe. "What's your name, baby girl?"

"Jane," I replied shyly while tucking a loose strand of hair behind my ear. This six-foot-six creature with broad shoulders had me feeling some sort of way. I was not going to lie. This nigga had my juices flowing on impact.

"I'm Bravo." He smiled, exposing a chipped tooth. "How long are you in Vegas?"

"Just a few days. What about you?" Truthfully, I wanted to walk away, but his presence was captivating. There was something about the light skin, sandy brown hair, and light freckles on his cheeks that made him interesting to me.

"I'll be here all weekend, celebrating my birthday."

"Is today your birthday?" From the corner of my eye, I could see Alicia waiting patiently for me to come the hell on. She was ready to test her luck on the sinful machines.

"Yeah." He nodded. "I'm twenty-four years young."

"Today is my birthday too."

"Get the fuck outta here!" He twisted his lips. "Say swear."

"I swear." I laughed.

"Well, we need to celebrate together." Bravo looked at his boy, then over at Alicia. "Is that your girl?"

"That's my girl, but she doesn't swing his way." I could tell Bravo was trying to set up some double-date type of shit.

"Oh, my fault. Tell your lady I didn't mean no harm." He shook his head.

"I'm not gay . . . She is." I laughed again.

"Whew!" Bravo exhaled. "Then I still have a chance."

"Boy, stop."

"For real, why don't you lock my number in and call me tonight? I have to make an appearance tonight at Tao. After that, we're turning up. I would love for you to join me." Bravo called off his number, and I stored it in my phone.

"See you tonight." I waved good-bye and headed over to Alicia, who had found a seat at a nearby dollar machine. She was already down twenty dollars. "My bad, girl," I told her.

"Do you know who that was?" she asked without so much as looking at me. Her eyes were glued to all the bright images on the screen.

"Bravo," I said, like he and I were old friends.

"Brandon 'Bravo' Ford, the starting forward for the Miami Heat!" Alicia exclaimed.

"He's a ballplayer?"

"Hell yeah! The number one draft pick of his year." Alicia was up on sports. Whereas I was clueless.

"Well, he invited us to his birthday party tonight at Tao." I shrugged.

"Then we need to go shopping." Alicia finally pulled her eyes away from the slots. "I know it's going to be some fine bitches up in there. I got to get right."

I shook my head. "First, we have this meeting, and then we can go shopping." No matter what, I was always about my cash flow.

"Fine." Alicia sighed.

The meeting that afternoon went smoothly with members of the Moretti Mafia. They were the shot callers of Nevada. Nothing went in or out of the desert without clearance from them. The gathering was set up by Mr. Pauletti in an effort to expand all our empires. Both families needed someone willing to run their dope clear across the country. Until today everyone they had propositioned had turned them down. Most men in my line of work were content with local shit. They were happy just being the king of their cities, but not me. I wanted to be internationally known. In order to do so, I had to take risks no one else was willing to take and fight twice as hard to prove my shit. With that being said, I was able to name my own price. And so I walked away from the table with a nice sum of money.

After shopping for two hours at the luxury stores in the Venetian, Alicia and I were dressed to the nines and ready to turn up. My make-up was beat, and my hair was on point. The black catsuit I wore exposed my cleavage and hugged my ass just right. It had been so long since I had gone out that I was nervous about it.

"This place is packed," Alicia practically screamed over the music after we entered Tao.

The place was filled to capacity with folks from all nationalities, and everyone was having a ball. It was unlike anything you would see at a neighborhood club. For starters, this club had to be at least twenty thousand square feet. It was painted in neon colors, which glowed in the dark, and the waiters and waitresses didn't appear to have clothes on, only body paint.

"Watch your step, miss." The attendant in a black shirt and red tie extended his hand to assist me into the booth overlooking the crowd. While Bravo had invited me to chill in his booth, I didn't want to look like a groupie. Hence, I had purchased my own. The price tag was damn near the cost of two arms, two legs, and ten fingers. The booth was big enough for a mob, but Alicia and I held it down.

All night long, we drank Ace of Spades like the shit was going out of style. I was fucked up but not sloppy. We danced to every song, including the ones we didn't know.

Ali even surprised me with a pink diamond necklace and tennis bracelet. The charms on both were half a heart with black diamonds that spelled BFF in the center.

"Thank you, Ali." I extended my arm so she could place the bracelet around my wrist. "Where is yours?" Usually, when someone gave you half of a heart, they had the other half.

"I didn't get one. You know I don't wear no girly shit like that." She frowned. Her jewelry preferences entailed gaudy Jesus pieces and shit. "Are you having fun?"

"Yeah." I nodded, with a smile. Truth was, I was having a good time. Sadly, the occasional image of my parents' dead bodies danced in my head. It was a day I could never forget no matter how hard I tried.

"One sip for the road?" She held up one of the metallic gold bottles surrounding the large gold bottle in the middle of the table.

"I can't." The room was already spinning. I had to quit while I was ahead. "I think I'm ready to go."

"Let's roll, then." Alicia downed the bottle and wiped her mouth. "Can we stop at the casino before we turn in, though?"

"Come on, girl." I laughed.

As we were leaving the club, my shoe got caught on a snag in the floor, causing me to trip. Under normal circumstances, I could've stopped myself from falling. Unfortunately, my coordination was a tad off. Bravo reached out and grabbed me before I tumbled to the floor. Thankfully, he was in the right place at the right time.

"Damn, Ma. I'm going to have to get you some brakes," he quipped.

"I'm sorry." I laughed.

"I thought you was going to kick it with me for my birthday?" He looked disappointed.

"I was, until I found out you were a ballplayer." I tried hard to keep myself from looking as tipsy as I felt.

"What's that supposed to mean?"

"I didn't want you thinking I was a groupie." I shrugged.

"Baby, I watched you and your girl buy more bottles than me. I know you got your own paper." He laughed. A few men walked by and dapped him up. They were all over six feet, so I knew they were probably teammates.

"If you were watching, why didn't you come over and say something?" Biting my bottom lip, I tried to appear sexy.

"Shit. Because I didn't want you to think I was no groupie," he joked, and we both laughed. "Look, the night is still young. Why don't you come get something to eat with me? We can go Dutch, if it makes you feel better."

"I'd like that." It was time for me to get back on the dating scene, so why not start with a man like Bravo?

Chapter Twenty-nine

After putting the smash down on an all-you-can-eat buffet, Bravo and I walked the strip and talked. He was a really down-to-earth guy, and I liked being with him. In an hour's time, he opened up to me about his childhood and family issues. I could tell some things were weighing heavy on his heart and he needed an unbiased ear to allow him to vent.

"I was the product of incest," he blurted at one point. He searched my face for a reaction, but I didn't provide one. "My uncle raped my mother when she was fourteen, and told her not to tell. She was afraid, because he's crazy." Bravo circled his index finger on the side of his head, demonstrating his uncle had mental issues. "Nine months later, she had me on the bathroom floor at school. Then she had some explaining to do. When she told the family, they called my mother a fast-ass liar. They wanted her to get rid of me, but she wouldn't, so they put her out. She was forced to do things she wasn't proud of just to keep food on the table. She made a lot of sacrifices for me, you know." Basically, Bravo was saying his mother had sold her body.

"Now that you're doing well, I bet she smiles all the time, because it means her sacrifices were well worth it." I could just picture his mother telling the family that had shunned her to kiss her rich ass.

"My mother died from HIV during my first year in the league." He got choked up from just articulating the deadly letters. "She had it since I was about twelve, and . . ." Tears streamed down his face. I felt his pain.

"It's okay, Bravo." I didn't know what else to do besides reach up and wipe his face.

"I'm sorry." He wiped his face and pulled it together. "It's just that she died on my birthday, so I always get a little emotional."

At that exact moment in time, I knew we were meant to find each other. Our stories were different, but a few of the chapters were the same. I went on to tell him about the loss of my parents on my birthday, as well as the lifestyle my father led. He didn't judge me, as I hadn't judged him. It was refreshing to find someone you could open up to without second-guessing their intentions.

"You've told me about your folks, but what's your story?" he asked as we approached our hotel.

"I'm a hustler," I replied honestly. If I was going to be open and up front with anyone, it would be him.

"There are lots of ways to hustle. Do you do hair and nails? Do you sell knockoff purses? Do you claim other people's kids on your taxes?" he joked. He followed me into the lobby.

"I push weight," I said as we headed to the elevators.

"Huh?" He stopped laughing and pushed the button for the elevator.

"I have a very powerful drug empire." I stepped into the elevator. When I glanced at the shiny gold interior, I could see Bravo's reflection. His mouth was hanging open.

"Get the fuck outta here!" He leaned against the elevator wall. "I wasn't expecting you to say that shit."

"I hope it's not a problem." I smiled modestly.

"Nah, baby, it's not a problem. I'm no stranger to getting it how you live. You just don't strike me as the type of female to be in the dope game."

"I'm not in the dope game. I *run* the dope game. There's a difference," I said, correcting him. Then we both laughed.

"Now that you told me, you have to kill me, right?" he teased. When I didn't respond other than to raise an eyebrow, he continued. "Damn. Can a nigga get a kiss before you body me?"

"Come here." I motioned with my finger. He licked his lips and walked over to me.

"You're beautiful." He leaned in and kissed my lips. A surge of electricity hit me like lightning. My nipples began to harden, and my stomach did two or three backflips. The way Bravo's tongue danced in my mouth made me imagine how his head game was.

"I want you," I panted, reaching for his pants, completely forgetting where we were.

"Jane, I've never met a girl like you," he whispered.

"And you never will," I responded as he picked me up. I wrapped my legs around his waist and pressed my nails into his back. Just then the door opened, and he carried me to his room. Ironically, we were staying on the same floor.

Once we were inside the room, it was on like *Donkey Kong*. The way we ripped each other's clothing off, you would have thought we were wild animals. In no time, Bravo had laid me on the bed and begun planting soft kisses down my body. With his teeth, he slid my panties down to my ankles. My shit was wet with anticipation, but I was also nervous. Other than Ace, I hadn't been with anyone. As Bravo explored my walls with his tongue, I attempted to push Ace to the back of my mind. I tried to remember how he had cheated on me and how it had made me feel.

"Umm," I moaned. This boy's tongue game was proper. He would've stayed down forever if I hadn't tapped his shoulder.

"You ready, baby?" Bravo pulled a condom from his pants pocket and made a show of sliding it down the large pole between his legs. Seriously, this nigga was a solid nine inches. I guessed that "big feet" myth was true in his case.

"I'm ready." With a smile, I braced myself for the impact. Slowly, he slid the tip inside, then pulled it out and repeated the motion two more times before going in deep. The pain was pleasurable, if that made any sense.

"Oh shit!" I moaned as Bravo stroked the fuck out of my body for over an hour. By the time we were done, I had lost count of my orgasms.

"That was good," Bravo declared as he rolled off of me and exhaled.

"Yes, it was. I needed that," I admitted.

"I could tell you were a little tight and tense. It must've been a minute."

"You're the second man I've ever been with."

"If we're being honest, you're the seventh person for me." He gazed over at me.

"Only seven?" I raised a brow. "As a professional athlete, I know you've got to be lying."

"Bible." He raised his right hand. "I ain't no ho."

"Sure." I sat up on the side of the bed. "You mean to tell me that you don't have a group of women throwing it at you?"

"I didn't say that. Women throw themselves at me daily. I have a stalker that sends me letters regularly, professing her love for me and promising to be the best woman I've ever had, but I'm not checking for none of them. Real talk, that shit with my moms had a nigga scared." He crawled toward me, then laid his head in my lap. "Besides, I'm a one-woman man."

"So why haven't you married anyone up, then?" I couldn't resist rubbing his wavy hair.

"I haven't found the right woman until now." He stared directly into my eyes.

"Bravo . . ."

"Look, Jane, I feel something that's undeniable with you. The way we opened up to each other speaks volumes to me."

"Don't you think you're moving too fast?"

"When I see something I want, I don't play games with it. I want you, but I'm willing to go at your speed."

That night we had sex three more times. For the entire weekend, the two of us were inseparable. The more time we spent together, the more difficult it was imagining going our separate ways. I had never thought I'd have a strong connection with anyone like this ever again, yet here I was, head over heels and beside myself. When the time came for us to part ways, but I didn't want to say good-bye.

"What's the matter?" Bravo was standing near the bed, putting the last items into his suitcase.

"I don't want our time to come to an end." I pouted, which was unlike me. I rarely let my guard down and acted feminine.

"It doesn't have to." After zipping the luggage, he walked over and wrapped his arms around me. "Come back to Miami with me, and we can keep this thing going." He kissed my lips.

"I wish I could, but I can't. I got business to handle. However, you can come back to Detroit with me, and we can keep this thing going," I replied, mimicking him.

"I got ball to play, baby, but I wish I could." He sighed. "Let me ask you something. Do you believe in love at first sight?"

"Honestly, I didn't before I met you, but now I can see it." I smiled.

"Janelle, I really feel like you and I are soul mates." He looked into my eyes. "Believe me when I tell you I am far from being a corny dude, but I really want to make you my wife. Something about you and me just feels right! I feel complete."

"Wow!" I was taken aback, yet I completely understood what he was saying, because I shared his sentiment. "I agree. It feels right."

"Fuck it. We're in Las Vegas. Let's do it." He pulled back from the embrace with a smile as big as Texas.

"Do what?" My eyes widened.

"Let's get married today!"

"Let's say I agreed. What happens next? I still go back to Detroit, and you still go back to Miami."

"Baby, let's just do it and figure that shit out later." Without hesitation, Bravo dropped down on one knee. "Will you marry?"

Staring down into his face, I saw nothing but a man with a good heart and pure intentions. I saw my Prince Charming; I saw the man I was sure my parents would've approved of. "My answer is yes, Brandon, but we can't get married here. I want to do it right. You have to meet my daughter and my grandmother. I want to meet your family too. Let's see how things go for a year or two, and I promise to meet you at the altar."

Satisfied with my promise, Bravo agreed to pump the brakes on marriage. However, before his plane headed back to Miami, he took me to see Ben Naviera, a world-renowned jeweler to the stars. From the moment we stepped into the ivory- and platinum-decorated store with tons of jewelry on display, Ben and his staff wined and dined me while we discussed the cut, clarity, and style of the engagement ring I envisioned. Of course, they showed us nothing but the best, and of course, I loved every single one of those rings. However, I settled on a six-carat princess-cut ring with canary and chocolate diamonds as access stones. I thought I'd have to fly back in to get the ring, but Ben assured me he would expedite the process and have it done while I waited.

"Are you sure about this?" I whispered to Bravo once we were finally alone in a private office. "This ring is expensive." Given the ring's price tag of roughly $350,000, I was beginning to have second thoughts about it. I'd never owned anything that expensive in my life. Not that I couldn't afford it, but I just wasn't into flashy things.

"Baby, true love is priceless," Bravo responded nonchalantly as his phone rang. It was one of his friends calling to say that they were heading to the airport and that he had better hurry up.

"I know you have to go. I can wait here," I told him after he hung up.

"Are you sure?" He appeared conflicted.

"I'm sure, but call me as soon as you land, and I'll do the same." After planting my lips on his, I tongued my man down for the better part of three minutes, until we both had to pause for air. After another kiss, he left me in the office alone.

I waited only about an hour for Ben to return with my ring. When he did, it was absolutely gorgeous. I loved the way it glistened and captured the light, bouncing it against the wall in what amounted to a light show. After collecting my paperwork, I headed back to the hotel to meet with Ali and catch our flight back to the D. I was the happiest I'd been in a long time, and I prayed my fairy tale would never end.

Chapter Thirty

After leaving Las Vegas, Bravo and I did our best to spend time together over the next few months. Due to his hectic schedule, I was the one who mostly caught flights to see him. Naturally, it was always sad to say good-bye, but truthfully, seeing him for only a few days here and there was perfect for me. I didn't need to be up under my man, and distance always made us enjoy each other more, in my opinion.

I still hadn't introduced Ju or Gran to Bravo, but I was planning on it really soon. Part of me was waiting to feel him and see if he really was the guy he showed me, and so far, I had yet to see any different. Most people probably thought we were crazy for moving at lightning speed, but it worked for us, so it didn't matter. Bravo was a guy with whom I could spend forever and maybe even have more babies. Even though he hadn't mentioned it, I was really thinking about retiring for good after we got married. For now, though, I was still on my gangster shit, and today was no different.

After pulling up to the James H. Cole funeral home on West Grand Boulevard, I cut the engine, grabbed my purse, and climbed out. For some reason, Richard Lennigan had called an emergency meeting with me today. Although I had him on retainer, I hadn't heard from him in forever. I hoped he wasn't going to tell me Ace was dead. As much as I despised Ace, I didn't want to think of him lying lifeless in a place like this.

"Janelle, thank you for coming," Richard said when he greeted me at the door. He was wearing typical lawyer attire—a suit and tie.

"Richard, what's up?" I squinted from the sun.

"Come on inside." He held the door open for me, and then he headed toward one of the ceremony rooms. My heart skipped three beats as I followed him. "I called you here on behalf of Ace."

"Please don't tell me he's dead." I could feel my heart drop to my stomach as we entered the ceremony room.

"I ain't dead yet," Ace said from the front of the room. He was dressed to the nines in a three-piece Italian suit and black loafers. His haircut was fresh to death, and the cologne drifting off his body smelled expensive. To his left was a prison guard. To his right was a pastor dressed in a purple and gold robe.

"What's up, then?" I asked with an attitude after realizing that he was okay. Ace looked better than I remembered. Nonetheless, I was still irritated by his presence.

"Janie, I know I fucked it up last time, baby, but I been hurting without you. Please forgive me and say you will marry me." He reached into his pocket and produced a red Cartier box. I was completely at a loss for words, but not for long.

"Anthony, I'm sorry, but I'm engaged to someone else." Raising my left hand, I flashed the oversize rock on my finger.

"What? Engaged to who?" Ace snapped. "Did you know about this, Richard?"

"No, I didn't." Richard shook his head.

"It wasn't for him to know!" I snapped.

"Janie, I thought you said you would be mine forever?" Ace actually looked wounded.

"You couldn't possibly think I would stay with a cheating-ass nigga like you! You fucked me over and thought I would stay loyal? Nigga, please."

"Janie, I made a mistake," Ace insisted.

"A mistake is leaving your keys in the car. A mistake is forgetting to put the clothes in the dryer. Falling into another bitch's pussy ain't no fuckin' mistake!" Until now, I had suppressed my anger. Seeing him brought it all back up to the surface.

"Baby, you've got to believe me when I say you're the only woman I love. I swear on my daughter." Ace tried to reach for me, but I swerved.

"It's too late. I found someone else, Ace, but I do wish you well." With a faint smile, I turned and headed out the door. I loved Ace with every fiber of my being, but it was time to move on. I wasn't a bitch who hustled backward. Never had been and never would be.

"Janelle, wait up." Richard emerged from the room and had to jog to catch up to me.

"Listen, if you want to remain on my payroll, you better remember that you work for me and not Ace!" I was furious. "The moment he took that plea, you were no longer his attorney!"

"I called the meeting only because I thought it was a good idea at the time. His friends went to so much trouble setting this up." I knew the only friends Ace had were the Pauletti men. With their pull, they had probably paid the funeral home, as well as the guard escorting him, to say Ace was attending the funeral of a loved one.

"Don't do that shit no more." Without another word, I brushed past him and walked out the door.

Later that night, Alicia and I were seated on the main floor at the Palace of Auburn Hills. The Heat was playing the Pistons; the place was packed. This was the third game of the playoffs, and the stakes were high. Each team had won a game; therefore, the winner of tonight's game would gain leverage. Although I was a Pistons fan, quite naturally, I sat behind the Heat in Bravo's team jersey, black skinny jeans, and wedge gym shoes. Alicia was dressed in the complete warm-up suit—sweatband and all.

"Girl, I got ten racks on these niggas!" Alicia was leaning forward in her seat, watching every play.

"You have a gambling addiction."

"I'm addicted to money!" Ali stood and clapped when D. Wade crossed over his opponent so hard, his ankles damn near broke.

"Anyway, did you hear what I was saying about Ace?" During the first half of the game, I had tried to catch Ali up about my day, but she had been uninterested. Sports were her life.

"I heard you."

"What did I say?" I smacked my lips.

"Jane, can we please just watch the game?" Alicia asked in a polite tone.

"Fine." Like a child, I crossed my arms and pouted. Alicia didn't pay me any attention, so I focused on Bravo. My man looked good on the court too. I couldn't wait to show him some postgame love tonight. He caught me looking, then pressed his index and middle fingers to his lips. I returned the gesture with a smile.

Finally, halftime came, and the DJ was cutting it up. The music was so hype, everyone in the stands was turned up to the max.

"I need to go pee," I whispered to Ali.

"You can't hold it?" she asked.

"Girl, come on!" Just as I stood, the DJ turned on a song that stopped me in my tracks.

"I think I'm Connie Briscoe . . . Jane Doe . . . two bad hoes in the streets getting dough." The crowd around us sang the entire hook word for word.

I looked at Alicia for clarification. She didn't respond; instead, she pointed up at the big screen. I'd be damned if my image wasn't plastered up there for the world to see. I didn't know what to do, so I sat back down. The crowd continued to sing, and niggas who didn't even know me began nodding and smiling.

"What the fuck is this?" I exclaimed.

"Some rapper named Jazzie J put a song out using your name," Alicia responded nonchalantly.

"How long have you known about this?" I didn't listen to the radio or watch television. Therefore, I was completely in the dark.

"It's been out for about a month. I thought you knew." She shrugged.

"How does she know me, and who the fuck is Connie Briscoe?" This shit had me confused. I didn't know if I should be flattered or pissed off.

"Connie is some old bitch out of Baltimore who did it really big back in her day," Alicia replied. "She moved weight through her housekeeping business for almost thirty years without being on anybody's radar."

"Damn." I was impressed. "I wonder what happened to her." Honestly, a bitch like Ms. Briscoe had my admiration, and I wanted to set up a meeting with her to pay homage.

"Someone in her camp snitched, and she got sent upstate for sixty years. She did only seven years, though, because she had a massive heart attack in lockup."

"Ms. Doe, can I get a picture with you?" some white guy asked after tapping me on the shoulder, completely interrupting the history lesson Ali was giving me.

"Not right now." I shook my head, but this bastard snapped a photo any fucking way. Without hesitation, I jumped from my seat, snatched his phone, and dropped it hard onto the floor. Although it cracked, the poor phone was still useable . . . until I stomped the shit out of it. You would've thought the man would be angry. But he turned to his friends with a smile, and they all cheered.

"I told you, she really is in the Mob!" the guy shouted. The entire section started clapping.

I rolled my eyes.

This song and all the attention it brought had me bothered. I felt in my spirit that something wasn't right. I just couldn't put my finger on it.

Chapter Thirty-one

The Miami Heat had beaten the Pistons 103–101. It had been such a close game that I had been on pins and needles the entire time. With twenty seconds left in the final quarter, my baby had been fouled. His 98 percent free-throw rate had saved the game. Although the Pistons were pissed, they still shook hands and played nice for the cameras during the postgame interviews.

"That girl is fine as hell!" Alicia damn near sprained her neck trying to look at one of the Pistons' cheerleaders as she passed by us. We were waiting for Bravo in the hallway outside the locker room. The three of us had dinner plans.

A middle-aged woman approached Ali and me. "Excuse me, ladies. My name is Lana Burke. I'm an event coordinator for the rich and famous." Swiftly, she produced a silver business card. "I hear congratulations are in order for you and Bravo. When is the big day?"

"Soon," I replied without taking the card. It wasn't my intention to be rude, but ever since word had spread about Bravo proposing, everybody had been coming out of the woodwork with big smiles and even bigger pitches about why we should hire them to do this or that for our wedding. Although we had money to spare, their rates were astronomical, and I was not buying into the hype.

"If you're not already working with someone, my company, LB Events, would love to coordinate your special day."

"What's your starting rate, Ms. Burke?" I raised a curious brow.

"This would be on the house, of course." She winked and pushed her card my way.

"So, everything we want is free?"

"Yes, everything, from the finest champagne to the most optimum table linens, would all be free."

"Wow! Now, you're talking my language." This time I took the card.

"Sweetheart, those are the perks of marrying a million-aire. Welcome to the good life!" She flipped her hair with a chuckle. "Call me soon. Ciao."

I wanted to follow behind the scented trail of Chanel perfume and tell her ass a thing or two about who I was and how I'd been accustomed to the finer things long before I met Bravo, but I didn't.

"It's all good, J. Don't let her get to you." Alicia knew me so well.

"I just hate people thinking I'm a ho who needed saving."

"Earlier, you were mad about the song telling the world you were a female hustler. Now you're mad these NBA folks don't know your pedigree. Pick a side and stay there." Alicia knew she was right. Therefore, she continued to chew me out. "You're either going to be known as the best female dope dealer in the game or a goddamned basketball wife. Which one makes you sleep better at night?"

"Fuck you." I hit the wall.

"What's wrong?" Bravo was standing in the doorway of the locker room with his street clothes on and his gym bag in hand.

"Nothing's wrong. Congratulations, baby." I leaned up and kissed my man. I never wanted him to know my troubles.

"Man, you a bad boy with them free throws." Alicia pretended to dribble and shoot.

"Thanks, fam. Hey, how would y'all feel if we took a rain check on dinner and went to the party they're having tonight for the win instead?"

"I'm game, especially if shorties like that will be there." Alicia pointed at some girl swishing past us, and we all laughed. It was nice to see Alicia in a good head space, laughing, wanting to party and even chase a few skirts.

"What about you, Janelle? Are you coming?" Bravo stared down at me with a look I hated to love. He knew clubs weren't my thing, but for him, I would make an exception.

"Yeah, I guess I'm in." Tomorrow Bravo was going back to Miami to get ready for the next game, and I wasn't going. Therefore, I wanted to spend as much time with him as possible.

After a pit stop at Coney Island for some grub, we went back to my place for a power nap. Bravo got most of the sleep, while I cut my nap short to rummage through my closet for an outfit. For the better part of an hour, I tried on various pieces, until I settled on a black fishnet top, a black bra, and simple leather pants. I'd just finished putting my earrings on when Alicia came to pick us up. Bravo was already dressed and sitting in the living room. Together, we opened the door and burst out laughing.

"Are you ready? We're about to turn up." Alicia was hanging out the sunroof of a stretch Infiniti truck.

"Did you really rent a limo?" I laughed.

"I sure did!"

"Hey, Jane," Rocky called and waved after rolling down the window. I could see Patrice sitting beside her, drinking Hennessy straight from the bottle. Usually,

I would've had a sidebar conversation with Ali about inviting our shooters out while we were with Bravo. The last thing I needed was to catch him up in some bullshit. However, my girls had been doing a good job. They deserved a reward, so I let it slide this one time.

"Bravo, meet Rocky and Patrice. Ladies, meet Bravo." I gave the introduction while climbing into the large vehicle with a leather interior.

"What up, doe?" Bravo sounded like a Detroiter the way the sentence rolled off his tongue.

"I can't believe how tall you are. Television makes you look shorter." Patrice stared Bravo up and down.

"I hear that a lot," he replied while grabbing a bottle from the ice bucket and fixing a drink.

Rocky began with a barrage of questions. "Do you know if D. Wade or Kalil Perry will be there? I wonder if Gabrielle will be there. What do you think, Bravo? Never mind that. Can we take a picture for the Gram?"

I gave Bravo an apologetic glance, and he patted my thigh in a manner suggesting everything was cool. Besides, I thought he was amused by my girls. Aside from Ali, he'd never met any of my people.

"Fuck the Gram. Let's go live on Facebook's ass!" Bravo geeked Rocky up as she readily pulled out her phone. For nearly fifteen minutes, I watched as everyone acted silly for the camera. I wasn't feeling all the social media, so I let them have at it.

"What's got you deep in thought over there?" Bravo whispered after catching me staring out the window.

"Have you heard the new Jazzie J song?" I blurted out.

"Yeah, it's kind of slick, if you ask me. There aren't too many people out here with their own songs."

"I don't like it, and I wish she had asked my permission before using my name in this urban street anthem. I think it brings the wrong attention." My head was pounding from the stress of this song. I had let it go at the game, but now it was back on my mind. That song had the potential to destroy everything I'd worked so hard to obtain. How would my Mafia connections feel about being attached to me now?

"Baby, I don't think it's that serious. In fact, I'd be flattered if I were you. People admire you. You're something like a big deal." He nudged me.

"I don't want to be a big deal, though." Rolling my eyes, I laid my head on his shoulder.

"Too late."

"We're here, y'all," Alicia announced before she downed the remainder of her bottle.

We all stepped from the limousine and formed a single-file line. As usual, the place was packed, and there was still a line of people waiting to get in. The minute they spotted Bravo, camera phones started flashing from every direction.

"Can we get your autograph?" a few provocatively dressed women shouted.

Bravo looked at me for the okay, and I nodded.

"Who should I make these out to?" Bravo asked with a smile.

"Um . . . ," said one of the ladies. After pausing, she added, "We were actually asking Jane Doe for her autograph. Sorry."

"Oh, shit, J. You got mad fans," Alicia said as she jumped up and down on the red carpet.

"Janelle, these ladies want you." Bravo sounded as shocked as I looked.

"Ladies, I appreciate the love, but I don't pass out signatures." I tried to sound as nice as possible, though I was irritated as fuck.

"Aww," they replied in unison.

"Hey, do you ladies want to come in with us?" Alicia chimed in.

"Oh my God, yes!" they chorused.

"What the fuck are you doing?" I mumbled.

"Trying to set up a threesome." Alicia rubbed her hands together and motioned for the security guards to let the women go past the velvet rope.

"I'm leaving!" I bellowed. After turning on my heels, I headed back toward the limo. Bravo swiftly put his arms around my waist and redirected me toward the club.

"She's just having fun, baby. Relax," he whispered. "Let's get a drink or two, take a few pictures, shake a couple of hands, and then we can leave, okay?"

I looked up at him with eyes that wanted to decline, but how could I? "Okay," I said, relenting.

Chapter Thirty-two

The Black Diamond Nightclub was popping and was filled to capacity with some of everybody. Alicia was cutting up on the dance floor with the groupies from outside. Patrice was up in the DJ booth, keeping a guy she went to high school with company while he mixed the music. Rocky was all up under some light-skinned ballplayer with buck teeth and sandy-red hair. Bravo was in a huddle with his friends, talking sports, and I sat in the corner alone, patiently waiting for the night to be over. I really wasn't trying to be in a sour mood, but my head was consumed with wild thoughts and ill vibes.

"Excuse me. May I sit?" a young Hispanic girl hollered over the music.

Without replying, I slid over on the velvet sofa and made room for her.

"I'm Estillita." She extended her right hand, while using the left to sip from her glass. "You're Jane, right?"

"Who wants to know?" I scoffed.

"Um, I do. That's why I asked." She rolled her eyes and then laughed. Nudging me playfully, she smiled. "Damn, girl. Lighten up. Why are you always so serious?"

"I'm not always so serious. Besides, you don't even know me like that to be playing."

"You're right. I don't know you, but I want to get to know you. That's why I came over here." Estillita finished her drink and sat the glass on the table.

"No offense, but I'm not trying to get to know you." I tried to slide over some more, but I had run out of room on the sofa.

"Damn. I guess you are a bitch, just like everyone says." She adjusted her skirt and stood. Before she could walk away, I caught her hand and pulled her back down.

"Who calls me a bitch?"

"The coach, the players, their wives . . . hell, everybody." Estillita rolled her eyes. "Nobody wants to be bothered with you, and no one wants you with Bravo, either. He's a good guy, and you're bad for his image."

"Wow!" I was shocked. Until now I had been in the dark about the way the team felt about Bravo and me. My usual reaction would be to put my gun in this bitch's mouth, but the last thing I wanted to do was prove everyone's theory about me.

"Come on, Jane. You can't really be shocked, can you?" When I didn't respond, she continued. "You are always frowned up, and you never make an attempt to be social. Everyone knows you're a goddamned drug dealer with your own money, but you can at least play the part of the happy fiancée when you're with the team." She reached into her purse and pulled out a vial of white powder. Casually, she poured a little on her hand and sniffed a quick line. "Don't look at me like that. This is probably your shit!" She closed the vial and wiped her nose. I wanted to tell her that it wasn't my product. I could tell by the top on the vial. However, I remained silent so as not to incriminate myself.

"Look, let's start over." I forced a smile and extended my hand. "My name is Janelle. I'm Bravo's fiancée. And you are?" Now, don't get it twisted. This bitch hadn't finessed me or made me feel bad about anything. However, the minute she had put that powder up her nose, I had realized I was completely overlooking a potential client who would spend thousands a week with me, especially if we had a rapport with each other.

"Nice to meet you, Janelle. I'm Estillita, Antonio LeCruz's wife and the vice president of the MHWA." With glazed eyes and a red nose, she smiled.

"Estillita, I'm sorry for coming off as rude. I'm having a bad day, but I am happy to meet you. What's the MHWA?"

"The Miami Heat Wives and Affiliates. We get together once a month to work on fund-raisers, sporting events for the youth, and"—she leaned in close to me—"to talk shit and get drunk."

"This sounds like something I need to be a part of. That way people can get to know me and realize I'm not that bad, after all." In all honesty, I could've cared less about these wives and affiliates. I just wanted to gain more intel on who else's wife in the organization needed my services.

"That sounds great. Our next meeting is Thursday. Put your number in my phone. I'll call and remind you." She handed me her unlocked phone. Quickly, I slipped the digits to one of my alternate phones inside and handed it back to her.

"I'll be there." I nodded and then excused myself to visit the ladies' room.

Unfortunately, the restroom closest to the VIP was full, so I headed down the spiral staircase toward the one on the main floor. When I was halfway down the staircase, this guy heading the other way practically ran into me.

"Excuse me, miss. I didn't mean to bump you. I sincerely am sorry," the guy said, his hands raised in surrender. I wanted to tell him that all the apologizing wasn't necessary, but I understood why he was doing it. The partygoers in Detroit were notorious for starting fights and sometimes shoot-outs just because someone bumped them or stepped on their shoes.

"You're good," I hollered over the music and proceeded to the bathroom. "Fuck!" The line was at least ten people strong. Although I could've stood and waited, there was something about going into a stall right behind the previous person that really made my skin crawl.

"Janie, is that you?" A short, chubby man with a purple fade and black nail polish stared at me with a grin larger than Texas. He was wearing an oddly fashionable python suit and the matching Guiseppes.

"I'm sorry, but who are you?" I plugged a finger in my ear to hear him over the music.

"It's me, Sonnie!" He paused to give me time to remember, but I didn't. "Now, I know you ain't going to act like I didn't slay your mother's hair for nearly two decades!"

"Oh my God, Sonnie!" I wrapped my arms around the guy my mother always referred to as my "special" uncle while I was growing up. Back then, he had long dreads and was a lot thinner.

"Yeah, bitch, you better remember." He snapped his fingers. "Look at you, all grown up, looking just like your mama." He shook his head. "That was my main bitch!"

"Yes, you were as thick as thieves!" I replied, recalling.

"You better know it too! What have you been up to, diva?"

"Just maintaining." I smiled.

"I see you're draped up and dripping with diamonds, so you're doing more than maintaining." He pointed at my ice.

"I own a few clothing stores, nothing major. What's been good with you, though?"

It was really hard to hear over the music. Therefore, Sonnie pulled me toward the back of the club and then into a back office. "I've been running this place with my boyfriend, Dale. What have you been up to, other than running clothing stores and such?" Sonnie turned on the light and closed the door. The space was sparsely decorated with a love seat and throw pillows. There were several boxes all over the place and a few pictures on the wall.

"I had no idea this was your spot. Ya'll got it looking good in here." My eyes roamed the walls until they landed on a familiar face. Immediately, my heart skipped two beats. After walking over to a gold frame, I rubbed my finger over my mother's face. She was so young and full of life.

"We took that in two thousand, at my very first hair show."

"Is that a waterfall ponytail?" I laughed. "And those pencil-thin eyebrows were a mess!"

"Forget what you're talking about. Those things were in, and we won second place that night." Sonnie walked over to the picture to admire my mother with me. "She was my best friend till the end, believe that!" I wanted to sit and listen to all the stories I knew Sonnie had about my mom, but just then there was knock at the door.

"Excuse me, Sonnie. The bar needs you for a second. The POS system crashed again," someone called through the closed door.

"I tell you this place would burn to hell without me." Sonnie patted my back. "I don't know how long this will take, but feel free to stay as long as you like, sweetie."

"Nah, I won't stay, but I will be back soon, so we can catch up. Is there a bathroom in here, though?"

"Yup. Right there. If you shit, make sure you spray and close the door when you leave."

After staring at the picture for a few more minutes, I went into the bathroom to handle my business. As soon as I washed my hands, I heard the door to the office open.

"Sonnie, I didn't shit, and you need some more tissue," I called out, but no one said anything. Thinking nothing of it, I opened the door, and to my surprise, the room was dark. Blinking rapidly, I tried to adjust my eyes so that I could see in the dark. Just when I thought I saw someone, something hit me in the stomach.

"I'm going to kill your ass! I swear to God, I'm going to kill you," a woman snarled. She tried to hit me again, but this time I saw the fist coming and dodged the blow. Thinking fast, I flew over to the light switch and hit the light. I couldn't fight fair in the dark if I didn't know how many people I was up against. "Bitch!" she growled.

The woman retrieved a gun from the handbag she'd been hitting me with and aimed it right between my eyes. I wanted to plead with her to spare my life, but when I looked at her face and remembered what I had taken from her that day in the park, I didn't dare. How could I?

"My son did nothing to you, yet you coldly took him from me with no rhyme or reason." Her hands trembled. "What did we ever do to you?" She walked slowly my way.

"You and your son did nothing to me." I felt a lump forming in my throat. "I'm so sorry." I was face-to-face with the biggest skeleton in my closet, and the shit was scary as hell. "Every day I think about what I did and—"

"Every day I *live* with what you did!" she screamed. "Do you know what it feels like to carry something in your womb for nine months, while dreaming of all the special moments you will have with your child, like birthdays, graduations, a wedding?" She pressed her gun against my forehead. "In one second you took all those dreams away, and now you have to pay for what you did!" Tears streamed down this broken mother's face, and before long, tears streamed down mine too. Everything she was saying was true, and it was time to face the music.

"Do it!" I whispered. "Please do it." Although I knew what I was leaving behind, this was the only way to make what I did right. A life for a life. Although I hadn't pulled the trigger, I was just as responsible for taking her child away from her.

Click!

The woman had pulled the trigger, but the safety was on.

Chapter Thirty-three

The minute I knew Vito's baby's mother had fucked up, I sent a quick elbow to her face, causing her to fly backward. Then I snatched the chrome .44, unlocked the safety, and pointed at her ass. She was bent over, holding her face, and blood was oozing through her fingers.

"You should've killed me, bitch!" I growled.

I grabbed a throw pillow from Sonnie's couch and put it over the back of her head. Before she ever knew what was happening, I let two shots off. Feathers flew all over the room as her body dropped like a bag of dirty laundry. Just like that, she was dead, like her son.

"Shit!" Staring down at her limp body, I thought hard about how the fuck I was going to get away with murder in a club full of people. There was no way I could just walk out of this office like nothing had happened. Not only did Sonnie know I was in here, but his waitress did too. "Fuck!"

Buzz. The phone vibrating in my pocket startled me. I answered right away. "Hello."

"J, where did you go?" Alicia yelled over the music. "Bravo is looking for you."

"Alicia, keep him with you, but tell Rocky and Patrice I need them now." I turned the lights off in the office and crept over to the door. After sliding it open slightly, I peeked outside to make sure no one was coming.

"What's wrong? Are you okay?"

"I'm good. Just send the girls downstairs, to the office at the rear of the club, under the VIP. Keep Bravo company for a while!" Without another word, I ended the phone call and waited on my goons.

Nearly fifteen minutes later Patrice and Rocky finally approached the door. Although they were intoxicated to the max, they were focused and ready to handle whatever situation I had for them.

"What's up, Jane?" Rocky asked after I cracked the door open a little more to expose my face. I was still waiting in the dark.

"Come on in."

Once they were inside the room, I closed the door and turned on the light.

"Oh shit!" Patrice was the first to notice the body on the floor, with half a face. "I don't even want to know what happened. Just tell me what you need from us."

"I need to get shorty the fuck out of here." I locked the door to the office. "I just don't know how."

"We need to evacuate the club." Rocky paced back and forth. "And you need to be the first one out."

"No, I'm not going to leave you guys with this mess."

"Jane, this is nothing we're not used to. You need to get your man and get the fuck out of here," Rocky said, pressing.

"The other times were different . . . no evidence, no witnesses. There's too many people in here tonight," I insisted.

"Jane . . . ," Rocky protested.

"Enough! Roll her up in the rug now!" I ordered. After placing the gun down on the couch, I went into the bathroom to find any kind of cleaning solution. Although I was sure Rocky wanted to force me out of the office, she didn't say another word. Instead, she and Patrice went about their task.

Just then the doorknob jiggled, and we all froze. Patrice grabbed the gun and aimed it at the door. Rocky turned off the light and took position behind the door, waiting to pounce. The knob jiggled again, until someone unlocked the door. Sonnie stepped into the dark room, closed the door, and fumbled with the wall until he found the light switch. The minute the lights came on, he damn near had a heart attack. I didn't know if it was the dead body on his floor or the gun in his face, but he was as pale as a ghost.

"What in all hell is going on here?" Sonnie looked at me for clarification.

"I'm sorry about all this." I walked over to Patrice and put my hand on top of hers to lower the weapon. "This bitch came in while I was in the bathroom, trying to kill me, so I had to do her," I admitted reluctantly. Truthfully, it had been my only option at the moment.

"Who is she?" Sonnie pointed at Patrice as Rocky came from behind the door. "Her too?"

"These are my peoples. They didn't have nothing to do with this. They were just trying to help me." I sat down on the couch and put my head in the palms of my hands. "If you call the police, please don't mention them, Sonnie. This is on me alone."

"Girls, can you leave me with Janie please?" Sonnie walked over to Vito's baby mama and took a seat behind his desk.

"It's all good. Just give me a minute," I said after noticing my goons didn't leave when asked.

"We'll be outside the door." Rocky eyed Sonnie suspiciously before relenting to my request.

Once the coast was clear, Sonnie sat back in his chair and stared at me. "What kind of shit are you really into?"

I played dumb. "What you mean?"

"Never mind the dead girl on my floor. Tell me why you got bitches trying to kill you in the first place."

"The bitch fucked my baby daddy, and we had beef about it. I whopped her ass, and she didn't appreciate it. She told me when she sees me, she was gone do me." I shrugged and shifted in my seat, trying to play it cool. "I guess she was serious. Thank God I got the upper hand."

"You are definitely your mother's daughter." Sonnie laughed. "I remember that when Monica lied, she always shrugged and shifted too." He sat up at his desk and peered at me. "Is this drug related?"

"What?" I frowned.

"Do you know your mother sold dope too? In fact, that's how she met your father."

"No, I never knew that."

"Julius worked under her rival, a nigga named Jah. He would send Julius to shake her down at least two, three times a week. It was an attempt to force her off the streets, but your mother wasn't an easy target. Besides, your father liked your mother, so he never robbed her. Instead, he used the time to flirt with her, and he paid Jah his own earnings to keep up the front. Once Jah found out that Julius was playing him, he went to shake Monica down hisself. Monica was ready for him, though." He sighed, with a smirk. "Funny thing is, that situation ended up much like this one, and she called me." His eyes locked with mine. "Together, we made her problem go away, just like we're going to make yours go away."

"So, you're saying you're going to help me?"

"Of course I will, Janie. I just need a small favor from you." Sonnie sat back in the chair again.

"What's up?"

"I know what you do, and I need in. Lace me with twenty pounds of raw a week to pump through the club, and I will help you get this body out of here undetected." He raised his right hand to God.

I sat silently for a second and pondered my options. "How many weeks are we talking?"

"Indefinitely is fair, don't you think?" Sonnie leaned over his desk and glanced down at the lifeless body resting near my feet.

"Forever is a very long time to front that kind of work, especially on a weekly basis. How about I front you five pounds a week indefinitely and we call it good?" Although I really had no room to negotiate, I still rolled the dice.

Sonnie played hardball right back. "Twenty pounds a week and we get this problem handled. I assure you it'll never be spoken of again. Or you can try your luck. Just remember, this girl was someone's daughter, sister, and friend. She will be reported as missing, and when the police come knocking, I have the civic duty as a business owner to tell them what I know and hand over any incriminating evidence that the cameras at my establishment may have recorded."

I wanted to remind him of the street law regarding snitches. Instead, I stood from the couch, walked over to the desk, and held my hand out. With a Grinch-like grin, Sonnie held his hand out, and I sealed the devil's deal with a firm shake. For now, I would play the game, but I had no intention of keeping my promise.

Chapter Thirty-four

After conducting business, Sonnie assured me my problem would be handled. Still, I left Rocky and Patrice behind to make sure that shit was cleaned up the way I liked it, and that there was no funny business.

"Baby, where have you been?" Bravo called. He was descending the stairs as I ascended them.

"I went looking for the bathroom and ran into my mother's hairdresser. He runs this place."

"You've been gone for an hour and a half, though." He made a show of checking the time on his watch.

"Did you miss me?" With my hand on my chest, I appeared shocked. "When I left, you were all huddled up in the corner with the fellas, not paying me any attention, remember?"

"Don't be like that." Bravo pulled me into his massive arms and tongued me down right then and there. Usually, I would've refrained from the PDA, but the more attention we got, the less attention people paid to whatever was going on downstairs in Sonnie's office. There was a round of cheers and whistles coming from everywhere. However, the moment was short lived, as several men bum-rushed us. They knocked me down the steps and commenced jumping all over Bravo.

"What the hell?" After getting my bearings, I stood to my feet and tried to make heads or tails of this mosh pit. Within seconds, a melee broke out around me. "Get off of him! Bravo, I'm coming." I flexed through the crowd, trying to get up the stairs to my baby. Security and his teammates had come to his rescue, though.

Pow! One shot rang out, and everybody hit the deck. I didn't know who had fired the gun, but it was just the break that club security needed to apprehend the assailants and escort them out of the building.

As one of them passed me, he spat, "Ace might be locked up, but he still got goons, believe that!"

In utter shock and disbelief, I looked up the stairs, and everyone that had been in VIP was staring down at me with hate in their eyes. I looked down the steps at the rest of the partygoers, and ironically, they were looking at me with excitement and admiration. It was a true depiction of where I was in life.

"Let's give it up one time for Jane Doe, a hood legend in the making!" the DJ hollered before cutting on the song that had become my unwanted anthem. On cue the entire lower level of the club went right back to partying and singing the lyrics of the song word for word.

Slowly, I forced myself up the stairs. It took everything in me not to run away from the club and never look back. I was embarrassed, I was pissed, and I was reminded once again that Bravo wasn't from my world. Still, I pressed forward until I found him sitting on the steps, holding his face. "Baby, are you okay?"

"These ho-ass niggas jumped me. Hell no, I'm not okay." When he removed his hands from his face, I could see that one of his eyes was swollen shut.

David Watts, the team's small forward, had the nerve to block me from touching my man. "Janelle, no disrespect, but I think you should leave," he said.

"Bravo, talk to me, baby," I begged, but he said nothing. "I didn't mean for this to happen. I swear on my daughter." Tears began to gather in my eyes. I didn't know what hurt more, him not talking to me or my knowing I was the reason why he would not be able to play in the playoff game tomorrow.

"Come on, Jane. Leave him be. It'll be all right," Alicia interjected as she came down the stairs.

"Bravo, please, baby, say something."

"I'll take him with me tonight. He'll call you when he's ready." David helped Bravo to his feet, and they walked away. I cried like a baby all the way down the stairs and out the club.

"Where are Rocky and Patrice?" Alicia asked as she pulled out her cell phone after we got into the limo.

Although I didn't even want to utter a word, I had no choice but tell her what had happened in Sonnie's office. I also told her about the deal I had had to make, but I assured her I would seal the loose end sooner than later.

The remainder of the ride to my house, Alicia tried to make small talk, but I wasn't in the mood. Instead, I rode with my eyes closed, in silence. After pulling up at my place, she offered to spend the night with me so I wouldn't be alone, but I told her I was cool. We said our good-byes, and I retreated inside.

As soon as the door was closed, I broke down sobbing. Tonight had taken just about everything I had. If it wasn't one thing, it was always another, and I was tired. Although I was built Ford tough, the thing with Bravo was the straw that had finally broken the camel's back.

After walking over to the custom sofa made of elephant skin, I reached beneath the seat and pulled out the J. A. Henckels butcher knife that went to my kitchen set. I didn't keep guns in my main house. The knife was meant for protection. Today, though, I pondered using it to kill myself. As I stared at the huge blade, my phone danced in my pocket. At first, I ignored it, but then I thought it was Bravo calling. To my surprise, it was Gran.

"Hello. What happened? Are you okay?" I said frantically when I answered. It was almost 2:00 a.m. My heart skipped three beats as I waited for her to say something.

Silence.

"Hello?" I said even more frantically.

"Mommy," Ju answered before she fumbled the phone.

I heaved a sigh of relief. "What are you doing up this late, sweetie?"

"Mommy." Ju giggled. I could hear Gran in the background, snoring. I knew then that she was playing with Gran's phone and had dialed me by accident, something she'd done once before. It amazed me the way the kids were tech savvy at such a young age.

"I love you, Ju."

"Love you," Juliana said while pressing buttons in my ear.

I dropped the knife on the floor and wiped my eyes, truly thankful I had taken her call instead of taking my life that night.

Chapter Thirty-five

Ding-dong!

The sound of the doorbell woke me from my slumber. At some point during the night, I'd dozed off while holding the phone. It was still in my hand.

"Ju?" I called out, but then I noticed my phone had died.

Ding-dong!

After sitting up on the side of the bed, I stretched. It was six in the morning. Still in the clothes I'd worn to the club, I shuffled across the bedroom, down the hallway, to the front door. "Who is it?"

"It's me." Bravo's voice crept through the door and caused my heart to skip a beat. Part of me wondered if he was there to take his belongings back or cuss me out. Either way I didn't care; I was just happy to see him.

After opening the door, I apologized profusely. "I'm sorry, Bravo. I really didn't mean for any of that to happen." Although his face was concealed by triple black Ray-Ban frames, it still looked pretty bad. "I'm so sorry, baby."

"I'm sorry too." After wrapping his massive arms around my body, he kissed my forehead.

"You have no need to be sorry."

"I never should have hollered at you like that in the club, especially in front of everybody. I also shouldn't have let you leave without me. For all I know, those guys could've been in the parking lot, waiting to hurt you."

"Baby, you did nothing wrong. You were pissed, and I don't blame you. This is my fault entirely." Looking up into his gaze, I swallowed hard. "You are a good guy, and I don't deserve you. Maybe it's best that we part ways now, before things get too complicated." Although I meant what I was saying, I didn't want to say it. I loved Bravo so much that I didn't want to see him hurt on the account of my bullshit.

"It's already complicated." He lifted my left hand and pointed at the diamond engagement ring. "I don't pass out rocks to just anybody. I love you, and regardless of what anybody thinks, I still want to spend the rest of my life with you."

"Baby, the way I live right now is reckless. I'm not fit to carry your last name. I don't even want you associated with my bullshit, especially after last night. I know the media is going to have a field day with the story."

"Gangster girlfriend causes the Heat to lose the playoffs." Bravo was joking, but I didn't laugh. "Baby, don't trip. You know I don't care about that. I can still ball with a swollen eye. Besides, the team doctor will have me all fixed up by the time I get off the plane tonight."

"It's not just about the eye. It's the song too. I don't want your colleagues looking at me sideways." Last night's events had changed things for me in a major way. I felt vulnerable and exposed. For the first time in my life, I wished I could be anyone but me. Sure, the song had given me fame, even a few celebrity fans, but at what cost?

"Babe, that song was dope." Bravo kissed my forehead again and then headed down the hallway toward the bedroom. "Enjoy the notoriety. Don't overthink it."

"I think it'll be a problem," I mused, following behind him. Once we reached the bedroom, I plopped down on top of the supersized circular bed and watched as he packed his bag.

"That shit was boss, babe." He began singing the hook just to irritate me. I wanted to punch him playfully in the arm but was distracted by the doorbell ringing. "That's probably my chauffeur," he said.

"Hurry up, then," I yelled before going to get the door.

When I opened the door, I was not greeted by a chauffeur. Standing there were several members of the alphabet gang.

"Good morning, Janelle Doesher," a Caucasian man with black hair and a graying beard said as he handed me a folded document. It didn't take a rocket scientist to know that I had just been handed a federal warrant.

"What can I do for you, Officer?"

"I need you to step aside while we search the premises," the federal agent demanded.

"This isn't even my house." I frowned. Actually, it was, but it was in Gran's name.

"Ms. Doesher, our warrant gives us the right to search any and all premises you have been known to frequent." At this point, the agent stepped into my foyer and instructed me to have a seat. His squad followed him in. "I want every toilet unscrewed and all the sinks too!" he instructed them before turning back to me. "Don't worry. This won't take long."

"Just don't damage my shit!" I retorted before flopping down on the sofa, as cool as a cucumber. There was nothing to hide, so I didn't even protest. Instead, I grabbed the house phone from the cradle and made a call.

"Hello, Janelle. What can I do for you this morning?" my attorney, Richard Lennigan, asked after picking up on the first ring.

"Sorry to call so early. The Feds just showed up at my crib with a warrant. I need you to come through and make sure everything is everything." The warrant was at least six pages of fancy verbiage and hidden agendas; there was no way I'd be able to read and process all of it.

"Sit tight! I'll be right there." Richard ended the call without uttering another word.

"Babe, what the fuck is all this?" Bravo stepped into the living room, wearing nothing but a scowl. "They won't even let me finish packing my shit!"

"My attorney is on the way. Don't worry." I spoke loud enough to be heard by every person in the room, so they knew what the deal was.

Highly irritated, Bravo trudged over to the sofa and sat down beside me. "I'm going to miss my flight."

"I'm sorry." We'd just gotten over the other shit, and now here we were again. Once more, my street life had interfered with his life.

"Janelle, are we good?" His whispered question was an indirect way of asking me if there was anything illegal under this roof.

"You know I never shit where I sleep," I replied, and he visibly relaxed.

"Cool." With a smile, he grabbed my hand and sat back on the sofa.

"I swear, I don't deserve you." Not only was Bravo an all-around good guy, but he always seemed to understand who I was, and he gave me the freedom to be me. It didn't matter to him what my profession was. All that mattered was that I kept my game tight and never got caught slipping.

While we waited on Richard, my phone blew up like crazy. Having read the addresses listed on the warrant, I was aware that all my associates' homes were being ransacked as well. I prayed like hell no one had anything hot in their cribs, but I would soon find out otherwise.

Richard walked through the door hurriedly. "Janelle, I got here as fast as I could."

Without a word, I handed him the folded document. I watched as his eyes examined the pages line by line.

"Where is the man in charge here?" Richard shouted.

"That would be me, Harold Gurney. Who are you?" The Fed walked from my kitchen into the living room, carrying a garbage bag filled with the contents of my refrigerator.

"I'm Richard Lennigan, Ms. Doesher's attorney. Tell me what cockamamy judge would expedite a warrant based solely on a goddamned rap song." As Richard went to bat for me, I nudged Bravo. I knew that damn song was trouble waiting to happen. He shook his head as we continued to listen in on the conversation.

"The contents of said song indicate that your client is the highest-ranking female narcotics distributor this side of America. Jane Doe is pushing more weight than elephant scales!"

"Agent Gurney, you and I both know that you're grasping at straws here. My client is nothing more than a hardworking, tax-paying business owner."

"Are you done with your speech, so I can go back to doing my job?" the agent asked.

Richard didn't bother replying. Instead, he got on his cell phone and made several calls.

Bravo had to leave without anything except the clothes on his body in order to make his flight on time. I hated to see him go, but I didn't want him to stick around for this. For the better part of the day, I watched helplessly as the Feds destroyed my home room by room. They flipped my furniture, tossed my bedding and, as promised, took apart all sinks and toilets, looking for flushed narcotics. They also broke the legs on a marble dining table, pulled an eighty-inch television down off the wall, and put several holes in my walls while looking for an imaginary safe. After all that, they still walked away empty-handed. To say I was livid would be putting it lightly. It would cost me hundreds of thousands of dollars to repair and replace my shit after this little visit. Someone had to pay, and I knew exactly who that someone was.

Chapter Thirty-six

The next afternoon I scheduled a flight to Los Angeles, California. It was time to pop up on the bitch who'd put my name in that song, but first, I had to tie up a few loose ends with Rocky and Patrice.

"What's up, Jane?" said Shawntae, the beauty bar owner and Rocky's cousin, greeting me from behind the desk. She appeared to be working on the schedule.

I stopped briefly at the desk to catch up with her. She was good people. She let us meet in her supply room from time to time. "How is your little man doing?"

"He's doing good." When she looked up from the calendar, I could see that her eyes were red and puffy. "I'm the one who's a mess." Her five-year-old son, LaVonte, had recently been diagnosed with autism. I didn't know much about the disorder except that it was a condition related to brain development. "I need to homeschool my son until I can find the best facility for him. I'm looking at the schedule now to see how I can still see clients and be with my son. I need the money to keep this place open, but he needs me too. Enough about me. How is your daughter?"

"She's doing good." I placed my purse on the desk, reached inside, and grabbed my checkbook.

"Janelle, although I appreciate what I think you're about to do, I don't do handouts." Shawntae shook her head.

"It's not a handout. It's a hand up." I wrote out a check. With a wink, I placed it in the pocket on her shirt. I was a firm believer in helping those in need. I couldn't imagine having to bear the burden that Shawntae was bearing. She was a strong person, but even strong people needed help.

"Thank you."

"You're welcome. Please don't hesitate to call if you need anything else." After writing down my number on a piece of a paper, I handed it to her, then headed toward the back of the building. Rocky and Patrice were already waiting there.

"Please tell me that shit is a done deal," I said.

"Yeah, we got shorty out of the club and cleaned up the office really good," Patrice said. She sat atop a stack of boxes, eating a banana. Rocky was leaned up against the wall.

"What are we going to do about your man from the club? The nigga played his part, but I wouldn't call him trustworthy. How well do you know him?" Rocky said.

"Don't worry, Rocky. I'll handle him as soon as I get back, but for now, move on with business as usual."

"Where are you going?" both Rocky and Patrice asked at the same time.

"I have to shoot a quick move, but I'll be back ASAP."

"Let us come with you," Rocky urged.

"Yeah, Jane, you are kind of hot right now. You shouldn't be making moves by yourself," Patrice insisted. She had a point, but I blew her off.

"I'll holla at ya'll when I get back." After walking over to my girls, I gave them each a dap and an envelope full of money for another job well done.

Late that afternoon I hopped on a plane to Los Angeles, California, by myself. I was so heated with this situation that I didn't need an entourage to help me with this one.

After getting into the first taxi I saw, I headed straight to see the label responsible for putting out the song with my name all over it.

"Welcome to Easy Street Records." A white receptionist with dreads and a nose ring smiled. "Do you have an appointment?"

"Is Eric Washington here?" I replied.

"And you are?" she asked in a polite tone, although she was being a smart-ass.

"Get the nigga on the phone and tell him Jane Doe is up front." I snapped my fingers in her face. Literally, I was three seconds from going ham on this girl just off general principle alone. The receptionist could discern the lunacy in my eyes. Without hesitation, she pressed the button beside her computer monitor.

"Mr. Washington, you have a visitor by the name of Jane Doe."

"Eric is in the massage room, but I can speak with her. Please send her back, Molly," a young woman said through the intercom.

"Miss, you go through those doors. Mr. Washington's assistant, Lorie, is in the second office on the left." Molly pointed, too nervous to get up and escort me. With much attitude, I pushed one of the metal doors open and went in search of my prey.

As I walked down the hallway, I couldn't help but stare at the bright orange-colored walls adorned with various pictures of a few music legends with Eric, a few gold records, and the key to his hometown of Birmingham, Alabama. Eric "Easy" Washington was a big, fat country boy with a degree in music. After serving as an intern at one of the most distinguished music labels for over a decade, he decided to step out into the world and do his own thing. To date, the nigga was responsible for more than one hundred singles that hit number one, "Jane Doe" being one of the latest.

Rather than entering Lorie's office, I kept walking and noticed a door with the words *massage parlor* on it. Willing to bet this was where Eric was hiding, I barged right in without bothering to knock. As I suspected, he was lying across a massage table, with his face down. However, to my surprise, the male masseur wasn't massaging anything. Instead, he was using his tongue to tickle and tease Eric's asshole. Quickly, I pulled out my cell phone and snapped a few pictures. That was when the door opened and Lorie hollered, "You can't be in here."

"What the fuck?" Eric snapped his head up. The masseur stood frozen, like he didn't know what to do.

"We need to talk," I barked. Slyly, I tucked the phone in my pocket, and no one was the wiser.

"You need to leave." Lorie tried to grab my arm, but I gave her a look that told her if she didn't back off, I would pluck her like a bugger.

"It's fine, Lorie," Eric said, dismissing the girl while reaching for his eyeglasses and sliding them on. The arms on the frame were so tight on his face, I thought they were going to pop at any moment. "To what do I owe this pleasure, Ms. Doe? Let me guess . . . you flew here personally to tell me you love the song, right?" He chuckled.

"Wrong, motherfucker!" I yelled. "I came to collect what's mine." If the song was going to wreak havoc in my life, I may as well be paid for it.

"And what's that?"

"I want a thirty-five percent cut of all the profits on that song."

"Psst." Eric smacked his oversize lips. "You've got to be joking."

"Are you trying to find out if I am?" With a straight face, I looked his corny ass up and down.

"What are you gonna do?" He sat up on the table and stared me down. "You are a public figure. Therefore, we have the right to use your name and likeness in anything we want."

"I wasn't a public figure until you made me one." Up until the release of the song, only Detroit locals knew my pedigree. The rest of the world knew me as Bravo's fiancée.

"It doesn't matter." He shrugged. "My lawyers will spin circles around you, if you dare take me to court."

"I don't do court. I get street justice. You should know that," I scoffed. "Break me off my bread, or you will reap what you have sown."

"Look, Ms. Doe, I'm not giving you a dime, and that's final." He motioned for the masseur to continue with the massage.

"The girl that raps this song has a show tonight at the Smoothie King Center in NOLA, right?" I asked nonchalantly. "Then she goes to the Verizon Center in D.C. next, and Scott Stadium in Virginia after that, right? With a sold-out tour like that, it would be a shame for the starring act to be a no-show." After looking up Jazzie J online, I had memorized her entire tour schedule. "Keep fucking with me and the bitch won't make it to sound check tonight."

"Okay, Ms. Doe. Let's talk about this percentage deal again." Now Eric was frazzled and concerned.

"No. That deal is dead. I'm done talking percentages. I need some real money, and I need it now." Slapping the wall, I made so much of a scene that he jumped nervously.

"How much money are we talking here?" After standing from the table, he tried to cover his puny dick, which barely hung over his balls. It was hard not to laugh.

"I need a million dollars."

"Shit!" Eric exclaimed. "Bitch, your ass is tripping."

"Bitch?" I repeated in such a tone that the masseur excused himself from the room hurriedly. "I got your bitch! Believe that." How dare this nigga test my gangster? Didn't he know who the fuck I was?

Reaching down into my bag, I watched as Eric ran to a corner to cower like a bitch. He thought I was going to shoot him, but that was too easy. As a substitute, I retrieved the burner phone I had bought earlier and made a call.

"What's up?" answered the person on the other end.

"Handle that bitch!" I spat and closed the phone. Those three little words were the reason Jazzie J's life ended that day with two head shots. See, I had killers everywhere, ready and willing to put in work just to be members of my team.

I faced Eric. "You should've asked to use my name or, at the very least, come off my bread. Now you'll never make another dime off your artist." She was about to be chopped into pieces and scattered across the Mississippi River.

Chapter Thirty-seven

After leaving the record label, I snapped the burner phone into two pieces and dropped it in the sewer system. Next, I took my waiting Uber back to the airport and paid the driver handsomely to say he had never seen me if he was asked. I didn't want to stay in Cali any longer than necessary. Thank God I was just in time for the last flight of the evening back to Detroit. The moment my flight touched down on home soil, I turned on my phone and called Gran to check on Ju.

"Janelle, some people came here and tore this house apart. What have you done?"

"I didn't do anything." I felt like a child being scolded.

"Don't go telling those tales. People just don't do things like this for no reason." Gran was extremely upset. "They came knocking on the door in the middle of the night and scared us to death."

"I'm sorry, Gran. It won't happen again, I promise." I felt horrible. Shit like this could've caused my grandmother to have a heart attack. "How is my baby girl, though?"

Gran must have handed Ju the phone, since the next words I heard were, "Mommy, I want to see you." Juliana's voice was so cute. It had been over three months since my last visit to Georgia. "Can I come to your house?"

"Yeah, I'm ready to come back to Detroit too! For good this time!" Gran yelled from the background. "This here just don't make no sense."

"Okay, okay." Although Detroit was the last place I wanted either of them, I relented. I really missed seeing my daughter every day, and part of me missed Gran's ass too. "Give me a little time to set up your living arrangements, and I'll have Blondie set up your flights."

After getting off the phone with Gran, I returned the calls of Ali, Blondie, Rocky, Patrice, and a few others. Just like I thought, they had all been hit with a search warrant. Everyone swore they were clean. For now, we had nothing to worry about. Still, I told everyone to lay low. My instructions were to change phones daily and to refrain from sending text messages. Hell, I didn't even want these bitches to blow a red light right now. We had come too far to get caught slipping.

Pulling up to my house, I noticed a black SUV parked at the curb. Instinctively, I was on the defensive, but when a backseat window rolled down and I saw Mr. Pauletti motion me over, I exhaled slightly. I climbed out of the car and approached the SUV.

"To what do I owe this visit?" I asked through the window. Though nervous as hell, I played things as cool as I could. I already knew why the boss was here, but I needed to hear him say it before I opened my mouth about anything.

"Take a ride with me, Jane." After unlocking the door, he opened it and then slid to the other side of the backseat to make room for me.

"Actually, I was just about to—"

"It won't take long, I promise." Everyone knew you never took a ride with a mobster, but I had no other choice. "Tell me what the fuck happened and why your name is all over the goddamned newspaper," Mr. Pauletti demanded after I got in the backseat with him. His driver, Matteo, pulled away from my house, pretending not to ear hustle.

"I don't know shit about the fight in the nightclub with the Miami Heat. That was all on Ace."

"What fight, Jane?" Mr. Pauletti sat back in his seat and stared me down in a disapproving manner.

"Wait, if you aren't talking about the fight, then what exactly did it say I did in the newspaper?"

"Never mind the headlines. I just need to know why the Feds are digging into your shit so heavy."

"Damn. Did they hit you too?" My eyebrows rose.

"No, thankfully, they didn't." He shook his head. "However, I need you to tell me why they came in the first place. I thought your shit was solid." Mr. Pauletti coughed hard into a beige handkerchief, leaving a little blood behind. About eight months ago he had called a meeting and had told all those in his immediate circle that he'd been diagnosed with stage four prostate cancer. Every time I had seen him since then, he'd seemingly lost more weight.

"Don't worry. My shit is solid. This Fed thing stems from some stupid rapper who made a song with my name in it. I had no idea until I heard it last night."

"Jane, if you want longevity in this game, you've got to stay out of the limelight." Mr. Pauletti was an old-school gangster: no photos, videos, or audio recordings. "I know it's hard to do with your celebrity boyfriend and this damn social media, but you've got to try. Or this is going to keep happening, until they pin something on you."

"You're right." I nodded. Over the time I'd known him, Mr. Pauletti and I had grown close. Once he had stopped looking at me as a female and had started seeing my value, he'd begun grooming me. He'd shown me how to monopolize the game with calculated moves and ingenuity.

"I'm not going to be here much longer." Mr. Pauletti coughed again. "Which is why I want to bring you to the table before it's too late."

"Where are you going?" I didn't follow what he was saying.

"Jane, this cancer is kicking my ass, and I'm tired. It's time to prepare the family for my demise." He gazed at me with weary eyes. "In my absence, Vincenzo, my right-hand, will take my seat. My son, Luis, will take his, and so forth. Once everyone moves up, there will be one seat at the table. It usually goes to an Italian male, but I want you to have it."

"Mr. Pauletti, I don't know what to say." Though elated at the news, I was saddened by the reason I'd received it.

"Jane, you've proved yourself from day one. Your drive and ambition have skyrocketed the family into a new arena. It's situations like this that make you a made woman. I want you at my table not only because I like you, but because I know in my heart you deserve to be there."

"Thank you for thinking so highly of me." I was nearly moved to tears.

"Come to the house tonight at eight. I'll announce it then." He winked. "In the meantime, please stay the fuck out of trouble."

"I know your son is going to be pissed."

"Let me handle him. All you have to do is show up." Mr. Pauletti extended his fist, something I'd taught him a while back, and we bumped knuckles.

Chapter Thirty-eight

The conversation with Mr. Pauletti had me on cloud nine. However, that all changed the moment Matteo dropped me back off at home. No sooner had I put the key in my door than the cell phone in my pocket vibrated. It was my attorney, Richard Lennigan.

"What's up?" I asked.

"Jane, are you sitting down?"

"No. Should I be?" Pausing on the doorstep, I leaned up against the house and waited for the bad news.

"The Federal Bureau of Investigation is requesting your presence at their headquarters ASAP."

"What?" was all I could say, as it felt as if the wind had been knocked out of me.

"Apparently, they discovered some incriminating information at one of your colleagues' homes. They want you to come in so they can give you the opportunity to clear your name before they come back to your house with an arrest warrant."

"If I go down there, will they arrest me?" Fear gripped my heart as I contemplated where to run and hide.

"I don't believe so, but if they do, I will bail you out right away." Richard paused, as if he could read my thoughts. "Janelle, you can't run from this. That would only make things worse. The best thing for you to do right now is go down there and hear them out. I'll be there with you."

"Fuck it! I'll see you in half an hour." After ending the call, I placed the phone in my pocket and jumped into the basic Toyota Camry parked in the driveway. I never drove the car, because it was Bravo's. He was supposed to have custom work done on the windows and wheels next week. However, today the plain ride was just what I needed to represent my humble lifestyle to the Feds.

Instinctively, I removed my diamond earrings, bangles, and necklaces while speeding down the freeway. I even pulled my hair into a bun and wiped the Victoria's Secret lip gloss off my lips. After finding a parking spot in the crowded lot, I decided to leave my Gucci bag in the trunk of the car. Then I headed toward the large federal building.

I spotted my attorney waiting near the entrance. "Richard, what do they have?" I asked as I approached him.

"I wish I knew. Agent Gerard was very vague on the phone." Richard held the door open, and we entered. You would've thought we were walking into Fort Knox with all the security checkpoints, the surveillance cameras, and the canines resting behind the desk.

Ten minutes later we were escorted up to fifth floor by an officer in combat gear who was carrying an assault rifle.

Agent Gerard was standing in front of the elevator when the doors opened. "Ms. Doesher, thank you for coming. Right this way. I hope it was no trouble." Agent Gerard led Richard and me into a small room with white walls, a glass mirror, and a white table.

"What can I do for you?" I inquired nonchalantly while taking a seat.

"Well, to be frank, we recovered detailed documents from the home of Jessica Johnson, with dates and times of each narcotic shipment for the entire state of Michigan this year for the AFM."

As he continued, I thought about what he was saying. After the twins were killed, Jessica was hired to replace

Tamia in the finance department. It was her job to schedule the eighteen-wheeler trucks for distribution. Once the drivers dropped off the shipment for the week, they would head to a separate location and pick up the profit from a stash spot. Eventually, they would meet with Jessica, who would send the money to a foreign account in the Cayman Islands. Our connection in the Caymans would in turn send us some clean money for our American accounts. The shit sounded complicated, but Jessica seemed to handle it with ease. Now I came to find out the stupid bitch had been keeping a record this whole time. Hadn't she ever heard of a goddamned paper shredder?

"What does any of this have to do with me?" On the surface I was cool; internally, I was hot!

"We know our findings are just the tip of the iceberg." The FBI agent smiled smugly. "Ms. Johnson is in custody and is facing some very serious charges. She's willing to talk, but we thought we would give you the opportunity to do so first."

"Nice try." Richard shook his head. "Jane, let's go. I'm sorry I wasted your time and mine."

"Don't you want to clear your name?" Agent Gerard asked, pushing.

"Unless my client is being formally charged with something, there is nothing to clear. Come on, Jane."

"Suit yourself." Agent Gerard shrugged.

"See you later, alligator." I waved at the agent before exiting the small room with my attorney, who'd just done a damn good job.

Once outside and away from the building, Richard explained what had occurred. "He's lying. If they had someone willing to rat on you, they wouldn't have called a meeting. They would've listened to their informant, tried to set you up, and worst-case scenario, they would've arrested you." Richard was sharp. I was happy he was on the payroll. "Look, go home, get some rest, and watch the inner circle these next few days. The FBI is nothing more than a bunch of pricks in suits, but the DEA is crafty. If this becomes a drug case, they will come for your head."

"Well, if they come for the queen, they better not miss!"

Chapter Thirty-nine

After bidding farewell to Richard and leaving downtown, I had to head straight to the Pauletti residence in order to make it in time for the special meeting. Becoming a made woman would be a beautiful end to a fucked-up day.

Upon arriving at the residence, I noticed the gate was wide open and the guard wasn't on duty. Something was off. Therefore, I approached with caution. Across the lawn, I saw a coroner's van and several people standing outside. I rushed toward them. Karla was standing alone on the lawn, in tears, with make-up running down her face.

I rushed to her side. "Karla, what happened?"

"He's gone, Jane." She cried into my shoulder.

"What?" I knew what she meant; I just didn't want to believe it.

"I went to wake him from his nap, and he was gone."

"Karla, I'm so sorry." As I consoled Karla, I cursed under my breath. This probably sounded selfish, but I was pissed. How dare he die before announcing my position? I knew without Pauletti's co-sign, I'd never get a seat at the table.

The coroner emerged from the house with a gurney. He stopped when he caught sight of us. "Ma'am, we're going to take him down to the morgue," he told Karla. "The body will be ready for the funeral home to pick up first thing in the morning."

"I'm going too," Karla insisted.

"You can't do that, ma'am. I'm sorry." Casually, the coroner rolled Mr. Pauletti's body bag past us. It was hard to believe I was just with him and now he was gone. The coroner loaded the gurney into the back of the van and closed the doors. He turned in Karla's direction. "You can come down in about an hour and properly identify the body, though." When Karla said nothing, he nonchalantly stepped inside his van and pulled away.

As the van went past the gate, Karla almost lost it on the lawn. She began jumping up and down in a tearful rage and didn't stop until she nearly collapsed. I wrapped my arms around her and directed her limp body toward the house.

Inside the foyer, Mr. Pauletti's son could be heard from a mile away going completely off. "I wonder if this is why my father called this meeting. Did he want us all to be here when he died?" Luis addressed four men in suits who were standing around the foyer. When he turned and saw me, he lost it. "Why the fuck is she here? Who called her!"

"Your father asked me to come," I said while I led Karla through the foyer to the sofa in the sitting room. After propping her feet up and making sure she was comfortable, I returned to the mobsters.

"Tell me, Jane, why in the world would he do that?" Luis asked, in disbelief.

"He told me that death was knocking on his door and he wanted to get us all prepared for his passing." I hated Luis with a passion, but I kept my cool and tried to have compassion for what he was going through. I knew all too well what it felt like to lose a father.

"Okay, I understand him making us prepared, but why would you need to be prepared? You're nothing but a mere street runner anyway." His tone was rude and condescending. The other men knew how wrong he was, but they still remained silent.

"I'm far from a street runner. As a matter of fact, your father was going to bring me to the table tonight." My revelation raised several brows, but not Vincenzo's, as he knew the plan.

"Bullshit! My father, God rest his soul, would never bring a nigger to our family table," Luis scoffed.

"It's true." Vincenzo nodded. "I swear on my mother's grave that your father wanted Jane at the Pauletti table."

"No! No! Hell no!" Luis barked. "There ain't no way in hell I'll ever bring a black bitch to this family's table."

"Who are you calling a nigger, bitch?" Before I could think about what I was doing, I reached all the way back and brought my hand forward so fast that I slapped the spit from Luis's mouth. One look at the blood on his lip and he tried to strike back, but Vincenzo stepped in.

"She ain't coming to the table!" Luis yelled as two additional men restrained him.

"You know I deserve that spot." My eyes practically pleaded with Vincenzo. There were levels to the game, and I deserved to move up a notch.

"Jane, you've done good, but I've got to say Luis is right. The family isn't ready for a female at the table. I'm sorry." Vincenzo put his hand on my shoulder and tried to offer a consolation prize. "You can keep your distribution ring going, though."

"No, I'm sorry," I sighed. "Without Mr. Pauletti, I can no longer do business with you." It was one of the hardest decisions I'd ever had to make. However, it was what it was. My team hustled harder than anybody's squad! We had come too far to be demoted and downplayed yet again. Whether they knew it or not, these men needed us.

"Jane, you don't have to leave. We love the work you do." Vincenzo smiled.

"Let me get this right. I'm good enough to place more money in your pockets than ever before, but not good enough to eat at your table?"

Vincenzo didn't have to explain. With my head held high, I walked away from the Pauletti mansion with a smile. Sooner or later, they would come calling. When they did, I would tax their asses severely.

Chapter Forty

After a grueling back-and-forth battle, the Heat had managed to beat the Pistons in Miami in game seven of the playoffs, thereby clinching the championship. Although Ali and I had flown into town this morning, I had decided not to attend the game. Instead, I had watched from the penthouse suite of our condominium building just off the waterfront. After the fight in Detroit, the Internet had gone crazy about my relationship with Bravo. Fans had started calling me bad luck, and some had even threatened to shoot me if I was seen anywhere near the arena. Though I wasn't scared of the threats, I hadn't wanted to bring my man any bad luck. So I had sent Alicia to hold it down for me, while I had curled up on the couch with my favorite blanket and a bottle of wine. I still wasn't much of a drinker, but the separation from the Paulettis had taken a toll on me.

"Jane, wake up." Bravo shook me from my slumber.

With a yawn, I stretched, and then I hopped off the couch in order to wrap my arms around his neck. "Congratulations, baby." Although I would've loved for the Pistons to win the championship again, I was elated for my man. This meant more money, a championship ring, and the opportunity for endorsements. "Come here. Let you show you how proud I am." I dropped to my knees, then pulled on the Hermès belt buckle around his waist.

"Stop, Jane." Bravo snatched away from me forcefully. "We need to talk."

"What's wrong?"

"I need to know right here, right now that you love me. I need to hear you say that you aren't just stringing me along, and that you will be my wife."

"I love you with all I have, Bravo. I want nothing more than to be your wife. What's wrong?" His behavior was scaring me.

"Nothing. I just needed to hear it."

"You're lying. What happened?" I knew my man was definitely withholding information.

"There is talk of me being traded." His eyes were filled with tears, and Bravo tried hard to keep them from falling. "Coach Jones pulled me aside and gave me the heads-up. The decision from the higher-ups will come within the next few weeks."

"How can they do that? Why would they do that when you just helped their team win?" Although Bravo wasn't the star of the team, he was definitely a valuable asset.

"My contract is about to be up, and in light of all the recent publicity surrounding us, they feel that my negative image will effect the team next season." Swiftly, he wiped his tears to keep me from seeing them.

"Bravo, I don't know what to say. I love you to the moon and back, and I want to spend forever with you, but at what cost? Losing a position on the team you've always dreamed of being a part of just to be with me is not worth it."

"Baby, I don't give a fuck about none of that, if what we have is real. All I need to know is that it's me and you against the world." Peering down into my eyes, Bravo begged for an answer. My head told me to lie to him, so that he could move on without me. However, my heart wouldn't let me do it.

"Until I draw my last breath, it's me and you against the world. I swear to God, I will make this right." In silence,

I laid my head against his chest, and together we cried. I didn't think him crying was a sign of weakness; I saw it as a sign of humanness. He was hurt, and I had caused that hurt, and I wanted nothing more than to fix this for him.

The next morning, I hit the ground running. The first call I made was to Estillita. She informed me the Miami Heat Wives and Affiliates was meeting at her home this afternoon to plan the celebratory trip to Disney World. I persuaded her to switch the meeting to the meeting space in my building and to let me handle all the details. Though reluctant, she agreed after a brief deliberation but warned me not to fuck this up.

I got dressed quickly and then did a little research on the guest list. After gathering the names of the women in the organization, I headed down to the third floor to knock on the door of Gunther Pratt. Gunther was a conservative gay man with impeccable style, and he carried the tea on everybody. In fact, he had a midnight radio show that revolved around dishing the dirt. We'd met on the way to the elevator several months ago. He had complimented my ostrich handbag, and I had complimented his ostrich shoes. We had joked about being twins and had been close ever since.

"What in the hell has got you up this early?" Gunther said when he opened the door. After stepping aside, he let me enter his sleek yet humble eighteen-hundred-square-foot condo. He was dressed in nothing but an oriental robe and a do-rag.

"I need some info on a few of these people." After shoving my list in his hand, I walked into to the kitchen and took a seat atop the high-top barstool.

"Now, you know I don't be giving up the goods for nothing, honey. What do you have for me?" Gunther shifted his weight to one side and patiently waited on my answer.

"Do you know Eric Washington is a member of the 'undercover brother' society?" With my arms folded, I watched as Gunther gleamed with excitement.

"Not *the* Eric Washington, the one that just got married a year ago?"

"That's the one, and I got the proof." After whipping out my cell phone, I gladly showed Gunther the pictures.

"Child, this is unbelievable, especially when he was the main one talking about hip-hop ain't hard no more. It's homo, with all these gay rappers and bisexual lyrics."

"You know people in glass houses are always the ones throwing stones." I shrugged.

"This is some heavy shit. What's your price for the story and pictures?"

"I'm not selling it. You can have it. I just need information on the people on that list."

Gunther was shocked. "Janelle, there are people that will pay good money for this. Are you sure?"

"It's all yours *if* you help me with the list."

"Bridgette Halley and Amber Davids are the face of S.O.C. It stands for Saving Our Children. It's an organization that was formed to protect children born under the influence of heavy narcotics."

"Damn, Gunther. I need some dirt, not the hero shit."

"These women are no heroes. They are heroin heads." Gunther busted my bubble and kept right on down the list. "Karen Tate, the director's wife, killed a pedestrian last summer, while driving drunk. The league covered it up by paying the victim's family a large amount of hush money. April Polish, the assistant coach's wife, appears to be holier than thou, but everybody knows she's been messing with the athletic director, Steven Dow, behind her husband's back. In fact, I heard April's third son is Stevens. The rest of these girls are pretty clean."

"How come you never reported on any of them on your show?" With these many skeletons in the closet, I was beyond shocked the radio station hadn't released this information ASAP.

"Look, there is an unspoken contract between the station and the Heat. We don't speak on them, and they don't sue us." Gunther smirked. "Why do you think we haven't reported that mess that you and Bravo have been going through? Speaking on that, off the record, are you okay? I heard about the Feds, girl."

"Yeah, I'm good. All that drama stems from the Jazzie J song with my name in it." Though I wanted to ask Gunther where he'd gotten his intel about me, I let it ride.

"Yeah, I heard the song. Did you know Jazzie has been reported missing by her family? She didn't show up for her concert." Gunther handed my list back to me.

"I can't stand the bitch for ruining my life, but I do hope she turns up, safe and unharmed." With my best smile, I tried hard to sound sincere.

I didn't know if Gunther bought my bullshit, but he didn't call me on it, either. Instead, we continued with small talk for another twenty minutes, until Alicia called to tell me she was downstairs. Now that I'd collected all my bones, it was time to put the rest of my plan in motion.

Chapter Forty-one

Alicia and I spent nearly three hours shopping and decorating the meeting space in my building. Neither one of us was crafty, but I'd say the coral, gold, and cream theme turned out very classy.

"I think we should decorate for the wedding. What do you think?" I said. With a chuckle, I smoothed out the table linen, then stood back and admired our work.

"Bitch, please. You better pay somebody. I'm tired." Alicia grabbed a bottle of water from the beverage table and gulped it down. "Why are we doing this anyway? We don't even like these hoes."

"They are talking about trading Bravo. I need to get these girls on my side to help change that." Quickly, I glanced at my watch. It was almost showtime. "Come on. We've got to get dressed."

"You go ahead. I'll stay in this." Alicia looked down at her white halter top and navy blue capris. "I may need to kick somebody ass, and I can't do that in my good clothes."

"Suit yourself." With a laugh, I left the meeting room and headed up to the penthouse.

As soon as I entered the penthouse, the smell of something amazing smacked me in the face. I peeked in the kitchen and checked on Chef Kristoff. He was standing over the stove, searing lamb chops. After giving him a thumbs-up, I headed to my bedroom and closed the door. The minute I began to undress, the phone rang. It was Sonnie. He'd been calling me off and on since last night, but I wasn't in the mood to talk. Then I got a text from Rocky, telling me to call Sonnie before he became a problem. "Fuck!" After sliding the coral bodycon dress over my body, I begrudgingly grabbed the cell phone and returned Sonnie's call.

"What is the problem?" I asked after he answered.

"I fulfilled my end of the deal, but you haven't. When am I going to get what I asked for?"

"Sonnie, I ran into an issue on my end. Can I call you when I get back to the city?" I absolutely hated to talk business on my phone, especially now that I was on the alphabet boys' radar.

"Janelle, I don't give a fuck about what issue you ran into. A deal is a deal!" he spat.

"You're right. My bad about that." Rolling my eyes, I continued. "My friend will contact you today and square things off. Plus, I'll lace you with extra when I get back."

"Good! This shit better start coming like clockwork, because I won't be calling back." *Click!* Sonnie ended the call abruptly. Squeezing the phone tightly, I heard a few cracking noises. With a huge sigh, I regained my composure and dialed Patrice.

"Hey," she answered.

"Take Sonnie that gift I promised him, and make sure you do it by tonight."

"For sure," she said.

I ended the call, tossed my phone clear across the room, and plopped down on the bed. With my head propped up by my hands, I sat there, feeling beyond pissed off and frustrated. The last thing I wanted to do was go entertain a bunch of phony bitches right now, but I knew Bravo was counting on me. Exhaling deeply, and adjusting the invisible crown on my head, I rose and slid into my gold Louboutins and left the bedroom.

Chef Kristoff and his staff were loading up the serving cart with food when I passed the kitchen. "Everything looks amazing," I called out and then headed back down to the meeting room.

As soon as I opened the door, I heard the light chatter and laughter that filled the room. Almost all the ladies had arrived and were seated.

"Thank you for coming, ladies," I announced. I smiled, but it wasn't reciprocated.

Karen was the first one to speak out. "What is she doing here?"

"Well, her fiancée is on the team. Why wouldn't she be here?" said another woman, one whom I wasn't familiar with, defending me.

"Not for long, if you know what I know," said a woman by the name of April Polish. She cleared her throat.

Estillita, who was standing next to me, took the floor. "Ladies, please don't be rude. Janelle went to a lot of trouble to host this meeting. She wants to get to know us, and I believe we should get to know her before we fire shots."

"We ain't firing nothing but shade. She's the one with the guns," some dark-skinned woman said before slapping a high five with her neighbor.

"That's real cute, Dominique." Estillita flipped the girl the middle finger.

"Ladies." I spoke loud and clear. "It's been brought to my attention that Bravo will be traded on account of me, and I don't think it's fair. I selfishly asked you to assemble here to beg for your mercy and to plead with you to speak with your husbands to see if there is something that can be done for my man. You know just like I do that he doesn't deserve this."

"You're right. He doesn't deserve this, and you don't deserve him. Bravo is a great man with exponential talent. He was headed to the top of his game until he crossed paths with you," April stated matter-of-factly.

"Look, I'm sorry, Jane. Maybe this was a bad idea," Estillita said, apologizing.

"Yes, this was a real bad idea!" Karen stood from her chair. "If you care about Bravo's future, cut him loose. That's the only way we will consider talking to anybody about renewing his contract."

Before I knew what was happening, Alicia came storming up from the back of the room and came to a stop right in front of Karen. "What did my friend ever do to you?" she screeched.

"Ali, it's cool." I had to pull her out of Karen's face.

"See what I mean?" Karen looked from Alicia to me. "We don't want your kind affiliated with us in no way, shape, or form."

"What's my *kind*?" I asked, seeking clarity, as Chef Kristoff and his team rolled the meal into the room.

"You know what you are. There is no need for me to tell you." Karen looked me up and down. "Come on, ladies. Meeting is adjourned." She snapped her fingers, and just like that, the women got up from their seats.

"Before you leave, please grab a goody bag with your name on it," I said and pointed to the favor table in the corner of the room. "I put a lot of thought into those bags, and it would mean a lot to me if you took them."

"Jane, I wouldn't give them shit!" Estillita tapped the toe of one of her Manolos against the floor. She was as livid as I should be.

"Don't worry. This will be good," I assured both her and Ali as the women grabbed their goody bags and began to open them. "Five, four, three, two, one." It didn't take long before the expressions on Amber, Bridgette, April, and Karen's face changed from smug to astonished.

"Thank you, Jane," most of the women said in unison, though there was nothing in their bags except for a few trinkets and a card.

"I've been waiting all season for Chanel to release these." The lady who'd defended me early on held a pair of hoops up to her ears.

"You ladies are most welcome." I smiled. "If you don't mind, please let me talk to these ladies in private."

"Are you cool, Karen, or do you need me to wait?" one of the flunkies asked.

Speechless, all Karen could do was nod her approval.

Estillita could barely contain herself. "What did you put in those bags?" she asked.

"You'll see." I winked.

After Ali and Estillita and the flunkies had left the meeting room, I smiled at the women of the MHWA as they stood around the room.

"What the fuck is this?" April hollered.

"It's your deepest, darkest secret coming back to bite you in the ass." I laughed. "See, while you bitches were pointing a finger at me, you forgot there were three fingers pointing back at you. If you don't find a way to keep my man on the team, this information will be leaked. If you help me, no one will know about this but us."

Amber finally spoke up. "Are you blackmailing us?" she said.

"Call it what you want. Just know that you've been warned," I replied.

"Since you brought this ghetto trash into our circle, I'm holding you responsible for this." With much attitude, Karen stormed past us and out of the room like it was on fire. The other women followed suit.

"I may be ghetto trash and a few more things, but I've never been a liar. I wouldn't suggest you call my bluff!" I hollered as the door closed behind them.

"Jane, I'm dying to know what was in their bags."
Estillita laughed.

"You'll find out soon enough if they don't make good
on the deal." I was a woman of my word. I wouldn't say
anything about the goody bags and their contents unless
it was necessary. "Come on. Let's eat."

Chapter Forty-two

Within five days, the decision came down from the Miami Heat owners to renew Bravo's contract for another five years. He was elated about the news and on his way to Disney World with the team to celebrate that victory and all their accomplishments. He wanted Ju and me to attend, but I respectfully declined. Not only was I sure the team members and their female companions didn't want me there, but I also didn't want anything to ruin his moment. Besides that, this wasn't the time and place for him to meet my daughter for the first time.

For the time being all was well with the world, or at least I thought it was until I got off the plane at Metro Airport. Parked curbside were Rocky and Patrice, who were waiting for me and Alicia, instead of the car service we'd requested.

"What's popping?" Alicia asked them as she peered up and down the terminal pickup and drop-off area to see if there was anything out of place. Silently, I did the same. It was unlike the girls to just pull up on us unannounced.

"Hate to pop up on you like this, fam, but we need to talk about Sonnie," Patrice responded as she grabbed both my and Alicia's bags and then tossed them in the trunk.

"The nigga been blowing us up and getting reckless with his messages," Rocky said as she got in the backseat with Alicia, while Patrice hopped in the driver's seat. I gave one more glance around the area and then got into the front passenger seat of the Gold 300.

"He's still tripping, although you gave him the work already?" I asked.

"Yeah, he blew through that shit and called three days later for more. I told him that his weekly stipend won't start over until Friday, and that's when all hell broke loose. This fool has been calling us nonstop, threatening to go to the cops," Patrice explained.

Rocky added her two cents from the back. "We need to put a handle on dude."

"Janelle, they're right," Alicia interjected. "We've come too far to let him blow the whistle."

"Sonnie is an old-school nigga, and he ain't a cop caller, believe that," I asserted. Reclining back into the seat, I closed my eyes.

"Okay, let's say he is bluffing. With us cutting ties with the Pauletti family and running out of product, we'll never be able to make good on the deal, anyway, so what happens next?" Ali said.

"Just tell us how you want to play this," Patrice said. She was ready, but I wasn't. Sonnie was like family. Though I knew he had to go, I wanted to be sensitive about how I did it.

"Let me think on this one. I'll give you the blueprint soon," I told them.

"Janelle, we don't have time. We need to do him now!" Alicia insisted, then punched the back of my seat. I wanted to turn around and give her a piece of my mind, but I wouldn't dare scold her in the presence of anybody, so I let it slide.

"Sonnie will be handled when I say it's time to handle him," I said forcefully.

The tension in the car was thick, and I knew they were frustrated with me for pumping the brakes on the plan, but it was what it was. I was the boss of this crew, and they all respected my position.

As we pulled up to the crib, I noticed that flower arrangements lined the entire driveway.

"Someone loves you," Rocky teased as we parked.

"Shit. My grandmother is in the hospital. Can I take one of those vases?" Patrice said. She didn't wait for an answer before stepping from the car to choose an arrangement. I followed close behind, curious about the sender of all these flowers.

"You know it ain't nobody but Bravo's lovesick ass." Alicia commented as she climbed out of the backseat and got in the front passenger seat.

"I don't know," I called over my shoulder. I leaned down to read the card on a few arrangements and noted that they were all from Ace. He was probably apologizing for that stunt his goons had pulled at the party. "Take what you want. I'll catch ya'll later."

Once inside my house, I dropped my bags at the door and headed straight to the bathroom. After the past few weeks I'd had, a long, hot soak in my oversize jetted tub was just what I needed to clear my mind of the clutter. Before the water could rise an inch in the tub, my cell phone went off.

"Hello," I said into the phone after briefly contemplating not answering the call.

"Janie, did you like my flowers?" Ace's voice was low yet powerful as he whispered. No doubt he was probably on an illegal phone hidden in his cell.

"Why are you calling me, Anthony?" Plopping down on the toilet, I waited for the reply.

"Do you love that nigga?"

"I do love him, and I would appreciate it if you would stop fucking with us. That shit you pulled at the club could've gotten somebody hurt for real!"

"Can you come and visit me?" He slid past my statement like I hadn't said shit.

"Visit you for what? Me and you ain't got nothing to discuss."

"I think I found a way to tap into the prison market. I'm talking hundreds of thousands, but I need a strong force on the outside to ensure shit goes as planned."

"I can't help you, Ace." I reached over the bathtub and cut the water off.

"I put you on with my family, and this is how ya'll do me?" he hollered. "They haven't reached out in weeks, and you just blow me off. Okay, I see how it is."

"You're getting reckless on this phone, and I'm about to hang up." I paused to let my words sink in. Ace hadn't been out of the game that long. He should've known better. "I'm no longer a part of the family. Your uncle died."

Reading between the lines, Ace was at a loss for words for nearly a whole minute before asking me what had happened, where it had happened, and when.

So as not to give up too much information on the phone that could be used to connect me with the Mafia, I simply replied, "Cancer."

"I've got to go." Ace hung up without saying bye.

I felt bad for him; he was as close to Mr. Pauletti as I was. I was sure losing another prominent role model in his life brought back the feelings he had had when he lost my father. They were both good people who had lived bad lives. Thinking of Mr. Pauletti and my father caused tears to fall down my face.

"You can be anything in the world, baby girl," my father would say when I was growing up.

"I know, Daddy," I'd reply. I'd always giggle, for no reason.

"So, what do you want to be, then?"

"The best goddamned dope dealer this side of the Dirty Glove!" I said aloud now and wiped the tears from my face.

If my daddy could see me now, I knew he'd be proud of his baby girl.

Chapter Forty-three

After much thought and careful consideration, I had decided the time to act on Sonnie was now. I'd gone a whole three months playing the game and going through the motions with him. The more work he got, the more he wanted, for free. He felt like he had the power, but things were about change. With no more patience with the situation, I had decided to invite him on a little outing.

"Damn, Janelle. Why are we meeting at night, out in this messy rain?" Sonnie shook his umbrella and removed his wet trench coat before walking into the warehouse I'd invited him to.

"I wanted you to be the first person to see my new baby. Excuse the plastic. I just had the floor done. In fact, if you need work done on the club, my boy Diego is licensed to do some of everything. He's super affordable and can get shit for the low." I smiled and turned on the light and pointed down at the hardwood. "He did the tray ceilings too. Do you like it?"

"With the exposed brick and the chandelier lighting, I love it, but, honey, why are we here?" Sonnie made his way over to the wall to cop a feel.

"It's a banquet hall. I'm going to call it Monica's Place." I beamed proudly as I took in the construction site before me. Though it was far from complete, I was already in love with my newest business. The banquet hall wouldn't really be a moneymaker, but it would provide a private meeting space for my crew and another way to clean our dirty money. Besides, it was named after my mother, so what wasn't there to love?

"You know, Monica lived for a good party, honey." Sonnie walked back over to where I stood and folded his arms. "This is cute and everything, but unless you're giving me a partnership in this business, then I need to get what I came for so I can go. My man and I have dinner plans in less than an hour."

"Damn, Sonnie. I'm trying to share a moment with you, and all you want is the work. You know, greed will get you killed out here in these streets." I laughed lightly so as not to alarm him with my true feelings.

"Well, I ain't dead yet. So, come on." I couldn't tell if he was on to me, so I played it cool.

"The work is in the back. Come on, so you can get it and go." Together, we headed to the back of the unfinished storage room.

"Is this your stash spot?" he asked nonchalantly, and I smirked.

"Yeah, most of it is here. Why you asking?" After opening the door, I let him enter the dark room first. Once inside, I started rummaging through a few boxes. "The light is somewhere on the wall. Hit it for me."

"No reason. Just curious."

"This one is yours." I turned around with Sonnie's box in my hands and had to laugh hard when I saw the gun in his hand. He even had the nerve to have a silencer on it. "So, this is how you do your best friend's daughter?"

"Janelle, it's always business, never personal." With a straight face, Sonnie smacked the box from my hands and put the nose of his gun between my breasts.

"Funny thing is, I was just about to tell your ass the exact same thing."

Pop! Pop! Pop!

"What the fuck?" Sonnie's eyes widened in surprise as he received three body shots from behind, causing him to fall. On his way down to his knees, Sonnie grabbed my leg and began begging like a bitch for me to call for help.

"I told you greed would get you killed." After snatching my leg away, I went over to the wall and hit the light. Rocky and Patrice were standing against the wall like nothing had happened. I, on the other hand, was ecstatic. See, I loved when a plan came together.

"What do you want us to do with him?" Rocky stared down at Sonnie as he gasped for air.

"You know that house Alicia bought on Pasadena Street to turn into a shelter for battered women?" I said.

"Yeah." Patrice nodded.

"Wrap him up good and take him over there first thing tomorrow. The garage needs to be repaved. The concrete should be there in the morning. My guy Diego will handle the rest." Just like that, my issue with Sonnie was handled.

Days turned into weeks and then into months. Before we knew it, a whole year had passed and no one had come to question us about Sonnie. In fact, his disappearance had been aired on the news only a time or two before it was replaced with a more pressing story.

Surprisingly, we still hadn't heard from the Pauletti family, either. I guessed they had decided to try their hand at hustling without me. My entire squad had begun to second-guess my initial decision. Several times they had asked me to call Vincenzo and apologize for leaving in such haste. These bitches actually wanted me to beg the Paulettis to break bread with us again. I wasn't the begging type, so I had politely declined by standing my ground.

Besides, I had money on top of money, so I wasn't the least bit worried about the downtime. It was actually a blessing in disguise, because I was able to spend my days with Ju and most of my nights with Bravo, who was thriving with the Heat now more than ever. Gran was working with me on my domestication skills, and I was beginning to get the hang of being a housewife. Alicia, on the other hand, was about to go stir crazy. She had her record company to fall back on. Even so, she was addicted to street life.

"This shit is for the birds." Alicia played with the food on her plate. We were seated in a booth at the Cheesecake Factory for lunch. I wasn't really hungry, so I had skipped right to dessert, White Chocolate Caramel Macadamia Nut Cheesecake.

"How's the label?" I asked to switch gears.

"It's doing well. We just signed a little boy out of Kansas. I swear he's the next Usher." Alicia pushed the meat loaf and mashed potatoes to the side.

"That sounds exciting!" I smiled.

"I guess." She shrugged.

"What's the problem?" I was sick of watching her mope.

"I'm tired of being idle. I'm ready to get back out there and finish what we started."

"I'm with you, but our hands are tied." I finished the cheesecake and gestured for the waitress. When she came over, I asked for another slice to go and the bill.

"I feel like we should start our own thing, you know?"

"You want us to go up against the Mafia? No thank you." I shook my head. One thing I knew for sure was that the Italians didn't play.

"We have enough connections. We have the know-how and the fucking staff. I say we at least try."

"Here is your cheesecake, ma'am. The bill was paid by the man over there." The waitress pointed across the room, and I almost shit myself. I began to kick Ali under the table.

"What the fuck is your problem? These are some thousand-dollar shoes on my feet." She looked at me as if I had lost all my marbles.

"Girl, look across the room." I pointed and waved at the man coming toward us.

"Get the fuck outta here," Alicia said through a fake smile. Of all the people we had to run into, it had to be Vincenzo.

"Jane. Ali. May I join you briefly?" He smiled. I wanted to flip this fake-ass nigga the bird. Instead, I simply obliged and slid over.

"What's up?" Alicia asked once Vincenzo was seated. "Long time no hear from."

"My apologies to you both. It was not my intention to let time get between us," Vincenzo said before cautiously surveying the room. "Jane, I was wrong to let you walk away. Luis insisted we could continue without you, but the truth is . . . things have gone from sugar to shit without you."

I finally spoke. "Why are you telling us this, Vincenzo?"

"We've been having some issues lately. Luis is costing me more money than he's making. He has fumbled a few deals and is on the brink of losing everything his father built. Jane, I need you back on."

"The only way I'll return is if you bring me and Alicia both to the family table." With no hesitation and a straight face, I stared Vincenzo down. Ali was my ride or die. I didn't want to sit at anybody's table if she wasn't at my side. Therefore, my demand was nonnegotiable.

"I can't agree to that, Jane." He shook his head.

"I thought Mr. Pauletti named you boss?" I declared.

"He did, but I can't make a decision like that without everyone's vote. There is no way Luis will vote in favor of this." Vincenzo sighed.

"I guess you have a decision to make. It's him or us." I stood and motioned for Ali to do the same. "Thanks for lunch."

"Wait." He pointed for us to retake our seats. "I may have a solution, but it involves some dirty work," he practically whispered.

Alicia, who was still seated, leaned in. "We ain't afraid of the trenches."

"One of the family rules is we can't touch a made man. However, since you two aren't technically in the family yet, you can handle Luis. Then we will have two seats, and I can bring you both in."

I sat back down and pondered Vincenzo's offer. I didn't like the fact that he was dumping his problem off on me. Then again, I didn't like Luis whatsoever, so I didn't protest. Taking his ass out to gain induction into the Mafia was like hitting the jackpot. Furthermore, I had killed niggas for a lot less.

"We'll do it!" I said.

Alicia looked at me with uncertainty but remained silent.

Vincenzo nodded. "I'll get you the specifics," he announced before exiting the booth.

"What if this is a setup?" Alicia asked once we were alone.

"I think it's more like a test." With a smile, I rose once again from my seat. Forgive me, but I couldn't wait to bring death to Luis's front door.

Days later, Vincenzo supplied us with information regarding Luis's daily routine, as promised. I knew everything from what time he left home in the morning to what time he returned to walk his dog at night. For days, I pondered his execution, wondering if it should be quick and simple, or long and torturous. Then Alicia and I went to work.

"There he is right there. Are you ready?" Alicia asked. She was sitting in the driver's seat of the stolen Volkswagen Jetta.

"I've been ready," I replied before exiting the car and heading down the street.

It was broad daylight on a Saturday morning. Most people were scattered around the farmers' market in Lansing, minding their own business. From a distance, I watched Luis enter the dry cleaners and emerge a short time later with two suits and three shirts. Next, I observed him as he went into the pharmacy. I walked inside a minute later, then followed a good distance behind as he walked from aisle to aisle before finding what he needed and checking out.

My palms began to perspire as I made my way to his car, following behind him. It was parked on a vacant side street. During the walk, I caught a glimpse of my reflection in a barbershop window. The dingy oversize clothing I wore gave me the appearance of a bum. My hair was covered with a nappy wig and a baseball cap. Shades concealed my eyes, and the black paper from a Reese's Peanut Butter Cup covered the bottom row of my teeth, giving the illusion that I didn't have any.

With a large bucket filled with clear liquid and a window wiper, I walked up behind Luis with my head down. Once he was inside his vehicle, I approached it and poured some of the clear liquid on the windshield. Instantly, he rolled the window down and began yelling. "What the hell is your—"

Luis didn't get the chance to finish before I tossed the remainder of the liquid on his face, shoulders, and chest. The familiar smell of gasoline was pungent. After removing a pack of matches from the pocket of my shirt,

I struck one, lit the entire pack, and tossed it inside the vehicle. Flames immediately covered Luis; his flesh began to boil. The scent was enough to make me sick. Yet the look in his eyes as he realized what was happening kept me planted for the show. He screamed and tried to open the door, but I blocked it with my knees. Normally, a man of his size had twice my strength, but panic caused him to buckle.

Terror compelled Luis to throw the car in gear and pull off on two wheels. *Screech!* His tires squealed as he went careening into the side of a nearby building. A few people that were rounding the corner scattered like roaches, until they realized what had happened. By then, it was too late. Luis's car blew up like in a scene from a movie.

Chapter Forty-four

With the thorn in my ass out of the way, Vincenzo inducted Alicia and me into the Pauletti family without opposition from the remaining members. We weren't greeted with hugs and kisses, but we were respected and given the space we needed to do us. Right away, we went to work. It was time to elevate the game and take the AFM to levels we were never meant to achieve. Our Mafia ties catapulted us into the big league. Within months, we had hired over three dozen female go-getters from all across America to operate our empire. The money was flowing in faster than we could stash it. Life was good on the surface. Regrettably, things were about to go from sugar to shit without ado.

"You know I love you, right?" Bravo said one night while on the phone. He was in Miami for training, and I missed him terribly. So much so that I had hopped on a plane earlier that day and had headed there to surprise him. I had invited my girls Ali, Rocky, and Blondie along. Patrice couldn't make it.

"I love you too, baby." I smiled at the thought of surprising him. "What are you doing?"

"A few of us got together at the coach's house to watch some game tape. I'm heading home now."

"Okay, baby. Call me once you get there." I ended the call and smiled again.

"You got it bad." Blondie giggled.

"Your nose is so open, a Mack truck could ride through that bitch," Rocky commented, then slapped fives with Alicia.

"Fuck all of you." I brandished my middle finger around the car.

"So, what's the plan for tonight?" Alicia asked.

"Bravo is on the way home. We're going to stop there so I can surprise him first. Then I'll have him call his boys, and we can go out." I put the car in park after pulling up to the entrance to our condominium building.

"Fuck his boys. I need a bitch!" Alicia laughed.

After exiting the vehicle, I handed the keys to the valet, and we headed inside. The girls marveled over the expensive building all the way up to the top floor.

"This place is nice. I bet you all kinds of rich people live here," Blondie mused as she ran her hand along the marble wall in the hallway. I wanted to remind her that she was rich too, but I was focused on getting into the condo before Bravo got home.

The smell of food and scented candles greeted me at the door to the condo. When I opened the door, I saw that the place was dark, but there was soft music playing in the background.

"Aw, shit!" Alicia cursed. She knew this wasn't a good thing. Bravo had no idea I was in town; therefore, the romantic atmosphere was definitely not for me.

Without delay, I walked into the kitchen, turned off the simmering pot, and grabbed a butcher knife from the holder.

"Come on, Jane." Blondie pulled at my arm. "This shit ain't worth the trouble."

"Fuck that!" I snapped, pulling myself free from her grasp. The noise got the attention of someone in the bedroom.

"Bravo, is that you?" a lady called out in a seductive tone before hitting the light and entering the living room.

"No, bitch. It's his fiancée." My breathing was slow and steady, despite the fact that I was enraged.

"I'm sorry. I wasn't aware he was taken." She gestured with indifference.

"How long have y'all been fuckin'?" Alicia asked while staring this ho over. She was dressed in her birthday suit and a pair of leopard Louboutins—my Louboutins.

"I think you'd better ask him," she told us.

"Bitch!" I dropped the knife, then forcefully wrapped my hands around her throat and backed her up against the wall.

"Jane!" Rocky called out, but I was in a zone. It didn't matter that homegirl's legs dangled or that her hands frantically tried to pull mine away. I watched as the light began to leave her eyes. Within seconds, she departed this world.

"Shit!" Alicia said once I dropped the deceased woman, allowing her body to hit the floor. Just then, the front door opened, catching all of us off guard.

"Jane?" Bravo dropped his keys and rushed over to me. "Baby, what's up?"

"Who is she?" I pointed. As if Bravo had just seen the bitch for the first time, he jumped back.

"What the fuck!"

"Who is she?" I screamed.

"I swear to God, I don't know," he sputtered.

"So, a random bitch just happened to let herself into your crib, undress, light candles, and cook you a fucking meal?" I reached down and picked up the knife.

"Jane, I've never seen this girl." Bravo raised his hands, then leaned in for a closer look. Upon further inspection, he frowned. "Babe, this is that crazy bitch that I told you about the day we met. Remember I showed you her letters a while ago?" He pointed to several places on her body that were branded with Bravo's name and jersey number. I remembered him showing me dozens of letters over the past year from this stalker, some of which included pictures of her tattoos. "I don't know how she got in here. I swear to God! Is she dead?"

"As a doorknob." Blondie laughed.

"Fuck all the jokes. Now that she's dead, how in the hell are we going to get her out of your apartment?" Alicia's startling realization caused the entire room to get nervous, myself included.

"I'll just call the police and say I did it." Bravo looked at me with so much sincerity that it touched me. "They'll have to believe me, because she's in my crib uninvited, and I have the letters to prove she was a crazy stalker."

"No, you can't do that." Though it did mean a lot that he was willing to take the heat, I wouldn't dare let him damage the reputation he tried so hard to uphold. "I'll figure something out."

"Just take me to the nearest Home Depot, and I got you covered," Rocky stated. This was right up Rocky's alley.

"Home Depot?" we all said in unison.

"I need some tools, cement, and a large bag," she replied, like it was nothing. I guessed she'd learned a few things from Diego.

"Jane, Bravo, you stay here. Rocky, Blondie, y'all come with me," Alicia said. Then she grabbed my keys, and they headed out.

Bravo didn't speak for probably fifteen minutes, as I watched him pace the floor. He didn't look at me, either. I knew he was freaked out by this entire situation, and I couldn't blame him. Women were supposed to be fragile and delicate, but I was neither. Previously, he'd been aware that I was a queen pin. Now he knew I was capable of murder. Perhaps, it was too much for him to handle.

"After we clean this up, I'll leave," I finally declared to break the silence.

"You don't have to leave." He sighed. "I'm not mad."

"It's okay if you are. I would understand, because it's one thing after another with me."

"Jane, I never pressured you about a wedding date. I figured we'd get to it one of these days, but now I think we should get married a lot sooner than later," Bravo blurted out. Before I had the opportunity to respond, he continued. "I don't know how this is going to play out. If the police knock on my door, I want to invoke my spousal right not to testify against you. I love you just that much."

He said all that as he gazed at me, and that was when I completely broke and began to cry. It was right then that I discovered the true meaning of love and loyalty. This was the kind of love my mom and dad had had for one another.

Chapter Forty-five

The very next morning, Bravo and I went to the justice of the peace and exchanged wedding vows. It was nothing fabulous or fancy—just us, the magistrate, and my friends. As I took my turn repeating the words of my vows, I couldn't help but feel weird inside. Though I loved Bravo, it was not ideal to be marrying a man that hadn't even met my daughter yet. I was sure he felt weird too, but he didn't say anything.

I felt selfish, because he was only doing it this way for me, and I felt like I owed him immensely for being so patient, understanding, and willing to see this thing out with me. Bravo had been nothing but a stand-up guy, and I felt like I let him down with every passing day. I wanted to do better for him, and I promised that I would do better as soon as I could. I also promised to have a big ceremony after the season, but for now, it was what it was.

Right after the ceremony, Bravo, my crew, and I climbed in Bravo's vehicle and headed to the airport. The crew and I were heading back to Detroit. Once we reached the terminal, everybody scooted out to give Bravo and me a minute alone.

"Brandon, I love you. I swear to God I do. Other than being a mother, nothing has made me happier than these past few minutes of being your wife. I know shit is all fucked up with me right now, but I swear I will fix things and get this train back on track. I thank you for loving me, and I promise to be the best wife I can be to you."

"I love you, Janelle. I knew what I was signing up
for when I asked you to be my wife. I don't want to put
pressure on you to be anything less than who you are,
because that is who I fell in love with. Go do your thing.
Call me when you touch down." Bravo planted several
kisses on my lips before Alicia practically pulled me from
the car. For the moment, all was right with the world,
and I was happy.

However, my joy didn't last long. The minute my crew
and I touched back down in Detroit, trouble was calling
my phone.

I pressed the ANSWER button on the dashboard in my
ride. Ali and I had just picked Ju up from Gran's new
house. "Hello?"

"It's Rah. I'm in trouble." Rasheeda was one of our
lieutenants in D.C.

"Fuck you mean, you're in trouble?" I said. I pulled up
to a red light and looked at Ali.

"I just got pulled over." She sounded extremely anxious.
"The police are behind me, running my shit now."

"So why the fuck is you calling me?" I barked out of
irritation. All my ladies knew never to call me if they got
in trouble; that was what we paid lawyers for.

"I'm hot," she replied, and my stomach dropped to my
knees.

"How much are you holding?" I sighed.

"The whole trunk is filled with uncut bricks of cocaine."
Rasheeda was about to do some major time; we both
knew it. There was nothing I could do.

Click. I hung the phone up just as the light turned
green, and then I rolled down the window and tossed the
phone into traffic.

"Why was she riding around with work anyway?" Alicia
wondered aloud. She was more upset than I was.

"These hoes are getting sloppy," I sighed before Alicia's
phone rang.

"Yeah?" she answered and then placed the call on speaker.

"We've been raided," replied the girl on the other end of the phone line.

"What?" Alicia asked while looking at me. Our luck today was nonexistent.

"The DEA just took down all three spots here in Philly."

"Where are you?" Alicia asked.

"Shit, I'm at my mother's house. I came over to bring her some money, and that's when it happened. They got over fifteen of my people in custody."

"All right. Lay low and keep me posted," Alicia said, then hung up. "What the fuck?"

"I can't believe this shit!" I hit the dashboard. "We probably should go underground for a while."

Alicia shook her head. "I can't. My record label is finally doing big things."

After years in the music industry, Alicia's company had really stepped up to the plate. Her new artist, Micky, was slaying every other female artist in the game. Her single "Baddie" was being played in heavy rotation on all the radio stations, and her album had just hit number one on the Billboard music chart. Tonight was the official album release party. Everybody important was coming in for the event.

Alicia went on. "If I leave now, what happens to everything I've worked so hard for? What happens to my artists' dreams?"

"Alicia, I hear you, but this is not a fucking drill. These niggas are coming for us. You'd be a fool to think we're untouchable."

Alicia nodded. "You're right. After the party, I'm going to go under."

"I'm sorry, but I'm not coming to your party. I can't risk it." In the rearview mirror, I looked back at Ju and hit a U-turn.

"Where you going?"

"I'm taking her back to Gran." There was no way I could escape with my little girl in tow.

"Why is this even happening?" Alicia grumbled.

It was a question I didn't have the answer to, but something in the milk wasn't clean. Someway, somehow, the AFM had been compromised by a rat in the organization. Unbeknownst to us, this shit storm was just getting started.

Chapter Forty-six

By midnight the DEA had raided fifty additional spots and arrested more than two hundred people in total. I found out through Richard Lennigan that Ali and I had also been hit with multiple charges, one of which was running a continual criminal enterprise. It was a charge created under the United States federal law that targeted large-scale drug traffickers responsible for long-term and elaborate drug conspiracies. Richard's advice was to turn myself in. He was delusional.

The moment news about the indictment came in from Richard, I grabbed my fake passport and ID, and as much money as I could, then hightailed it to New York. There was no one I knew there, and it was such a big city that I knew I'd get lost easily. Days passed before I finally cut on the television. Other than ESPN running a speculative story about me and my legal issues every now and then, the media outlets were pretty dry about my story.

After a week I took my chances and mailed a letter to Bravo. Once again, I had to apologize for my fucked-up situation invading his professional life. A few days passed before he mailed one back, forgiving me and asking if I was okay, as usual. I didn't write back this time. I just needed him to know I was sorry.

Though things were going well, I left New York after three months. I didn't want to overstay my welcome. Next stop was Los Angles, California. Staying in bigger cities made me feel safe. Again, I sent a letter to Bravo,

and again, he sent one back. After two months there, I
headed to Texas. Moving from state to state like a rolling
stone was beginning to take its toll. But the pressure was
real, and my back was against the wall. I felt sad and
depressed. I wasn't able to talk to my daughter, Gran, or
Alicia. I often wondered about each of them and prayed
for their safety. Bravo hadn't heard anything about Alicia,
and of course, he had no way to contact Gran. Them
not talking was intentional: I didn't need Gran asking
questions that he would feel pressed to answer.

By the time I reached New Orleans, I was lonely.
Instead of sending my typical check-in letter, I sent
Bravo instructions on how to get to me. He didn't hesitate to go through the all the necessary hoops to get here.
I was sitting in the living room, staring out the window at
partygoers on Bourbon Street, when I heard the door to
the room open. I'd left instructions with the front desk
to give him a key upon arrival.

"Baby," Bravo called out. He sounded worried yet
excited.

"Thank you for coming," I exclaimed as I sprang from
the couch. I ran over to him and kissed his lips. I was so
happy to see him.

"Come on. You know I don't need to be thanked. I wish
I could have come sooner. I miss you."

"Me too," I replied with my head down. Being an outlaw
on the run was no fun. I was tired of living like a hermit. I
was tired of looking over my shoulder, and I was tired of
living without my loved ones.

"Janelle, I never tell you what to do, and I never will,
but we can't do this forever. You need to go home and
just face the music." He finally dropped his bag on the
floor and took a seat on the couch. "These people are
calling you armed and dangerous. The last thing I need
is for someone to call the cops on you and they come,
guns blazing."

"If I turn myself in, I will be going away for a very long time."

"Years in jail don't have shit on a burial plot."

Bravo was right, but I still had to do things my way, so I changed the subject. "Look, why don't you go take a shower and freshen up? I have dinner being sent to us from Oceana. Then we can make love all night, before you head back."

Bravo looked like he wanted to continue the conversation, but then he decided to let it die. As he went to take a shower, I went into the bedroom and pondered what he had said. Though I didn't want to die, I knew prison for the rest of my life wasn't even an option. Perplexed about what to do, I was overcome by the urge to call Gran. I needed to know that she and Ju were doing okay. It had been so long since I had heard her voice that my hand was quivering.

"Praise the Lord this Saturday night." Gran's voice seemed normal. Other than sounding a little sleepy, she appeared to be fine.

"It's me. Is everything okay over there?" I said as I took a seat on the bed and lay back again the pillows.

"Janelle, baby, is everything okay where you are?" Gran was now alarmed.

"I'm good. Just needed to hear your voice." I sighed. Guilt was weighing heavily on my heart. I had been on the run for so long that time had gotten away from me. My daughter was getting older, and the space between us was becoming wider. "How is Ju?"

"She's fine." Gran yawned. "She got a letter the other day from her father. Did you know he was granted an early release?"

"No, I didn't know that." It was nice to hear Ace's good news, but I wasn't concerned with that. "Can I speak to my daughter?"

"It's eleven o'clock. That child has been asleep awhile."
Gran yawned again. "She has a big day tomorrow."

"What's happening tomorrow?" I sat up in bed.

"Tomorrow is youth day at church. Juliana has a solo in
the children's choir."

"My baby is singing." The smile on my face was huge.

"She sings at the eleven o'clock service. Do you think
you can make it?" Gran asked.

"I'll see you there. Don't tell Ju. I want to surprise her."
In my mind, I knew this was the wrong decision to make,
but my heart was going against the grain. I had already
missed so much of my daughter's life. I wasn't about to
miss her big solo debut.

I told Bravo my plan, and he offered to come with me
the next morning, but I declined. After dinner we made
love over and over, until he was fast asleep and snoring
loud. While he rested, I took a shower and packed my
things. Then I left him a note and headed to the airport to
catch the 6:00 a.m. flight back to Detroit.

The flight arrived on time. After renting a car with my
alias, I nervously drove toward my destination. During
the entire ride, my mind told me to turn around and
leave, but I couldn't. I wanted my daughter to know
she was important enough for me to risk my freedom. I
wanted her to know she mattered.

Just before eleven o'clock, I entered Green Pastures
Baptist Church, wearing an enormous smile. The devil
himself couldn't steal my joy today, or so I thought.

"Welcome to our youth day." A shapely woman handed
me a program, then led me into the sanctuary. Oddly
enough, I hadn't been to church since the shoot-out with
Chucky.

"Oh, there's my grandmother." I pointed to Gran and
then walked over.

Her eyes widened and she smiled when she saw me. "I'm so glad you could make it, baby." She patted my hand, and I took the seat next to her.

"I missed you." I leaned in and kissed her cheek. The gesture came just as my daughter walked onto the stage. Fretfully, she fumbled with the mic before scanning the crowd. I waved, and she waved back. The pianist had hit only one note when commotion arose at the back of the church.

"DEA! No one move!" someone yelled.

I heard the words, and my heart sank. Not only was I about to be arrested, but it was going to happen in front of my baby too.

I didn't want to cause a scene or start a riot. Calmly, I raised my hands in surrender and stood. My eyes remained on Ju as she watched in horror as her mother was handcuffed. I wanted to yell out and tell her I was sorry. Sadly, I was unable to utter the words.

"Mommy!" Ju screamed into the mic before breaking down in tears.

"Gran, please tell her I love her," I whispered.

"Janelle, I'm sorry. I called them for your best interest. I had to," Gran said, apologizing. "I wanted it to go down safe like this with your father too, but it didn't."

Initially, I didn't know what in the hell she was referring to. Then, all at once, it hit me. Gran had known my father would be home on my birthday. She had called the police so that he would be arrested. However, he had started shooting, and they had killed him. All these years, I had speculated about who was responsible for tipping off the police. To find out my grandmother was the culprit hit me in the gut. And now I was going away, and my daughter would be solely in her care. What was I going to do?

Chapter Forty-seven

When I got down to the federal building, I was sent into an interrogation room and handcuffed to the table, and there I waited for six hours straight. They wanted to break me down mentally before the interview. At last, two agents came in and attempted the bad cop–good cop scenario. However, they didn't get very far before I shut it down by requesting my attorney. At that time the conversation ceased. Richard was away from his office. In his stead, he dispatched a colleague to inform me of the bail hearing first thing in the morning.

"Richard is going to request bond, but the DA will most likely deny it, Jane. They consider people with your means a flight risk," the middle-aged man explained.

"I can't do jail. Tell Richard to find a judge that takes bribes." I was willing to pay anything for my freedom.

"I'll pass the message along. Until then, try to get some rest, okay?" He stood from the table and patted my shoulder. I wanted to get up and walk out with him, but the handcuff on my right wrist prevented that from happening.

"Fuck!" I hit the table with my left hand.

Later that night, I was placed in a small room with another woman. For the most part, she was cool. Thankfully, she stayed to herself. The only time she spoke was when she asked if I was going to eat the hot dog and Tater Tots we were served for dinner.

"No," I said. "Have at it." I nodded to the tray.

"Thanks." She stood and grabbed my food. "I'm Grace."

"Jane." I nodded. The last thing I needed was a friend, but I wasn't going to be rude.

"Oh shit. You that Mafia bitch, huh?" Grace smiled. She was a big woman with five cornrows to the back.

"I guess." I hunched my shoulders.

"Yo, you a bad bitch, for real!"

"I'm sorry, Grace, if I sound rude, but how do you know so much about me?" I sat up on the side of my bunk and looked down at her.

"Shit. It's all in the indictments." Grace tossed a few Tater Tots back before continuing. "If you ever want to know who told on you, what they said, and how much of a pardon they got for snitching, just read the indictments."

"Where do you get them from?" I asked.

"I pulled that shit up online during my library time, but you can get them from your attorney."

"Thanks." I lay back on the bunk bed and stared up at the ceiling. Part of me wanted to know who had put me in this predicament, but then again, part of me didn't. Once I knew, there was no telling what I was capable of.

The next morning I was delivered to court for my bail hearing. As promised, Richard was waiting, with a smile.

"I need five minutes with my client," he informed the officer, who nodded. Richard took me to the side of the courtroom. "How are you holding up?"

"I'm cool, but I'll be even better if I can walk out of here this afternoon." I scanned the small room out of habit.

"I was up all night working on this. I believe everything is going to play out in our favor." Richard smiled.

"For your sake, I hope so."

"Janelle," someone called behind me. I turned to see Gran and rolled my eyes.

"When does Ace get out?" I asked Richard, totally ignoring the old bitch behind me. After what she had done, I could no longer consider her family.

"I'm not sure. I'll have to look into that."

"If I don't walk out of here, I want you to get Juliana to him the minute he hits the bricks. In the meantime, she should go and stay with Bravo." I hated to pawn my daughter off on a man she'd never met, but in this instance, it was what it was. I knew Bravo would do right by her in my absence. All I needed was for Richard to fulfill my wishes.

"Speaking of Bravo, there he is." Richard nodded as my man entered the courtroom.

He was wearing a black suit and dark shades. Although I couldn't see his eyes, I knew he was looking at me by the smile on his face. I wasn't in a smiling mood. Nevertheless, I did return the gesture to let him know everything was all right.

"Come on, Jane," Richard urged. Then he led me to our position behind the bench.

"Docket number J-five-four-one-two-three-seven-five. The State versus Janelle Doesher," the bailiff announced, stating my case for the judge.

The female judge looked tough as nails. I was nervous that this was not going to work in my favor. "Prosecutor, you may proceed."

"Your Honor, the defendant has been charged with running a continual criminal enterprise. She has access to millions of dollars in drug money, private planes, and Mafia ties."

"Objection!" Richard snapped. "My client is a business owner with ties to the community. You can check my client's bank accounts and federal tax returns, Your Honor. Millions of dollars in drug money is quite a stretch! As for Mafia ties, I would like to know where the prosecutor obtained his information. Is it on paper? If so, I would like to see it."

"He's right, Mr. King. Do you have proof of the alleged millions or the Mafia ties?" the judge asked the prosecutor.

"Well . . ." The prosecutor stalled.

Richard immediately took the opportunity to interject, "The DEA has raided practically every residence and place of business belonging to my client, looking for money they believed my client was hiding. They came up empty-handed each time." Richard sighed. "Ms. Doesher has a daughter, Your Honor. Please don't punish the child by keeping her mother locked up until the DA can try to build a case," he pleaded.

The judge nodded. "All right. I've heard enough. Bail for Ms. Doesher has been set at three hundred and fifty thousand dollars. This amount is to be paid in full immediately." The judge looked at me but spoke to Richard. "Mr. Lennigan, please advise your client that she is not to leave the state of Michigan at anytime from now until the end of the trial." The judge pounded the gavel, and just like that, it was over. I was free.

"Thank you, Richard." I hugged him tightly.

"Don't thank me. You paid the judge personally one hundred thousand dollars," he whispered. The moment I started playing in the big league, Mr. Pauletti had advised me to set up offshore bank accounts in the Cayman Islands. To date, I had over twelve accounts, one of which was specifically used for Richard. It held his retainer, as well as any other money he would need for my case, including bribe money.

"So, what's next?" I asked as we headed out into the hallway, where Bravo waited.

"They're probably going to expedite the trial date because you're a big fish, Jane." Richard laughed. "Knowing them, I would be surprised if we didn't go to trial in less than two weeks. They have at least ten people willing to testify against you already."

"Damn." I shook my head. "I wonder who started this domino effect anyway."

"If memory serves me correctly, it was someone by the name of LaShay." Richard could've bought my ass for a penny right then.

"Blondie?" I was sure I sounded as if the wind had been knocked out of me. Never would I have suspected this from her.

"Apparently, she called the police after a domestic violence situation at her home in Atlanta last year. When the police arrived, her boyfriend told them she was a high-level narcotics dealer. They searched the home and found a closet full of cocaine and money. She was looking at six to ten years behind bars, until they propositioned her to flip on her supplier. When she dropped your name, they dropped her charges and gave her one year to hand over as much information on you as possible."

Richard had said a mouthful, and I was nauseated. Not only had Blondie been privy to pertinent information, but the bitch had also been there when I killed the woman in Bravo's condo.

"Fuck!" I kicked the wall.

Bravo came over and stood at my side. "Baby, what's wrong?"

"I'll tell you in the car," I replied as Gran walked up and put her hand on my arm. "Don't fucking touch me!" I screamed, causing several people to stare. "I trusted you! You were blood, but now you're nothing!"

"I saw you heading down the path of self-destruction, just as I had watched your father do years ago. When those people kicked in my door, I knew I had to do something before the streets killed you," Gran cried.

"Save those fucking tears! Where is my daughter?" I didn't want to hear one more word from her ass today.

"Please, Janelle, don't take Ju from me." Gran wrapped me in an embrace. Instead of resisting, I leaned in and whispered, "If you want to wake up to see tomorrow, you will tell me where my daughter is."

"She'll be getting out of school at three," Gran whispered, then backed away, with the fear of God on her face.

Then I went to get my kid.

Chapter Forty-eight

After Juliana was tucked in bed, it was time to discuss my next moves with Bravo. I hated to have him involved in my shit *again*, but he was already in knee-deep and didn't even know it.

"What's up, babe?" he asked as I entered the kitchen, where he was putting up the dinner leftovers from Popeyes.

"I need to talk to you really quick."

He turned to face me. "I'm listening."

I took a seat on the stool by the kitchen island. "Richard told me that Blondie was the one who started this whole thing. Rather than taking her rap like a boss, she threw me under the bus." I sighed.

"Blondie is an informant? Since when?" Bravo was just as stunned as I was.

"For over a year is what I'm told."

"So that means she probably told the cops about the situation at the condo." Fear immediately consumed him.

"Probably." I nodded.

"Janelle, I can't go to jail, baby. What about my career?"

"So far the police haven't come for you, and I don't think they will."

"We don't know that for sure." Bravo was obviously shaken.

"If they wanted you, they would've shown up at a game or a practice session. Hell, your entire work schedule is all over the Internet and the television."

"So, what are we gonna do?"

"I have two options, but I don't think you're going to like either one." During my night in jail, I had pondered the matter and had come up with several ways I could get myself out of this jam if given the opportunity.

"Go on." Bravo leaned against the cabinet and folded his arms.

"I'm going to leave the States and change my identity for good." I stared at him.

"That sounds like only one option."

"Actually, that part is nonnegotiable. The options are either you come with me or you stay here."

"What about my team, my career?" Bravo asked.

"Baby, I love you with everything I got, but me and my daughter are outta here. I would love for you to join us, but I wholeheartedly understand if you can't. You have been nothing but accommodating to me. If you chose you this one time, I would have no choice but to respect that."

"Can I think about it?"

"Sure." I nodded, knowing then that Bravo was not on board with my decision to leave.

"I'm going to bed. Care to join me?" he said.

"I'll be up in a few."

After he left the kitchen, I went over to the refrigerator and grabbed a bottle of white wine, then headed to the couch. Normally, I didn't drink straight out of the bottle, but today was an exception.

As soon as I plopped down and cracked the wine open, there was a knock at the door. I looked from the bottle to the door and decided to take the bottle with me. I opened the door and was caught totally off guard. Standing in the rain was Ace.

"Hey, what's up?" I said.

"I'm fresh out, and the first person I wanted to see was my daughter. I hope you don't mind. I got the address from your grandmother." Although Ace needed a shower and a shave, I was digging the rugged look.

"She actually went to bed about an hour ago."

"It's been a long one, huh?" He pointed to the bottle in my hand.

"Yeah. Something like that." I smiled and stepped onto the porch.

"How are you holding up with everything going on?" Ace took a seat on the step and patted the spot beside him. "I'm not going to bite."

I hesitated before taking a seat. The last thing I needed was baby daddy and husband drama. "I know." I smirked. "It's just that my husband is inside."

"So, you actually did it, huh?" I could tell Ace was hurt. Yet he managed to keep a straight face.

"I did." I nodded. "He's a good guy, Ace."

"That's good. I'm happy for you," he lied before grabbing my wine bottle and turning it up.

"Now that you're out, what's next?" I knew Ace probably had some elaborate hustle up his sleeve. That was just how we operated.

"I want to spend time with my daughter and chill." He leaned back. Under the moonlight, his eyes were mesmerizing. I had to look away to keep from falling victim to his spell.

"*Chill*? I can't believe that's even in your vocabulary." I laughed.

"After doing those years, I came out with a new outlook on life. The street life ain't where it's at. Because of my lifestyle, I lost the woman of my dreams and precious time with my daughter."

Ace and I continued to talk for nearly two hours about our past, and we also finished two bottles of wine. We laughed a good while and even shed a few tears. It felt good to be in his presence again, even as just friends. I loved Ace and always would. Life had a funny way of switching up the game.

Chapter Forty-nine

Just as Richard had predicted, the trial started the very next week, after jurors were selected. Opening statements would be delivered today. I sat there, sharp as hell in a Valentino pencil skirt and a ruffled blouse, and I had a pair of black Gazelle frames on. My hair was pulled up into a loose bun, and my lips were painted a pastel pink.

The prosecutor stood and faced the jurors. "Ladies and gentlemen of the jury, we are here to prove that the defendant, Janelle Renee Doesher, is a cold-hearted criminal ringleader. You will hear testimony from various acquaintances of Ms. Doesher regarding her criminal enterprise, also known as the AFM. Under her leadership, the members of her organization were instructed to steal, lie, and even kill! Over the past year, we have seized narcotics, weapons, and millions of dollars in dirty money. It is imperative that we put this monster away, but we need your help to do so." The prosecutor headed back to his side of the room; then Richard stood for his turn.

"A *monster* by definition is 'a large, ugly, terrifying animal or person found in mythology or created by the imagination—something especially fierce that kills people.' Monsters are often featured in folklore and fairy tales. My client is *not* a monster." He pointed to me, and I tried my best to look innocent. "Janelle Renee Doesher was a young woman left to face the world alone after losing her parents at the tender age of sixteen. Has she made a few mistakes? Absolutely. Has she been in trouble before? Sure. However, she is no monster. She merely played the hand she was dealt and rose from the ashes of her situation to become a beautiful, well-educated business owner."

He went on. "As the prosecution stated, you will hear testimony from various acquaintances of my client as it relates to her character as well as to certain events in her past. However, he failed to mention that most of his witnesses were pardoned for their own participation in these alleged crimes in exchange for their testimony. I ask that you to keep this in mind when deciding the fate of my client. Thank you." With a nod toward the jury, Richard retreated to his seat.

The game had begun.

The first witness to take the stand was none other than my grandmother. Just the sight of her irritated me.

"Ms. Doesher, for the record, please state your relationship to the defendant," the prosecutor said while glancing down at a yellow notebook.

"She's my granddaughter." Gran smiled.

"So, you have no reason to want to harm her with your testimony, is that correct? In fact, the only reason you're here is to help her by putting an end to her madness."

"Objection! He's leading the witness!" Richard yelled.

"I'll allow it." The judge frowned. He was not the same judge I'd bought my get- out-of-jail-free card from last week. In fact, Richard had told me that Judge Hemsly was a hard-ass known for throwing the book at people. The state was playing hardball.

"I love my granddaughter. I saw her going down the same path as Julius, her father, and I wanted to put an end to the cycle of corruption," Gran replied.

"What relation is Julius to you?" the prosecutor asked.

"He's my son and Janelle's father. He was a drug dealer too, and Janelle idolized him from the moment she was born." Gran went on to speak about my time at her home and the two instances when I was arrested. Eventually, the prosecutor was done with his witness, and then it was Richard's turn to go at Gran.

"Ms. Doesher, how do you know that your granddaughter is an alleged drug dealer, as you put it?" Richard looked from Gran to the jury, attempting to create reasonable doubt about her testimony.

"Well, I wasn't sure until after my home was raided and the agent from the Drug Enforcement Administration told me," Gran answered.

"So, the police told you, but this is not something you know for a fact, from your own experience with your granddaughter?"

"I guess not." Gran sighed. "I just assumed."

"Ms. Doesher, I don't have to tell you what happens when we assume." Richard looked at the jury. "I'm finished with this witness." He took a seat next to me as I watched Gran leave the stand and limp away in defeat.

"The prosecution calls Donna Redding to the stand," the prosecutor announced.

I was completely blindsided, but I remained cool. I hadn't spoken to Donna in years. Who knew why she was even here?

After taking the stand and swearing to tell the truth, Donna was seated.

"Mrs. Redding, how do you know Janelle Doesher?" the prosecutor asked.

"Several years ago she hired me to accept stolen packages on her behalf." Donna fidgeted.

"What kinds of packages?" the prosecutor queried.

"She would pay for things like televisions, Kindles, laptops, and clothing with stolen credit cards. Then she would have them sent to abandoned homes, where I would get paid to sign for them."

"How long did you work with Ms. Doesher, and why did you stop?" The prosecutor looked at the jury. I already knew where this was going, so I whispered a few things in Richard's ear.

"I worked for her for about six or seven months. I stopped after one of the delivery drivers was killed."

"Are you referring to Neal Duncan?"

"Yeah, I believe that was his name. He and Jane had an altercation after he threatened to blow the whistle on her operation. I remember hearing her ask him to meet her later that night."

"Did you ever see Neal deliver any more packages after that?" The prosecutor smiled.

"No. In fact, it was all over the news that he and his wife had 'committed suicide' that night." Donna made air quotes with her fingers.

"I rest," the prosecutor said, turning the floor over to Richard.

"Donna, you do realize that you're under oath, right?" Richard said.

"Yes, of course," Donna declared with a slight attitude.

"Okay, so when the prosecutor asked how you knew Janelle, you said you were hired by her to receive stolen packages. But, in fact, you were a longtime friend of her mother."

"Yeah, her mother was my friend." Donna nodded, and the jurors began looking at one another.

"So why didn't you just say that?" Richard folded his arms.

"Objection!" the prosecutor yelled. "He's badgering the witness."

"Sustained. Move on, Mr. Lennigan," the judge instructed.

"On the night you say the story about Mr. and Mrs. Duncan committing suicide was all over the news, where do you remember watching television?" Richard asked. He lost me with his question. However, I was confident his line of questioning would benefit me.

Donna shrugged. "I don't know. It was years ago."

"Well, I have a sign-in log from Saving Grace Drug Rehabilitation Center, where you checked in."

"What's your point?" Donna was aggravated now.

"Is it safe to say that you were high on the night in question? Therefore, your memory could be a little distorted?"

"I know what I heard! Jane threatened that man, and then he miraculously killed himself."

"At the time, Janelle was what? Seventeen? Do you really think she was capable of murder? And did you know that Neal Duncan had a gambling problem? He was hundreds of thousands of dollars in debt, and his home was being foreclosed on by the bank. If that's not enough to commit suicide, then I don't know what is."

"I guess you're right," Donna said, relenting.

Richard rested his case.

The remainder of the afternoon went by just as smoothly as the beginning had. The prosecutor called a few more character witnesses, and Richard slew them as well. When court was adjourned for the day, I left the courtroom with a huge smile on my face.

"Jane, we had a good day, but don't celebrate prematurely. Today was just the beginning. I assure you things are going to get tougher as the trial proceeds," Richard told me as we strode down the hallway.

"I hear you," I said as we emerged from the courthouse.

The media was swarming the place like vultures, and when the journalists and their entourage caught sight of me, they hurried in my direction.

"Jane Doe, how does it feel to be the first woman who is internationally known for her handiwork with the Mafia?" a young black woman inquired.

"No questions," Richard responded.

The journalists paid him no mind and followed me all the way to the waiting town car out front, shoving their cameras and microphones in my face as we went.

Chapter Fifty

It was day two of the trial, and things had definitely taken a turn for the worse.

"Please state your name for the record," instructed the prosecutor.

"Gary Douglass." Gambino sat there with remorse all over his face.

"Mr. Douglass, how do you know Ms. Doesher?" the prosecutor asked.

"Jane is a client of mine." Gambino tried to be brief, but the prosecutor wasn't having it.

"For the record, what do you sell?"

"I sell guns, sir." Gambino looked down at the floor.

"When was the last time Ms. Doesher purchased weapons directly through you?"

"A few years ago."

"Did Ms. Doesher tell you why she needed guns?"

"To end a beef with this cat named Chucky."

"Can you elaborate?"

"Supposedly, Chucky killed one of Jane's friends. Jane went back at him but ended up killing his son and grandson. Chucky found out Jane had fled to Atlanta, so he sent some thugs to get her, but they failed. That's when she came back to the D and hit me up. She took the guns she got from me and went to handle old dude." Gambino was singing like a goddamned canary.

The prosecutor smiled. "Your witness."

"Mr. Douglass, were you there when Chucky was killed?" Richard asked and lifted a brow.

"No."

"So how do you even know that my client is the one who killed him?" Richard looked at the jury.

"Because she told me that's what she planned to do."

Gambino had practically placed the nail in my coffin. Richard looked as if he wanted to continue, but then it seemed as if he realized there was a possibility of Gambino hurting my case even more, so he decided not to question him further.

The prosecutor called his next witness. Just when I thought things couldn't get worse, I damn near shit when Eric Washington took the stand.

"Mr. Washington, please explain to the jury your last encounter with Ms. Doe," the prosecutor requested.

"She barged into my office and demanded a cut off the Jane Doe song that my client Jazzie J had on the airwaves at the time. When I said no, she basically told me that Jazzie J would not be performing at any future events."

"Are you saying Ms. Doesher killed Jazzie J?" The prosecutor feigned shock.

"I haven't seen Jazzie from that day to this one, so you tell me," Eric replied.

"I am done with the witness."

"No questions for this witness, Your Honor," Richard announced from his seat.

By the close of the second day, things were not looking good. My confidence was out the window. I wished like hell I could talk to Alicia, but she was still underground. I missed my girl. It felt as if I was all alone and had no one to talk to. All my other friends either had turned against me or were behind bars for not snitching. The world was cold, dark, and lonely. Bravo was here physically, but mentally, I knew he had checked out. The media had begun to dis him for his association with me. He had started to lose fans and friends. The Miami Heat had even put him on a leave of absence while they determined if they wanted to break his contract or not. He tried to pretend it didn't matter, but I knew better. Playing ball gave him joy, and I had taken that from him.

While he was away that night, I removed a pen and paper from the desk drawer and wrote a note to him, which I left on his pillow.

> *Dear husband,*
> *Thank you for the time we've spent together. Thank you for the laughs we've shared. Most of all, thank you for loving me, flaws and all. I hate that our journey has led us down this rough road. I hate that I brought us to this. More importantly, I hate what loving me has done to you. You don't deserve what my love has put you through. I hope you can find it in your heart to forgive me. Then maybe, just maybe, we can meet again in the next lifetime.*
> *Please forget about me and move on.*
> *XOXO*
> *Jane Doe*

With tears in my eyes, I removed my wedding ring. After placing it atop the note, I grabbed Ju and a few belongings, and then we headed out. Once in the car, I pondered where to go. For the first time ever, I didn't have a single person to turn to. As if God sensed my dilemma, he sent an angel directly to me via a phone call.

I answered on the first ring. "Hello?"

"Hey, Janie. It's Ace. I was calling to see if you could bring my daughter over sometime this week." He sounded nervous. "I know you have a lot going on with the trial and everything. Maybe it's a good idea for her to get to spend a little time with me, just in case . . ." His words trailed off. I wanted to be mad at him for thinking negatively about my situation, but he was right. The probability of my going to prison was a fact I had to face.

"Can I come now?"

"Um . . . yeah. Come on over." He cleared his throat and provided directions.

When Juliana and I were pulling into Ace's driveway, my cell phone began ringing. Bravo was home and had received my note. I didn't answer his call, because I didn't need him trying to change my mind.

"Mommy, where are we?" Ju asked from the backseat.

"We're at your daddy's house, baby," I said before I stepped out of the car and opened her door.

"Why are we here?" She peered at me with the very same eyes as her father.

"Because he wants to see you." I sighed.

Ace smiled from the porch. "Hey, there's my little girl," he called.

"Hi, Daddy," Ju said in her sleepy voice when she reached the porch.

"What's wrong? You don't miss me?" he asked her.

"Yeah, I do." Ju nodded.

"Well, come on in and get some pizza."

"Pizza!" Ju took off running into the house.

Ace took one look at me and realized something was up. "What's wrong?"

"Everything," I sighed.

"Jane, we'll get through this, no matter what." Ace wrapped his arms around me. It was his hug I'd been in need of for a very long time.

"Mommy, this lady in here has a puppy," Ju called from the doorway. She was holding a small Yorkie with curly hair. Before I could say anything, a woman came to the door, smiling.

"I hope she's not allergic," she said.

"No, it's fine," I said as I wiped my eyes and smiled. Ace had found someone new. I wanted to be hateful and jealous, but how could I?

I turned to Ace. "Thanks for the talk. Tell Juliana I'll be getting us a room at the Marriott up the street and will be back to pick her up in an hour." With my head held high, I walked to my car, climbed behind the wheel, then pulled off.

Chapter Fifty-one

Day three of the trial was by far the most draining. Throughout the day, we had to hear testimony from various members of my organization. Each of them took the stand and recounted for the jury what their roles were in the AFM. Some of them described certain scenarios in which I had instructed them to do specific things, like transport narcotics, count money in stash houses, or even discipline a worker for getting out of hand. The majority of the scenarios weren't too intense. I wasn't worried until LaShay, aka Blondie, took the stand.

"Ms. Henderson, please state your role in Ms. Doesher's organization," said the prosecutor.

"I was a lieutenant in the AFM," she answered. She spoke without looking at me.

"As a lieutenant, please describe your duties." The prosecutor leaned against his table.

"I was responsible for managing the entire Atlanta division of the AFM."

"Sounds like you were high in command. Did you have someone over you, or did you receive your orders directly from the defendant?"

"I reported to Jane directly." Blondie looked at the jury.

"So, it would be pretty accurate to say that the two of you were close, right?"

"Yes, we were close."

"As a close friend of hers, would you say 'Queen pin' and 'murderer' are accurate depictions of Jane?" the prosecutor asked.

"Yes." Blondie nodded.

"How do you know?"

"Well, I was present during at least three murders she committed."

"Do you remember details of these murders? If so, can you elaborate?" The prosecutor took a seat.

"Well, the first two murders involved a set of twins. One of them was shot in the head, and the other one was beaten to death by Jane with a baseball bat." As Blondie spoke, I could see the jury cringe from the details she was providing.

"What about the most recent murder? Can you elaborate?" the prosecutor asked.

"A while back, we arrived at the condo of her boyfriend, and there was a nude woman inside. Jane confronted the woman for being there. One word led to another. Then Jane choked the woman until she was lifeless."

"What happened afterward?"

"Her accomplices cut up the woman's body and disposed of it in several black duffel bags. After filling the duffel bags with liquid cement, they tossed them somewhere in the Miami River." Blondie shrugged after relaying the events.

The prosecution turned the questioning over to Richard.

"Ms. Henderson, why didn't you call the police after witnessing this murder?"

"Because I was scared," Blondie lied.

"Really? You didn't look scared when you were spotted on the hallway footage of Ms. Doesher's then boyfriend's condo. Interestingly enough, you were filmed carrying a black duffel bag from his home." Richard looked at the jury. "I would like to enter video footage from that fateful night into evidence."

"Objection!" The prosecutor stood. "His video is inadmissible, because he didn't provide me with a copy first, Your Honor."

"Your Honor, I received this footage by carrier at eight o'clock this morning. There was no time to provide the prosecutor with a copy," Richard retorted. "I have the carrier's documents right here."

While Richard grabbed his papers and the video and handed them to the judge, I sat back with a smirk. I was glad I had been up front with him about what I knew Blondie was going to say. All I had asked was that Bravo's name be kept out of court documents if possible, although I was sure people would make their own speculations.

"I'll accept the documents and the video footage," the judge said, then handed Richard his papers back. "The court will now watch the video."

After the bailiff started the video, the jury watched in awe as Blondie was seen carrying a duffel bag from the condo.

"My client is nowhere to be seen, Ms. Henderson," Richard noted.

"She was there, inside the house! Jane killed that lady!" Blondie was getting loud.

"Unfortunately, there is no footage of inside the home, so your testimony is hearsay. However, what we all see here is you, and only you, carrying one of the duffel bags you told us minutes ago had parts of a dead body inside them." Richard sighed. "I'm done with this witness."

"Ms. Henderson, you may step down," the judge said, dismissing Blondie. "According to my witness list, she is the last witness. Is that right?"

"Yes, Your Honor," the two attorneys said in unison.

"Given the holiday tomorrow, we will reconvene on Monday for deliberation. The jury is reminded not to discuss this trial under any circumstances. In addition, the members of the jury are reminded not to watch any news reports regarding this case!" After issuing these warnings, the judge dismissed everyone.

Chapter Fifty-two

Instead of heading home, I decided it was time to put plan B in motion. My fate was about to be sealed by twelve of my peers. At this point, the vote could go any way, and I wasn't one for taking losses. With the help of Vincenzo, I hopped on a jet headed to California. Of course, this was a complete violation of my bond. Yet desperate times called for desperate measures.

"Are you sure about this, Jane?" Vincenzo asked before we took off.

"I'm sure." I sat back in the seat and tried to calm my nerves. What if the police were waiting for me when we landed? What if something happened to the jet and we couldn't return on time? All these questions flooded my mind until we landed five hours later.

"A car is waiting right outside the doors to take you to your destination. I'll be right here when you get back," Vincenzo instructed.

"Thank you." I tried to smile, but my nerves prevented it.

"Mr. Pauletti vowed to look out for you and Ace after what you've both done for our family. Although he's not here, I'm keeping his word."

I stepped outside and into the waiting car and headed to Beverly Hills. Luckily, the jetport was less than an hour away. When the car stopped, I was greeted by several people in white lab coats.

"Right this way," one of them said. They ushered me inside a building.

"Ms. Doesher, before we get started, I wanted to show you something." The doctor led me into a room in the back of his office. Standing before me was my identical twin. Everything about her resembled me, other than the moles around her neck. "Meet Kelly."

"Wow." I reached out to touch her face . . . my face. The moment the indictment had come in, I'd called Vincenzo and requested assistance with my plan B. My idea was to have a plastic surgeon alter my face and body to look like someone else's. In the meantime, Vincenzo would find someone of my same build and complexion, then would give her my face for the trial. For her sacrifice, her family would be paid well. That was why it was impera- tive for me to be free on bond. The jury could damn well find me innocent, and all of this would be for naught. However, I didn't think the trial would end in my favor.

"Are you ready?" the doctor asked.

I nodded.

For several hours, I lay on an operating table in the back office, while the surgeon trimmed my nose, raised my cheekbones, and extended my chin. Next, he gave me larger breasts and a round, fuller ass. When it was all done, I was sore, but the pain wasn't overwhelming. The thought of having a new lease on life made all the nips and tucks worthwhile. Hours later, the town car drove both me and my look-alike back to the jet, where a nurse was waiting to fly with me in case of an emergency. Vincenzo had provided me with fake identification and passports for myself and Juliana.

Three days was not nearly enough time to heal. None- theless, today was showtime. This morning, I dressed my twin in some of my designer attire while I opted for a wig, baggy jeans and a T-shirt to conceal my bandages. Vincenzo didn't think it was a good idea to go to court today, but I had to be there in person when the jury decided my fate—well, Kelly's fate.

With my new face and body, I was rolled right into the courtroom by my personal nurse, Ann. "Good morning, ladies," a guard said, nodding and staring at Ann as we took up position in the back of the room. The fact that he didn't recognize me put a smile on my face.

"Good morning," Ann and I replied in unison.

The place was packed with media and spectators. From my seat, I observed Kelly as she took her seat beside Richard, who didn't even seem to notice the swap. He was saying something to her, and she nodded. Just then, the jurors entered one by one. My stomach hit the floor.

"Has the jury reached a verdict?" the judge asked.

"Yes, we have, Your Honor." The forewoman handed a manila envelope to the bailiff, who took it to the judge. Once the judge opened the envelope, took out a sheet of paper, and read the verdict, he handed the document back to the bailiff, who handed it back to the forewoman.

"Very well. Before the jury reads their verdict, please let me remind everyone in the courtroom that I will fine anyone who has an outburst, as this person will be guilty of contempt." He looked around the courtroom. "With that said, men and women of the jury, how do you find the defendant, Janelle Renee Doesher?"

A heavyset African American lady with full lips and a burgundy Afro, who was giving off an Angela Davis vibe, offered a sympathetic glance in the direction of the defendant's table. I knew what she was about to say before she even released the words into the atmosphere.

"We, the jury, find the defendant, Janelle Renee Doesher, guilty on all charges of murder and running a criminal enterprise."

Instantly, the smile on the prosecutor's face could be seen a mile away.

"Ms. Doesher, do you understand that you have been found guilty on charges that carry twenty years to life in prison?" the judge asked as he peered over his glasses.

My look-alike nodded.

"She understands, Your Honor," Richard replied.

"Very well. Now that you've been convicted, the court will set a sentencing date within the next thirty days. Do you understand?"

My look-alike nodded again just before two officers took her into custody. I knew the minute they took Kelly into booking, her fingerprints would raise a red flag. Therefore, I needed to get the fuck out of Dodge ASAP. Inconspicuously, Ann rolled me out of the courtroom in silence.

It was both a sad day and joyous day. The jury had just killed Jane Doe. However, they had given Janelle Doesher a second chance. This time, I wasn't going to waste it. I had come, seen, and conquered the life of being a gangstress. It was now time to live the life of a woman who had been given the opportunity to be born again.

"Where are we going, Mommy?" Ju asked as we rode to the airport.

"We're going on vacation."

"Is Daddy coming too? What about Gran and Bravo?" Ju looked hopeful.

"I think this trip is just for me and you, pumpkin." I wouldn't dare tell her that the people she had come to love would no longer be a part of her life.

"Okay, I guess." She pouted. The remainder of the ride was silent as Ju stared out the window.

I took the opportunity to close my eyes and reflect. When we pulled up to the awaiting jet, someone tapped on the car window. I opened my eyes to see Ace standing there, with two roses and a smile. He handed one to Ju and one to me before assisting me out of the car.

"Janie, I messed up once, but I swear, if you just give me one last opportunity, I'll never mess up again. I love you with everything I have. Without you and Juliana, life just isn't worth living. I don't care how many niggas you've dated or what ballplayer you married. He could never be me. We were meant to be together, Janie, and you know it." Ace poured his heart and soul out, reminding me of why I loved him in the first place.

"I'm ready to give us a second chance." I smiled. "This time, let's do this the right way."

Ace went in for a kiss but stopped when his phone beeped, indicating a picture message had come through. We both looked down and saw an unknown number. Ace was puzzled as he pulled the picture up. However, I knew exactly who it was from. It was a picture of a beach, with a message written in the sand. *See you on the other side.* This was Alicia's way of saying she was alive and well. Sooner or later, our paths would cross again.

As for now, my family and I were headed to Rio de Janeiro.

The End

Notes